SOUTHERN BLOOD

THE AMERICAN VAMPIRE SERIES

SOUTHERN BLOOD

VAMPIRE STORIES
FROM THE
AMERICAN SOUTH

LAWRENCE SCHIMEL AND MARTIN H. GREENBERG

CUMBERLAND HOUSE
NASHVILLE, TENNESSEE

Published by Cumberland House Publishing, Inc., 431 Harding Industrial Park Drive, Nashville, TN 37211-3160.

Distributed to the trade by Andrews & McMeel, 4520 Main Street, Kansas City, Missouri, 64111.

Cover and interior design by Joel Wright.

Library of Congress Cataloging-in-Publication Data

Southern blood / edited by Lawrence Schimel and Martin H. Greenberg.
        p. cm. — (The American vampire series)
    ISBN 1-888952-49-0 (pbk.)
    1. Vampires—Fiction. 2. Horror tales, American—Southern States.
    3. Southern States—Fiction. I. Schimel, Lawrence. II. Greenberg, Martin Harry. III. Series.
    PS648.V35S68 1997
    813'.0873808375—dc21   97-15897
                                                      CIP

Printed in the United States of America
1 2 3 4 5 6 7—02 03 01 00 99 98 97

For R. K.,
my dark rhinoceros,
who has a fondness for southern
(and other) creatures of the night.

—L. S.

Contents

Introduction

The American South, perhaps more than any other region in the U.S., is haunted by the past. Ghosts of history, of the dead, of wars and lineages, of slights to honor all linger vividly in the minds and lives of southerners.

For most any statement about the South, the opposite statement is oftentimes equally as true. That having been said, it is generally acknowledged that the South is a region rich in superstitions, both petty and grand, that arise from the many difference sources and traditions that make up southern cultures; one of the strongest and most popular of these is the myth of the vampire, returned from the dead to drain life from the living.

In a region notorious for its blue-blood aristocrats, for intensely segregated social hierarchies based on bloodlines and race, it is hardly surprising that a creature that lives off the blood that fuels both life and lifestyle in the South should find such resonance. It is hard for anyone living in or visiting the South to avoid noticing the tension between the new and the old, but the vampire strikes a chord for both newcomers and those whose roots are deep in the region, instilling fear (and sometimes envy) into all their hearts.

To speak of The War in the South refers not to the recent World Wars or Korea or Vietnam or Desert Storm, or any of the other major and tragic battles of this century that's nearing its end, but to the Civil War, when the Confederacy ceded from the Union, fiercely independent and willing to fight for what it believed was its rights. The War of Southern Independence pitted brother against brother, a terrible dilemma that faced each side—to fight and to kill for what they believed in at great personal cost to themselves and their families.

The existence of any vampire, especially those newly turned vampires, is often a similar dilemma—an internal civil war as human and vampire natures battle and clash. The struggle to remain human, to find humanity amidst the necessary carnage they must wreak for their own survival.

Some vampires, of course, abandon their humanity entirely. But the southerner is often too tied to the past, both his or her own and that of the region, and the southern vampire likewise retains that link to humanity and history. Codes of honor, of class, of lineage and pride remain important even for these undead creatures—and the men and women they prey upon. They are therefore both unnatural and very natural creatures to us, literally and figuratively. Flannery O'Connor writes, " Of course, I have found that anything that comes out of the South is going to be called grotesque by the Northern reader, unless it is grotesque, in which case it is going to be called realism."

Southern life (and fiction) has always seemed to focus on the small-town existence despite the presence of such major cities as Nashville, Atlanta, Louisville, and others. The one notable exception seems to be New Orleans, less a city at times than a nexus of commerce and culture, of decadence and excess, perched at the mouth of the Mississippi.

The stories in *Southern Blood* concern both the rural lives of southerners as well as the city-dewllers; they span many ages of the South, from the War to the present. Their themes are sometimes those of family life and tensions, of North against South, of new against old; their tones are sometimes gothic and romantic or contemporary and mundane. But always these stories deal with these creatures of the southern night, warm and inviting and heavy with possibility.

—Lawrence Schimel

Acknowledgments

This book would not exist without the assistance of Stefan Dziemianowicz, which is greatly appreciated by both editors.

John Helfers also provided invaluable help in compiling and processing this project.

Thanks are also due to many others, for suggestions and other help in tracking down some of the stories included, but especially to: Margaret Carter, Greg Cox, Ellen Datlow, Keith Kahia, and Mark Kelly.

SOUTHERN
BLOOD

She thought New Orleans would be a nice vacation.
But when night falls . . . the South shall rise again.

The Carpetbagger

BY SUSAN SHWARTZ

Legs askew, the dead woman lay in a doorway off Bourbon Street. Her head rested on a battered kilim bag and her eyes stared up like a camera set for time-lapse photography. Gradually the images trapped in the glazed lenses faded—the krewes passing, gaudy and raucous, Rex on his horse, Isis with her crown; men flaunting evening gowns and women wearing almost nothing at all below bobbing breasts; the flight and flash of plastic necklaces; and the avid pale face of her last cavalier.

Constrained by her New England upbringing, she had found it hard to scream, but after the sun plunged like a counterfeit doubloon into the brown water, her eyes had met the eyes of a man in weathered gray. He wore a hat with rifles crossed upon it, a saber, and a fringed gold sash, a Mardi Gras clone of Ashley Wilkes.

Not at all like Ashley then , but like the sailor in the *Life* photo at the end of World War II, he grabbed her, spun her around, and bent her back until she fell splayed upon her spine: and that too was nothing all that abnormal for Mardi Gras.

"How's this for a taste of your own medicine you bloodsuckin' Yankee?" Cold lips against her throat reeked gunpowder and bad blood.

Oh Jesus, just my luck if he's got AIDS, she thought. People danced on by, still screaming Mister, throw me something, letting the good times roll as she tried to roll him off her.

His face changed. She saw the gunshot-ruined mouth, bone and fangs protruding. His teeth sucked scream and blood and breath out of her throat.

She had time before her sight faded to wonder what she had done to deserve . . .

Silence, despite the jazz drifting from the bars.

Stars and streetlights shone down into her eyes. The transvestites picked their ways past her, cruising the Quarter, and the Mississippi rolled on: silent times for one more victim. That's what happened.

Hoofbeats down Bourbon Street: helmeted police with hard bellies, Tabasco tempers, and faith in law, order, and LSU football clattered in a dead march side by side.

Midnight. Mardi Gras is over. To your scattered bodies go.

A water truck whirred behind them, crunching discarded go cups, sprinkling the dead along with the rest of the trash lying in the way: water over the damned.

Easter isn't for weeks yet. What we have here is premature resurrection.

Tears of wretchedness cleaned her face. The dead woman turned her cheek where it rested on her bag and vomited a puddle of reddish brown.

Jesus, the crazy hadn't even bothered to steal her bag. The contempt of that plucked at her nerves. She would have screamed if she had had the strength and no sense left. She fumbled in her bag: wallet intact, cash intact, plastic intact.

Was she?

Fucked over in New Orleans. God. This sort of thing would have been bad enough at home with swabs and doctors, bright lights, the stink of stale coffee and her own unshowered flesh, questions from female cops, as invasive as a second rape, if rape it was. Among the bubbas—didn't the cops beat up on people down here?—it would probably be worse. You could scare hell out of yourself down here, if they didn't get you first.

"Did you know the man, miss?" She could just hear the litany now.

She shut her eyes. That face before it changed and shattered . . . the night before, she'd gone with friends to The Dungeon, just a few doors down.

"You don't want to go to Pat O'Briens; it's for the tourists. And the line for Preservation Hall is just too long. This is neat, you'll like it."

They ventured in at the narrow door, paid up, then headed down a sloping passageway lined with f'rgodssake cobblestones, and over a bridge across an artificial stream. Seriously weird, but not as weird as the picture of the horned and hooved patron on the wall. She was honestly tempted to throw the bounder a cake to let them pass.

Smoke and rock and roll assaulted them. So did The Dungeon's vibes. Very simply, they were the worst she'd ever felt.

"The hell with our three bucks. Let's go!" she nudged her friends.

But her companions were already shrieking at the choice of house drinks: Witch's Brew or Dragon's Blood. The man behind the dark, cramped bar wouldn't say what was in them. They should have gone back to O'Brien's or Preservation Hall. Wasn't as if tourists weren't here, too. You could tell them in their grown-up toddler clothes. You could tell the regulars, who wore dark shirts and pants, almost like New Yorkers. The few women among them had big hair, dyed, fried, and pushed to the side.

She wanted to leave now.

One man wearing gray and an Aussie hat swung down from where he sat near the dance floor, held out a hand.

"Go on!" one friend whispered and gave her a sly push. She saw herself in the mirror, out of place, dancing alone, her eyes enormous.

"You from up North, little lady?" His voice was honey over acid.

"Near Boston."

He danced tense and fast. Under the hat, he was pale, trim beard over a weak mouth, held angry-taut. Well, she could always retreat to the Ladies' Room; Board of Health rules meant they'd have one, wouldn't they?

"After 2:00 A.M., women drink free. You'll like that, won't you?"

What she didn't like was his hostility, only half disguised by the questions.

"I can buy my own drinks."

"Little Miss Independence. I just bet you can. All you Yankees, come down here with your own money, actin' like a queen. What you going to do here, anyhow? Kick up your heels in those Sunday school teacher clothes, then go back home and be a virgin?"

Jesus, why did she have to be the lucky one again? It wasn't an Aussie hat the man was wearing after all: she spotted some kind of Southern thing on the crown. A Confederate die-hard, wouldn't you just know? That war'd been over for a hundred years; but you couldn't tell down here. They' were still fighting it, them and their sacred Cause, aided and abetted by book publishers. No wonder the place was such a mess. They were still fighting a guerrilla war against the Reconstruction.

She turned and left the dance floor. "I'm out of here," she told her friends.

This long after midnight, she knew to find a cab back to the Quality Inn. The driver, hunched over the wheel, had a slow islanders accent. "Lady like you shouldn't be walkin' around here alone. Shouldn't be alone. They's all kind of lowlife."

He drove off, made some turns, and she was lost. Down the road, past a darkness in which she saw blurs in which long structures with pointed roofs emerged.

"Now, doan' you go in there—" It was St. Louis Cemetery Number 3, where Creoles, carpetbaggers, Cajuns, and voodoo queens lay above ground, their bodies protected from the seep of Lake Pontchartrain and the Mississippi for the short years till they decomposed. Whitewash, plastered over brick, coffins stacked within, tomb upon tomb, the dead yielded place to more recent dead and to the predators who hid among the green, shadowed lanes.

Her driver's eyes glazed sideways and his hand went to touch something round his neck. "They hide behind the tombs. You starin' at some angel and they' jump out at you!"

She tightened her grip on her bag, an expensive new one made out of a Turkish rug, and promised not to go there or go anywhere alone. She tipped him, and he waited till she readied the lobby before he drove away.

Yes, she had seen a pale face, twisted with anger beneath the shadow of a hat. And knew it before it changed. She wondered if any cop would buy that.

What did you suppose a Louisiana mental hospital would be like? Probably a snakepit. Like the bayou.

Sit up, why don't you? She struggled up, then rubbed her hands over her face to smear away the tears. Her fingers looked dark, as if she had worn mascara; and she knew she hadn't. Dark tears? She must be a worse mess than she thought.

She leaned out beneath the streetlight. The yowls of karaoke and rum-sodden drunks overpowered the blue notes of a jazz trombone, wailing like a train in the night. How pale her hand looked in the dark. She knew she'd caught some sun up on the levee by the Aquarium the other day, drinking Hurricanes and watching the dirty umber Mississippi flow by. Weird river, with its centuries of freight; weird city, like the shards of mirror in a burnt-out funhouse. By the waters of Babylon. Buy the waters of Babylon—and anything else they could try to sell her.

Again, she rubbed her eyes. Her tears were tainted almost red. Jesus.

She pulled a mirror from her bag to see the damages. And she saw precisely nothing at all. Oh, she saw the street, the pools of filth dissolving in the water from the truck. She saw the shopfronts. Saw a drunk embrace a post. But of herself, her reddened hands, her ruined clothes—not a trace of a reflection.

She could put a name for the type of creature that died, then rose and couldn't see its face in its mirror.

God.

That wasn't the name.

So, saying "God" wouldn't choke her. Maybe she wouldn't react to holy water, crosses, or garlic either. Amazing.

She rubbed her throat, at the rawness there from the bite. Her mouth tasted of salt and worse. Gagging, she made herself look down. She had retched, bringing up a tiny pool of blood. Dregs.

Apparently, draining her the rest of the way hadn't been worth the trouble.

Come to New Orleans! her friends had urged. We can eat our way cross town. Let the good times roll—they make an industry of it!

That wasn't all New Orleans had turned into a cottage industry. She had taken the quaint old streetcar up St. Charles to the Garden District.

"Can we see Anne Rice's house?" some idiot had called, to suppressed snickers. The writer lived here, behind a gate, amid lattices of painted iron and green trees and sunlight, glaring on the banquettes.

Sunlight. She would never see the sun again.

She forced herself to her feet, her eyes darting to the sky. When was dawn? Thank God, she had her watch. What if she went out calling to the Garden District now? Excuse me, ma'am, but I've had this accident, you know; and I was wondering—do you have a spare coffin?

Right!

If she had to be a monster, why'd it have to be a vampire? They were such a Goddammed cliche.

There. She had said the word.

What time was it? Her eyes darted frantically from her watch to the night sky. Hours left till dawn. That wasn't a real long lifespan, was it?

But she was dead already. Or undead. And she would die again unless she could think of something.

For God's sake, think of something.

I don't want to be a vampire. Want to go home! She doubted that North American Van Lines carried coffins. After giggling that she'd probably run off with a man in romantic New Orlean's, her girlfriends would have reported that she'd vanished: they'd track her down, when she used her plastic to pay for something like that. And what would she do, even if she could get home? Would an emergency ward test her for porphyria or give her standing appointments for transfusions? Did shrinks have office hours at night? For certain, she would have to hit up the weirdo shrinks at Cambridge Hospital for this. Well, John Mack had switched from shrinking Lawrence of Arabia to saucer people. He'd be sure to get another book contract out of her.

When they gave up on her, would they at least sterilize the stake they brought into the operating room?

You can't sit here all night, panicking under the streetlights.

Think it through.

She needed a place to rest. She needed a place to clean up, assuming running water didn't send her into screaming fits. The dregs of her own blood and the spoor of the one who changed her assaulted her nose. So that much was true: her senses were more keen. Maybe she could track him, could ask him why. I'll kill him. So help me God, I'll kill him.

Did she really think that was safe?

Safe? Was anything? She laughed. Several blocks over, dogs began to howl.

Well, did she have a better idea?

Food, perhaps. She was desperately hungry. There was nothing left in her to throw up. You can eat your way across town, they'd told her. Cajun cooking. Creole cooking. Dinner at Antoine's, yeah, sure; and she'd love to hear what Frances Parkinson Keyes sweet wimps said about vampires, too: probably faint on the spot. Beignets with a veritable blizzard of powdered sugar at Cafe du Monde. Sometimes you get the beignet: sometimes the beignet gets you. It had gotten her for sure this time.

It's much too rich! the well-fed types would cry at food down here, lifting hands in mock horror. Lettuce-eaters, all of them, examining each leaf as if a slug lay beneath it, maybe poking it with a fork just in case. Center-parted hair, sallow, muscles gone to ropey lines down arms and calves—but damn, they ate healthy. Bloodless.

Something, not her stomach, lurched hungrily.

If she could not eat, she would have to feed. And find some answers.

She started off down Bourbon Street, passing drunks and hookers like a wisp of dark cloud. Well, she had always had a talent for invisibility. It might help her now. A black man, rolling like a sailor too long from land, stopped. He shrank into himself, trying for invisibility. The salt of his flesh and blood lured her. His pulse thudded in her ears: alive, afraid, terrifyingly magnetic. The woman with him drew herself up and placed her own powerful frame between them. Go away.

She went.

Listen to that. The morning of Ash Wednesday, but The Dungeon's inmates still partied hearty. Perhaps she could put thumbscrews—no, she thought with a chuckle that appalled her too—perhaps she could put the bite on it for information. No one tried to collect $3.00. The bouncer actually stepped back. His belly under its ripped T-shirt twitched visibly.

Her feet felt every roughness in the cobblestones as she crossed the bridge. Another myth: running water didn't hurt. If the Ladies' Room wasn't empty when she entered, it cleared out fast as she washed. The sight of wall and towel dispenser and the rest of the room where her reflection should have been turned her slightly queasy. Maybe that was hunger, too.

When she was as clean as she could get (her clothes were beyond redemption), she walked into the bar. She half expected to see, beneath his slouch hat, the face of her attacker the vampire. The other vampire.

"He changed you. Why did he change you?"

The voice was breathless, magnolia over scraped slate, and it came from a woman crammed into a black leather—no, vinyl—dress. She was powdered pale, if sweaty, and she wore a ribbon around her neck. Black ribbon, not yellow.

Oh God, this vampire even had wannabes. She knew the type: the professional neurasthenic who read romance and popular history and quoted it like Gospel when she wasn't fluffing back her hair, or who combed genealogies to make herself look good. Eager to party, but the most stalwart virgin in the sorority house.

Tonight, though, the chittering spite—"he changed you?"—annoyed her. And it was even possible that "he" had left a message with this creature, who knew enough to recognize what she was.

"What do you know about him?"

"He say's he'll make me like he is, when I am stronger. I am so sensitive, so delicate, he say's. And then we'll be together forever." Exaggerated rapture. Not so much a wannabe as a groupie.

The woman laid one bruised hand on an ample breast, hiked up beneath her dress. Under the creaking heated vinyl, her heartbeat thudded.

The groupie stared at her with that look such women got when they eyed what they considered their physical inferiors, rendering them invisible with a flick of their eyeliner.

"Why did he pick a wicked little nothing like you? And a Yankee to boot! You just don't think you'll do as he say's. But you won't have a choice! You'll want to. And it will serve you right!"

She hadn't time for this. With a scream of rage that sent shards of mirror cascading down the walls, she pounced upon the woman. Her teeth closed on the ribboned neck, near the wound the vampire had left: she smelled him as well as stale perfume.

Don't drain her.

If she drained this woman, she would never learn the message she sensed driven like a stake into her clouded mind. A shop on Royal Street? That was all?

In disappointment, she released the woman, who sagged against the bar, her eyes appealing for rescue. Not even the bartender moved.

"You're not worth draining. You haven't got the guts to rise again. That's not protection you're bragging about, that's contempt."

The woman pushed away from the bar with surprising angry strength. She shoved her back easily.

"Look at you! You despise your own life. I want mine."

Not "wanted": I *want* mine. How had she survived her own transformation? Maybe the very force of that desire had pushed her back beyond the edge.

She glanced about the room. No one screamed. No one even moved. But their eyes glittered, not with fear or loathing, but with desire. She could feel the heightened pulses, the quickened heartbeats. They repelled her even as they drew her closer. Even the small amount of stolen blood had made her glow like a candle to these pathetic, sodden moths. One drink, one drunk. She didn't want to want them. But, God, she was starving.

She made herself laugh and hit a scornful high note that would have turned Mozart's Queen of the Night bloodless with envy. Gathering her new strength about her, she stalked out as if a cape indeed trailed from her shoulders. The bouncer held his arms out before the crowd, trying to protect it.

The first time in her life she made an exit, and it had to be Final Exit time. Damn.

She could not have drained that female rabbit. But the paltry sip of blood she had taken would not sustain her for long. Disgusting: there might be some glamour to being the Bride of Dracula, but none at all to being a vampire groupie.

She headed toward Royal Street and prowled until she saw a shop that matched the image she had seized. An antique shop, selling not Creole memorabilia, but guns, bullets, pictures, papers, swords: costly relics of the Civil War.

In the window lay a yellowed newspaper with crumbled corners, its print uneven and broken the way type was back in the 1860s and 1870s. Although the shadow of a tattered Stars and Bars half hid it, her changed eyes made it easy for her to make out a restrained headline. Beneath it was an engraving of a body lying across a floor, a blanket thrown across it to conceal—what? A shattered head?

Beneath the picture ran the story, which could have happened today: a man broken by the war, fighting in disguise in the West, but returning at last to his home and his old identity to take his life.

He had failed even at suicide. Suicides sometimes rose; and his anger had no doubt pushed him beyond the peace of death. No doubt, too, his people, those rational, blond people who never let anyone forget how reasonable they were, had despised what they would call mumbo-jumbo, worthy only of slaves or immigrants. They had not taken precautions; and so he had risen.

Gave new meaning to "the South shall rise again," didn't it just?

Why had he chosen her? She was a Yankee, therefore, as he saw it, his enemy. Maybe he thought to play the old hatreds out beyond the grave. She was strong enough to make the change, and there would be, even beyond the grave, some satisfaction in binding an enemy to his will. It probably even helped that she was female.

You still want to die, Mister? You tell me how I can find you and drive a stake through your heart. Assuming you've got one.

Could you just imagine? If every suicide rose—think of Faulkner's Quentin Compson as a vampire. I don't hate the South I don't I don't. She wondered how they'd have worked it out in Cambridge when Quentin threw himself off the Andersen Bridge into the Charles amid the odor of the honeysuckle, not the beer, sweat, rum, and tainted magnolias of this city, precarious beneath the level of the water. The Compson blood had thinned out; at least this way, he'd restore it after a fashion.

She'd always wondered if he and Shreve were lovers. Buried in one coffin, roommates again, to rise and let straight-arrow Shreve live for the first time. Right.

Wasn't as if you didn't find that theme in the South, either; just look at Blanche's husband in *Streetcar* here in New Orleans. Another suicide. She should write this, publish it; but she never had—never had the nerve, and never would now; oh, but it was funny.

God, she was losing it . . . Soon it wound be dawn, and she had no leads at all, no place to stay. What was she going to do? Wait out till dawn and then fry? It wasn't as if she outlived centuries so she could just fall away to ash. Maybe she was a wicked little nothing, and maybe it wasn't much of a life that she'd had; but she'd wanted it, never more than now. And she was damned if she was going to lose what she had left because someone had been too cowardly to stay alive and let an old grudge die.

What would become of her?

The panic she had suppressed flooded in on her the way some hurricane in years to come would make Lake Pontchartrain burst its levees and inundate this gumbo Atlantis.

"Oh help me, God!"

Dogs howled descant to her howl of anguish. The glass front of the store next to the gun shop shattered. A burglar alarm began to shriek. The white of old lace and muslin billowed from the darkness, to be restrained by iron grating.

Clean, fragrant cloth—yes! She tried the grates. The lock yielded to her new strength. She seized the gown that had caught her eye. Police would surely come soon. She peeled out of her soiled clothes (Sunday school teacher clothes, he had called them) and pulled the dress over her head, eased its genteel folds down over her waist, then squandered a moment smoothing her hair. The dress would have cost more than a month's salary.

She wished she could see herself—pale, glowing skin, dark hair, Giselle rising from the grave, not to save life, but to seek it. Her friends would giggle: just think, she'd met someone and stayed out all night! Tomorrow, maybe, they'd get round to panicking. They wouldn't miss her long; she was a spare. Next of kin would get her insurance. No, no home for her.

Where to? She would need a place to stay, some place safely dark. What about that rusty, torpedo-shaped thing in Jackson Square by the Cabildo? A submarine, it looked like. It would be dark inside. Yes; and she'd bet money she didn't have that it was sealed, so people could not climb inside and screw, just to say they had.

As she wandered down Royal, she thought she almost fit in here now, here, in this dancing dress that might have belonged once to some Creole *jeune fille bien elevee* who would not have been let out this late at night. It made sense. New Orleans spent more than half its time steeped in the past. Living and dead slept close together, and time here was twisty. It flowed sideways like a cat, to rub against the living or jump them, out of the shadows, and sink in claws and fangs.

She could go to the cemetery the driver'd warned her to avoid. Surely, no mugger could harm her now, or even meet her eyes. Perhaps there might even be some familiar name there, some scalawag or Yankee trooper whom a fever had borne off, and she could find houseroom. She would rather not lie among strangers.

She shut her eyes, seeking the thread of awareness that she'd heard (when she bothered to think of it) must draw a vampire to her creator. She found nothing. It hardly seemed fair just to leave her on her own, but it didn't seem as if chivalry worked for vampires. This was his turf. He knew how to hunt and track and stalk. He might even enjoy it. Besides, she was . . . oh God, she was so hungry.

She would have to feed. She was afraid.

"Excuse me, Mademoiselle. Miss, are you all right?" At a respectful distance, addressing her with respect: heartbeats, blood, sweat, life. Inclining forward in a half-bow, careful not to spook a woman all in white who should not be out alone before Ash Wednesday's dawn.

Go away.

He was coming at her: dark, reserved, more European than Southern. One of the Creoles, then, who mostly kept to themselves unlike the more boisterous Cajuns. Why did he have to be out, strolling back, no doubt, to some discreetly inherited flat in the Pontalba Buildings or to an even more discreet house whose iron grilles barred it from the riffraff of the city? Confident, or why would he investigate an alarm all by himself?

Hunger made her dizzier than she thought she could be, yet still keep her feet. She sensed the cleanness in his blood along with some subtle cologne and the starch in his shirt. He wore a wedding ring. Even worse, a family man. She shrank away.

"Were you hurt? Did the thieves touch you?"

What a reward for his kindness, to drain him till he died.

She shrank back. It was the wrong thing to do, she saw that in a flash; now he thought she had been raped and he'd want to help her.

Carefully, he stepped toward her. Slowly. He could not know how that tantalized her. He held out his hand. "Let me help you."

She shook her head, mute.

Dear little one, rest easy.

She never could. Her back touched the wall. His outstretched hand touched hers.

God help her; she could not help herself. She pounced.

Grabbing him with that strength she had not gotten used to, she bent back his head for the unnatural kiss. She would take no more, she promised herself, than would fill a go-cup.

His blood had all the savor of the food here: bell pepper and red wine and rice and meat. Oh God, make that a big go-cup. The blood tide flowed over her, bright memories frothing in its wake like bubbles in sparkling wine. A dark-eyed son, a shy daughter. Generations passing serenely despite upheavals beyond the iron grilles, years and years in which the dead and the living danced together, Spanish and French—*Vive l'Empereur.* Casting a cold, punctilious eye on the blond invaders, withdrawing further into the land itself, a land of camellias, of sun upon the river flowing past white homes, tumbling down in these latter years; a land of shadows in the bayou, of *feu follet* and *loup-garuo*.

Breast against her breast, his heartbeat making her even more drunk, he knew her, knew what she was, knew how she had come there. Anger at the lanky enemies fired the blood she drank. They fought at our side, but they are still strangers.

J'ai peur, maman. Mother, I'm scared . . .

His eyes rolled up, and he knew she could not restrain herself. Hail Mary Mother God and Into Thy hands rang in his fainting mind. His pulse beat like angel wings.

In that moment, understanding blossomed in his mind, and a terrible compassion. Poor little one. Just tonight? *Fais dodo, chere*. It was Cajun; it was rowdy; and it stopped her dead.

She wrenched her head away, holding him lest he fall.

"Dear God," victim and vampire said at once, in different languages.

She released him. He took a step or two, testing his ability to walk, then returned. Of course: she might leave him if she chose; but he must wait to be dismissed.

"Hey! Excuse me, you two. Did either of you see anything?" She whirled, but the man with her pressed her back and turned more slowly to face a large policeman, brother to the cavalry on Bourbon Street. His partner waited silent by his side. Could she take them both?

"Good evening," said her victim. He drew himself up, the perfect gentleman. "I very much regret, sir, but no. I was walking this lady home when we heard a noise. I am distressed I brought her down this street. What if the thieves had seen us?"

She followed his clue and took his arm, edging behind him. Don't overact.

The police straightened, touched hatbrims.

"But of course I should be glad to give you my card if you have further questions. Perhaps tomorrow, since today is a Holy Day?"

He moved his hand. Aristocrat or not, the policeman raised a hand: stop right there.

"Your name and address will do."

He gave it. Prosperous, well-connected, judging by the policeman's response.

"We may send a man around tomorrow, sir. But if you say you saw nothin' . . ."

"Neither I nor this lady. Now, if you will excuse us . . ."

He turned and escorted her away.

"Thank you," she whispered.

He touched his throat. "Of course I shall assist you," he said, his voice husky.

"I am sorry," she whispered.

"This is very terrible," her victim said. "You were a guest here."

"I am sorry," she said again. She had spent her life apologizing for inconsequential things; here, beyond the end of it, she saw how foolish those earlier regrets had been.

"So am I." Her victim reached out to her. He shimmered in the sudden flood of tears in her eyes. Then victim, knowing her need, comforted vampire, and she forbore to weep blood tears upon his shirt.

At length, she stood aside. She shivered. Though she had fed, the air was turning grey. He nodded.

"Those upstarts. *Canaille* with this money and their guns, their boots and their loud voices. And we had to listen to their bitterness when the war ended—a double bitterness, a double theft when the other thieves came from the North. And you, a guest, are threated thus . . ."

Another feud, then, passed down the generations, not against the Yankees or modern tourists, but against the strangers who had barged in and actually bought this entire area without their consent, trampled all over it with the barbarian they hailed as Old Hickory, and turned a sultry, almost European city into something more vulgar, if just as sinister.

"I thought . . ."

"Because he was born here, and you were not? What is the likes of him but a Scalawag to us?"

They were allied now by blood: she had an image of centuries of dark-haired men and women, profoundly loyal to family, silent in the face of outsiders, but quick to seize advantage. "Remember how long we have lived here. Do you think you are the first? You are not the first."

It happens in the very best of families. She almost laughed.

The Carpetbagger   15

An older tradition by far, for which the Code Napoleon was still the law whenever the code duello was not. And this was what she, sensing his cleanliness and his strength, had made her servant.

For how long? Until his fear of her outweighed his fear of death? Or longer? He had said he was bound by honor as well as blood, that she was not the first.

Perhaps his people had a way of handling this, handing down the knowledge—and the bond in the blood—from son to son (the spare, not the precious heir, perhaps) out of love for the man who first brought home the pledge. Maybe they had a family tradition: the special friend, with children as they grew up permitted to stay awake past bedtime to be presented to their night-time *Tante*. Down the generations: tending the vampire's coffin alongside the quiet graves.

It might just work. All those vampire stories had to come from somewhere.

He eyed her shrewdly. "You are wondering if your life, even as you are, is worth the price. I should remind you: our Church teaches us that life is to be preserved. Even as . . ." A gesture with one hand, so graceful that she almost saw ghostly lace swirl from his cuff. Life even for such as she. Apostle to the Undead. He smiled. She had not made a witless servant.

What did she want? Revenge? A stake through her maker's heart? He had left her one clue: the newspaper. And in it, the vampire's name, his history, his death.

"If he controls me . . ." A wind brushed the folds of her gown, her hair where it flowed over her shoulders. Almost dawn. Swiftly, she told him about her maker, his suicide, his rise from the grave.

"He had his life in the sun, and he despised it. And he hates this other existence too. So he chose you—someone he could treat as an enemy, someone he could take out his anger on; but someone strong enough to make him lose again. Because he wants to lose."

Like her maker, she would sleep during the day. But this man, so ready to serve her, so sure that her enemy was his, and had been his family's enemy for centuries: he could check court records. He could search the graveyards, probably did, at any rate. And he could enter a tomb by day, open the coffin, bring out stake and hammer . . .

He eyed her shrewdly.

"Do you want to give him what he wants?"

She flinched.

"I do not wish to kill," she said. "It strikes me as a paltry sort of vengeance."

He nodded respect and waited.

"He wants to die? Let us not oblige him. When we find his grave . . ." She knew her eyes glowed like coals, because the living man stepped back. "Do not stab him or burn him. But wrap his coffin in chains." A memory of old stories came to her. "With silver locks. And trap him till doomsday."

He smiled and kissed her hand. In the shadows and damp of before dawn, the gesture did not seem absurd.

She heard stirrings as New Orleans woke from a drunken sleep and returned to life. Ships' horns boomed over the river. Why should she not survive, dancing down the generations with this ally and his family? This seemed to be a useful city for casual violence and ancestral feuds. Why not, for vampires—even for the likes of her?

There would be an investigation when people missed her. Highly placed as this man's family was, she could evade it. They would protect her, would help her contrive financial means of her own. She could survive. She could.

"I must hide before dawn," she said. If worst came to worst, surely some of the tombs had been forced open. Or she could force her own way in. Bodies didn't last long in the city's heat and humidity: she would have her choice.

He touched his breast pocket. "My family has such a place, locked and tended. I will drive you there." Room in the inn, after all.

"I've heard the graveyards aren't safe," she objected. "No one will attack me, or if they do, I think they will run the instant they see me. But once I am . . . Safe . . . You . . ."

His laughter startled her.

"After surviving tonight, how shall I succumb to what you call a mugger? Come with me. Hurry."

The victim held out his arm. The vampire took it.

His discreet black car whirred over the road. The necropolis rose out of the waning night, whitewashed tombs, some crumbling into their original brick, a morbid slum four coffins high. She opened the window, trying to discern the live-in-death from the mere dead and living. She smelled only mud and wet vegetation. The dead were stored above the level of the water.

Some day, she knew, a hurricane would drive Lake Pontchartrain down upon this place, living and the dead together. Coffins would stir upon the face of the waters, the living clinging to the dead. Then, they would find her.

Perhaps. First, survive the day.

They hurried, a guide and his anemic Juliet searching for her tomb, through the shadowed lanes of the cemetery, past a tumbled angel, a whitened Gothic arch, a low-branched tree. The setting moon glinted on a plastic necklace, a glinting fake doubloon, tawdry images of the sun. She must preserve her memories of the sun as best she could. She would not, she thought, forgive that in a hurry. Anger made her shiver.

"Not far now," whispered her guide.

If thieves or killers lurked beneath the bulk of the chapel to the left (she heard their breathing), they sensed her rage and forbore to strike.

She would not let the Creole carry her carpetbag. It seemed hardly fitting.

Drawing a tiny key from his breast pocket, he opened the door and bowed her inside a tiny chapel. He crossed himself. A veritable Creole Chartres, she thought.

The approach of dawn was making her dizzy.

Visibly, he wavered. She suppressed a laugh. What should a gentleman do? Hold open the coffin lid of *grandmère* for this stranger guest?

"I must learn to do for myself," she said. She held out her hand again for his salute. He shut the door behind him and locked it. She would want an inside lock. That first of all.

Yes. She would learn to speak the husky softened French of her protector. And she would make herself at home here in the heart of this city of the dead. Perhaps her enemy would find her, or perhaps priests or police. Though she had not wanted life like this, she wouldn't let them take it from her. At least, not yet. By God, she'd lead them a chase and have herself a dance or two or five. Perhaps, she would dance one night outside that writer's home, and maybe be invited inside for tea or I-never-drink-wine. Or just talk. She would have many years for talk.

That was settled, at least for now.

She chose a coffin at random and opened it. Empty, or all but. The bones did not disturb her, but perhaps she should have one all her own. She whispered thanks and made herself lie down.

So much could go wrong. The tomb, the coffin, her servant, her enemy, her vengeance—she could not shut the lid upon herself, could she?

She must.

Darkness reached out to draw her down. *J'ai peur!* She cried out to it, a frightened child. A memory from the night floated back into her mind. *Fais dodo, chere.*

There, my dearest. There.

Now rest.

Whimpering at first, the vampire sang herself a lullaby. As the deadly sun came up, she learned to sleep.

Susan Shwartz is editor of the Sisters in Fantasy anthology series and author of many novels, including *Silk Roads and Shadows, Grail of Hearts, Heritage of Flight,* and others. She wants to give special thanks to Margaret Rousseau and Walter Jon Williams for their story.

Vampires, country music, and Ivy League boys don't mix.
It just isn't done . . . is it?

Claim–Jumpin' Woman, You Got a Stake in My Heart

BY ESTHER FRIESNER

*H*onestly, Binks, old man, we'd just love coming over for cocktails. You've simply got the wrong impression. Everyone in our—I mean my—old set does. Awfully white of you to overlook what people are saying. People will say anything for effect; they'll do anything for love, but that's another story. Mine, in fact.

Go on? Of course I'll go on. The whole sordid tale, if you like; it's your quarter. In spite of this *ghastly* hour, I'm still awake enough to know the real reason you've tendered us this invitation. You want the dirt. *Quelle* cowinkydink, Binks. You're dying to know how it happened, aren't you? They all are, but let's keep this just between old frat buddies, *n'est-ce pas?* It's hardly cocktail party chat. For Gawd, for country, and for pity's sake, don't tell the alumni office. No knowing how Mother Yale will react to the news, even if I do keep giving the old girl a shitload of *dinero* every year. I always did think *alma mater* meant one mean mother.

Well, all right, you can tell whatever you like to the little woman, but only because Whitney and I go *way* back. I was sleeping with her first. In fact, you owe me one, Binks. Without me, there never would have been a Whitney to glide down the aisle to your eagerly waiting arms. And on the flip side, I wouldn't be in this—situation—if not for your wifey.

She broke my heart, did Whitney M. Webster—yes, I know she's Whitney M. Webster-Winston now. Binks, but this was two years ago. We were in our senior year at Yale, it was Christmas break, absolutely *no way* on earth for us to know whether we'd gotten into Harvard Law, and the obligatory holiday pop-in on Mums and Dads about as tempting a prospect as a drug-free vasectomy. You remember how it was. I simply did not need my woman calling me up on *Navidad* morning to say, "I'm just *frightfully* sorry, Tripsy, but our engagement is off. I've found someone new." And not a word more; she rang off.

Christmas Day, Binks! When any *sane* woman knows a man is firmly lodged in the bosom of his family, and suicide looks like a damned pleasing prospect: To say nothing of the hangover from Dad's special Yuletide-recipe Bloody Marys. The Bloody's red, and you turn green; so festive. I was not prepared. She should have known I'd do something stupid.

Which I did. I made some excuse to the near-and-dear and *flung* myself into the Beemer. Drove *all* the way from Chestnut Hill to Webster's Mills, Georgia, in two days flat, just to—

What's that, Binks? . . . Yes, I said Webster's Mills. You won't have heard of it. Whitney never went back after *that* Christmas—not that I blame her—but the year of which I speak, she was spending the holidays there, at the ancestral *pied-à-terre* with her Daddy. Not that Bentley Webster ever stayed sober long enough to realize that his little girl wasn't another D.T. spawned by an overdose of Chivas and the swimsuit issue of L. L. Bean. Surely by now you know that it's a tradition for Bentley to get as high as a Macy's parade balloon every Thanksgiving, and stay right up there until the big apple comes down in Times Square on New Year's Eve. Of course, having *seen* Webster's Mills, I must say there are worse ways to view it than completely blotto.

It's an utterly hideous little pimple of a Georgia mill town, no bigger than a polo pony's poo-poo, but it was good enough for

Whitney's great gumpa to start up the textile plant that kicked off the family fortune. . . . Oh, thought they were Old Money, did you? That's not the only secret your little wifey's got to tell. Ask her about her darling Mumsy some time—the one you've never met because she's always . . . doing a little charity work in Bermuda, isn't it? Or else ask Whitney M. Webster-Winston what the M. stands for. You'll be surprised. So will I, if she tells you the truth.

All that's beside the point. I certainly don't bear the girl any grudges. Now. Two years ago, it was another kettle of *coq au vin.* Lord, Binks, I wanted to kill her! Then marry her. I didn't see any problem with that, because when love walks in the door, logic flies out your gonads, particularly when the object of your tender feelings has such a superb set of hooters. Passion blinds a man. You know what I mean; I've seen you at The Game when the Bulldogs bite it. Once you even got ketchup on your ecru Versaces; don't deny it. Well, I was so peeved about Whitney that I didn't even bother to put the mud screen up when I pulled the Beemer into the center of Webster's Mills.

Which center is, *in toto*—I kid you not—the Bop 'n' Burger Drive-In. People actually *eat* there, though I don't think it's food. It was nighttime when I arrived. A pink-and-yellow neon hamburger twirled lazily round and round at the top of a twenty-foot-high puke-green pole high above that symposium of sorghum fanciers. Below, what wasn't cinder block and asphalt was plastic and chrome. The sound of a jukebox wailed clear across the parking lot. There was nowhere to hide from the strains of "Take Me Closer to Jesus, Elvis." My Gawd, do they *still* manufacture that many denim-blue Ford pickups? I swear, Binks, somewhere someone is making a fucking *fortune* stonewashing trucks. How else could they all have that same air of prefab shabbiness? Between those venerable vehicles and the dented red two-door Chevies cluttering up the Bop 'n' Burger, the old Beemer stuck out like a virgin at Vassar.

Now, mark me, old man, ordinarily I wouldn't be caught dead in such a place. Kitsch went o-u-t simply *ages* ago. But I needed directions. A man can't very well lay his torn and bleeding heart at the feet of *La belle dame sans* timing if he doesn't know where said feet currently are. Whitney's mailing address over break was just The Aspens, Webster's Mills, Georgia, so I did have to do the odd spot of inquiry.

I leaned against the hood of the Beemer while contemplating which of the locals would understand a question phrased in grammatical English. The atmosphere was not conducive to clear-headed thought. The smell of paleolithic grease emanating from the Bop 'n' Burger kitchen was appalling. The whole parking lot reeked of it. And then, cutting through the miasma of deep-fried possum and sludgeburgers, there came a flying wedge of Tabu cologne that nailed me right between the eyes.

"Take your order, honey?" she said. You may have heard of Georgia peaches, Binks. Well, they're nothing compared to the Georgia honeydews this lady was attempting to conceal under her red cotton blouse; badly. You know I'm a gentleman. I didn't intend to ogle the Edams, but I couldn't help it; they were on eye level. I wondered whether Webster's Mills made a habit of spawning the Fifty-Foot Woman, until I realized that my hayseed Hebe was mounted on a pair of roller skates.

"Actually, I'm just trying to get some information," I told her, to which she replied: "This ain't Ma Bell, sugar. You just order you a Cocola, I'll be real happy to point you any which way you want to go."

Coca Cola; yes, Binks, I know. But for better or worse, that was how I met Miss Rubilene Nash. My mind was on other matters than correcting her quaint pronunciation. She was a vision of delight, old man, either in approach or retreat. Is your Whitney still the ruthlessly articulate girls'-rights advocate I once knew?. . . *Quelle dommage*. Well, then you know she would never have approved of Miss Rubilene's carhop outfit. Why do they call them carhops, anyway? One good hop in *that* rig-out, and more than Atlanta would burn.

I managed to hold on to some of the old Apollonian calm when she came skating back with my beverage. After all, I told myself, I was the jilted swain come to pound Sweet Reason back into dear Whitney's skull. It lacks a certain note of moral superiority if one's mouth is full of love's most persuasive rhetoric for one girl while one's loins are full of school spirit for another.

"The Aspens?" she repeated once I posed my question. "You don't mean Bojo Webster's place?"

"The Aspens, dear girl, is the residence of Mr. *Bentley* Webster," I informed her. "And his daughter Whitney," I thought it prudent to add.

"Oh, Whitney," she said. "You must be him." Her lips pursed out in a manner that would have been too delicious but for the fact that she was looking at me as if I were an especially cute and furry road kill.

"Him—I mean *he*—who?" I asked. Perhaps she had me confused with a different squashed cat of Whitney's acquaintance.

No such luck. "You're that Yale fella Whitney dumped," she informed me. Her golden brows knotted with the effort of recalling my name. "Gordon Franford III?"

I nodded. Despair made me heedless—my Gawd, if the working classes in this guanoburg knew the details of my recent *contretemps d'amour,* what did I have left to lose? I told her to call me Trip.

Never did I see such sympathy in female eyes, Binks; not that I felt like being the object of rural pity. "You poor thing," she said. "Driving all this way for nothing. Honey, unless there's two Whitney Maybelle Websters in this world, you have lost her, and you have lost her for good and all."

Yes, Binks, I've let your little helpmate's secret go whoopsy: *Maybelle.* Perhaps Whitney never saw fit to tell you the too-romantic tale of how her parents met. Mumsy was a waitress at one of the finer resorts on Hilton Head, when Daddy showed up at the bar a teensy bit borneo. When he took out his money clip to pay the tab, the lady saw what she liked, and married it before Bentley sobered up. You *do* know Whitney's words to live by? Either she gets things her way, or somebody dies. Got *that* single-minded spunk from her Mumsy. Also her charming middle name.

But to return: I was not raised to take defeat lightly; not with that much mileage on the Beemer. I drew myself up, adopted an air of dogged determination, and said, "I'll be the judge of that, young lady."

Whereat the toothsome Miss Rubilene burst into giggles. "'Young lady'?" she repeated. "Oh, sugar, if you only knew!"

I didn't. I assumed her mirth stemmed from my perchance inappropriate pomposity coupled with the obvious fact that she looked only a year or so younger than I. Still, *la coeura sais raisons que la raison ne connait point,* so I continued to make an ass of myself.

"If you don't know the way to The Aspens, then I'll thank you to say so," I informed her. "I haven't all the time in the world."

She looked chastened at that; sad, at any rate. "Honey," she said, "I could send you off on a wild-goose chase to The Aspens right now, but that wouldn't do you a lick of good. You want to see Miss Whitney, and Miss Whitney's not there. She's right here in this town, not a coon's spit from where we're standing. But if you know what's good for you, you'll leave her be, hustle those cute little buns into your fancy car, and hightail it back up North while you still can." And before I could register any pleasure at her evaluation of my *derriere* (it's all that time I spent on the Yale crew; tightens up the old gluteus whatzits so well), Miss Rubilene went on to say: "She's Randy Russell's woman now."

The hell she was, I said, which only evoked another of those *poor, ignorant boy* looks from her. Before she could explain, the anthropoid ape who owned the Bop 'n' Burger came out of Hell's kitchen to yell at my winsome informant to quit fraternizing with the damyankees and take orders from the Phil Donahue Fan Club currently cluttering up the parking lot and leaning on their klaxons for service.

Before she whirred away, she managed to whisper to me, "I get off work 'long to'ad midnight. You wait for me, and I'll do what I can to help you. Don't try scooting off on your own after that girl of yours, or you'll be real sorry. My truck's over there. Meet me by it." A scrape of skate wheels, and she was gone.

I strolled over to check out said chariot. It was a sky-blue pickup with a Confederate flag sticker on the windshield and a stuffed Garfield hanging upside down from suction-cup paws in the rear window. There was an "If You're Rich I'm Single" bumper sticker over the tail pipe, and one saying, "This Is My Other Car," for aesthetic and philosophical balance. Thank Gawd it had no gun rack, or I'd never have been able to pick it out of the crowd. I glanced into the back and noted that the lady was obviously a gardening enthusiast. Either that, or the Webster's Mills locals take it literally when they say they're going to dish the dirt.

It lacked but three hours of midnight. It wouldn't have been any skin off my tan to wait for Rubilene. I should have scouted out a local roach motel and checked in for a few hours' bidey-bye in the meanwhile. However, when have you ever known me to do the sage thing, Binks? I was the one who signed up for Organic Chem in freshman year when anyone with half a brain took Gut Psych to fulfill the science requirement. I confess, the undertone of doom in her voice when she spoke of Whitney and this Russell person intrigued me. It was like some divine Wagnerian motif to remind the audience that the gods were going to fall in the Rhine any hour now; so why bother. I should have waited to hear more.

Not I. Now I knew that my rival had a name; Randy Russell. How too, too goober. From the way Rubilene spoke with such assurance of the hopelessness of my cause, I gathered that this Russell was a known quantity in those there parts. What is named and known can be hunted down, like a wild skeet. I didn't wait. I drove to the nearest gas station and asked the pump jockey whether he knew the whereabouts of one Randy Russell.

Binks, if you could have seen the fond, lobotomized grin that o'erspread those zitful features, you'd have thought I was offering the lad the chance to evolve into one of the higher primates. "Cowboy Randy Russell," he breathed. "I got just about all his albums. Wish I had me enough money to buy a ticket to his concert tonight, though." He said no more, but gazed at me meaningfully. The implication was clear: aphasia *can* he cured for about twenty dollars in most civilized societies. Isn't science wonderful?

Quasimodo Jukes recked without that fine old Yale tradition that requires all her students, even unto the least of us, to learn how to do research. Usually I'm hard put to deduce breakfast, but love is a great smartener-upper. A concert, was it? And nearby, I should venture to guess, else why would this walking testimony to inbreeding seem so sanguine about obtaining the bribe from me and being able to attend said musical that very evening? Too, hadn't Rubilene just said that Whitney was —how did she phrase it?—less than a coon's spit away? Though I didn't know how far said beast could hawk a lugie, I still had clues aplenty.

I feigned stiff joints, got out of the Beemer, and strolled over to the front window of the filling station while Gasoline Alley Oop continued to blither on about how he had a bad memory for times and places, but might be subject to the electroshock of ready green. I let him natter away. Where there are concerts, my dear Binks, there are also adverts for the same posted in plain sight at most local businesses. Sure enough, there among the cans of thirty-weight reposed a placard advertising Cowboy Randy Russell's Homecoming Tour, with a gig at the East Webster's Mills Melodrome in—good Lord, it had begun at nine o'clock! And no doubt Whitney would be there, eyes ashine with socially misplaced *tendresse*. If I wanted to find her and dissuade her from what *had* to be the world's biggest *mesalliance* since Leda and the Swanson TV Dinner, I knew I'd best make tracks. I thanked my informant and absolutely *floored* the Beemer. Pity, really. Now I shall never know his full critical opinion of my Mums's morals.

Oh, I had no trouble finding the Melodrome, despite the fact that East Webster's Mills lies north of its patronymic town. It looked like a converted bowling alley. Either that, or all the best odea shall soon sport a giant phosphorescent duckpin atop their CURRENT ATTRACTION signs.

Parking was at a premium. Whoever this Cowboy Randy Russell was, I reasoned he must be pulling down a tender dollar. Perhaps Whitney hadn't lost quite so much of her sanity as I suspected, but still . . . a Country-Western singer? Even for New Money, Whitney should have had some pride.

I bought an SRO ticket from a very bored young box-office bimbette and entered the gates of Orphic Hell. The Melodrome was one of these theater-in-the-round bits, where, if the audience didn't like an act, there was no possible escape for the luckless performer as they swarmed the stage from all sides to pick his bones. Cowboy Randy Russell did not seem in any such immediate peril. He sat atop a backless wooden barstool in a puddle of klieg light and grinned at the applauding mob over the hump of his white guitar.

You know, Binks, we men have it all sewn up. When a woman gets as many wrinkles as Russell showed, it's time to look up the number of a good, expensive, discreet plastic surgeon. He was, I believe the term is, *craggy*. Rugged. Weathered and browned as an old saddle, or a cruise director. He had blue eyes of a piercing brightness found only in Louis L'Amour books. The obligatory Stetson atop nigh metallic golden curls, and his smile caused snow blindness in the first four rows. Truly *primo* teeth. He must have been the most popular boy in the bunkhouse until he learned to fight. You could smell the horse sweat clear back to the cheap seats.

"Thank you, folks, thank you very much," he said. "Now, I'd like to dedicate this next number to a very special little lady who couldn't be here tonight." My heart plunged into my Reeboks. Had I come so far—paid cash money—to hear *this*? That Whitney wasn't there? But then he went on to say; "Now, I don't mean for you to get the wrong idea. The lady in question's just a good friend, and we go way back together, but there's only one woman in my heart. A man can't ride two horses with one set of chaps—ain't that so, Miss Whitney?"

I heard a familiar giggle from the front row as he lavished a fond gaze upon my—I mean *your*—beloved. Yes, there she sat. I could catch only a glimpse of the back of her head, but I knew it was she. It was the only head of hair present untouched by mousse or Miss Clairol, and sporting a darling little navy grosgrain bow.

Cowboy Randy Russell shifted the white guitar and thumbed his hat farther back on his head. "So this here song's for my old pal and good drinkin' buddy, Miss Rubilene Nash, wherever she may be tonight; 'If Jesus Drove a Semi.'"

> *If Jesus drove a semi, he'd steer it straight and well.*
> *He'd pick up lonesome hitchhikers bound for the road to Hell.*
> *At each and every truck stop, an angel gets aboard.*
> *It's eighteen-wheel salvation on the semi of the L—*

What's that, Binks? . . . Yes, it *was* necessary to sing. I shall never forget that song so long as I—Anyway, my voice isn't *that* bad. The notes of the second verse were still echoing in my ears as I walked out of the Melodrome like one entranced.

Outside, a breath of cool air washed away the last dregs of

Cowboy Randy Russell going on about paying the tolls to Heaven and splitting gas costs with his Savior. I was able to think clearly again, and the first thought that crossed my mind was to snoop about and see whether I couldn't be waiting for the happy couple backstage when the concert was over.

There was no problem about it. The twenty I'd saved on useless information from the grease monkey now went to slick the palm of the bubba guarding the stage door. He pointed me at Cowboy Randy Russell's dressing room as soon as he was able to get his hand out of his pocket. I believe I told him that I was the Singer's cousin, though I'd wager that, for another ten, he'd have let me through had I claimed to be the Angel of Death making a house call.

I moved quickly, not wanting to run into any other backstage personnel who might require additional *baksheesh*. The door to Cowboy Randy Russell's dressing room had a chintzy star on it, silvered plastic, but no lock. I slipped inside and turned on the lights.

There she sat, perched on the edge of the sleekest, blackest, most tasteful and elegant coffin I'd ever seen. Rubilene Nash uncrossed her excellent legs, slid to the floor, and said, "Didn't I tell you to wait for me?"

I'm afraid I was still gaping at the body box. You will recall the stories about the great Sarah Bernhardt catching forty winks in a casket, but a Country-Western singer? Astonishment froze me, though I swiftly defrosted under a *numero uno* case of the creepy-crawlies.

"You *can't* mean—" was all I managed to utter.

Rubilene nodded.

"But that's—*kinky!*" I said, my mind still limited to commonplace speculations. "He and Whitney do it in *there?*" I extended a trembling finger at the blue satin interior.

"Of course not!" Rubilene exclaimed. She gave me a look of revulsion. "You Yankees just have the filthiest minds. Do it in a *coffin?* Lord! Cowboy Randy Russell may be a no-account, two-timing, womanizing, undead sumbitch, but by God, he ain't no *pervert.*"

Undead, the lady said. Just so. You'll understand why I laughed in her face then, won't you, Binks?

She was even prettier when she was angry. She also had a good right cross, quite staggering even when all it delivered was an openhanded slap. I stopped laughing. "You don't believe me," she said. "Fine. I don't care do you believe or not, just so long as you get the bell out of this room before he comes back. If you don't, you're dead."

I recouped some poise and pulled up the only chair in the room. Slinging one leg athwart the other, I gave her rather a cool reply, viz: "I am a Yale man. *We* don't do vampires."

Rubilene rolled her lovely eyes. "I swear, you won't be worth the rope to hang you, boy. You want proof? All right, I'll see can I find some; only, you better be a speed reader is all, because if you're not out of here before the concert's over . . ." She made the sign of someone cutting off more than my allowance, then flung herself into the large steamer trunk at the foot of the coffin.

I confess to a mounting *malaise*. Consider: This woman had doubtless abandoned her paying job to follow me here and warn me off. Either there was a real vampiric threat to my welfare—in which case I had better do my damndest to recall how they disposed of Langella in the Broadway production of *Dracula* and I don't think it was bad reviews—else Miss Rubilene Nash was several pearls short of a strand, in which case I was in questionable circumstances of personal safety by being alone with her that way. I was debating flight, when she heaved a thick album out of the trunk and pitched it into my lap.

It was a scrapbook. Some of the reviews dated back over thirty years. There were many photographs among the newspaper clippings. In each and every one, Cowboy Randy Russell was clearly identifiable, surrounded by gaggles of sweet young things. He was also just as clearly the same age, whether snapped in 1950 or 1980. "I thought vampires didn't register on film," I remarked, trying to keep a choirboy tremor out of my voice.

Rubilene snorted. "Cowboy Randy, he's *show* bidness," she said. "You don't just give up being photogenic over a little thing like unnatural life." She spoke with an expert's conviction. I had to believe.

Thirty years, Binks; almost forty, and he hadn't aged. There is just so much that Minoxidil and Retin-A can account for. I stood up, still holding onto the album. "How has he managed to get away with it? Surely someone else must have noticed—? Those closest to him: his agent, his manager, his—toadies? I mean, roadies."

She sighed. "And cut their own throats? Sugar, Cowboy Randy Russell's box office. Long as a man keeps on a-hauling in the green, ain't no one going to ask, like, *uncomfortable* questions 'bout his looks. By the time *do* they think to get suspicious, he maybe fires them and gets new folks on too stupid to find their ass with both hands and a road map. And his fans wouldn't give a gold-plated shit even was he dead and buried, long as he keeps singing."

I considered the phenomenon of Elvis Everlasting and had to concur.

"But you're on to him" I said

She nodded. "I told him I'd caught wise," she said."I guess that's what broke us up, him being dead and all. He just laughed."

I was stunned. "He knows you know," I said, "and he lets you live?" From what I gathered during an all-night Halloween film festival at Yale, vampires were notoriously tidy when it came to tucking away those who discovered their secret. Permanently.

"You heard him out there," she said. Her lips curved into an embittered smile. "Called me his *pal*. Used to be I was more. I guess you know how when you swear to your *pal* as how you'll keep all his secrets, it's binding."

Uh-oh, I told myself. A woman scorned, that which Hell hath no Fury like. I pictured the Stetson-sporting beast pulling up to the Bop 'n' Burger and ordering a patty, *ever* so rare, then sweeping poor Rubilene off her wheelies. A celebrity, after all; a Country-Western singer. Poor child, stars in eyes one minute, fangs in her throat the next. And then *el dumpo supremo*. Between the pain of a broken heart and the fear of a broken neck if she squealed, no wonder Rubilene kept silent.

Besides, who in this civic chancre would ever believe her tale of vampires, even if they saw the fatal scrapbook? The *Enquirer* hadn't covered the story yet, nor had *Reader's Digest* touted "My Most Unforgettable Ghoul."

"I'm sorry," I told her. I meant it.

A single tear trickled down her cheek. I lifted it with a fingertip and battled manfully the urge to kiss her. However, doesn't Whitney go on about how *real* men aren't afraid to give in to their emotions now and then? Let no one dare brand me an MCP. I took the lady into my arms and helped my yang side happen.

She pushed me away, but not immediately, and she didn't smack me again. In a deliciously breathless way, she said, "Why, aren't you the sweetest thing." There was a momentary look of cool cunning in her eyes—that special female fluoroscopic vision that can count the contents of your wallet through four layers of clothing—but she doused it quickly. She was a wise woman, my dear Rubilene, and subtle as good wine.

"No need for you to feel sorry for me, sugar," she said. "Though I do appreciate the attention. I'm glad I got shut of Randy before it was too late. I'm just afraid your Whitney isn't going to be so lucky."

Too late indeed. You *do* know the drill when it comes to the hemophagocytic hoi polloi, don't you, Binks? A nip or two does no more harm than mild anemia, but chugalug over the limit, and the victim turns vampire, too. Now I ask you, could you see poor Whitney flittering around the night sky, sucking total strangers? People who were just Not Her Kind? *Princeton men?* Besides, she looks such a bowwow in black, and Bloomie's is so seldom open after dark. Hello, eternal life; ta-ta, charge cards. *Not* a good trade.

I asked Rubilene whether she was certain in her apprehensions. She nodded vigorously and said, "He's going to make her his bride. That means he'll have to take her all the way, make her like he is. He sealed that when he gave her a ring on Christmas Day." And she gave me one, too, but it wasn't quite the same. Rubilene shivered. "He's been taking the change nice and slow, kinda savoring it, like, but it can't go any farther 'thout she crosses over. Tonight's the night."

Whitney, the bride of a C&W vampire. My own girl, trapped with that man—that monster—that *music*—for all eternity. The mind boggled. "I must save her," I told Rubilene. "Quickly, where can I get a stake?" She suggested the Grill Room of the Dew Drop Inn on S.R. 47-A, until I explained my strictly vegetarian intentions.

"Through the *heart?*" she exclaimed, making the same face Whitney does when something strikes her as euw, gross.

"It's the only way," I maintained, having flashed on the final scene from *Dracula* in this, my hour of need. I cast about the dressing room, but found nothing remotely stake-ish. Determined, though stupid, I instructed Rubilene to run out and fetch me something apropos while I hid behind the curtains, ready to spring out and prevent the villain from sealing his unholy purpose in Whitney's blood.

Yes, Binks, I *did* talk like that. I was upset.

Rubilene protested, but I stood firm. There were a pair of gingham drapes dangling from the wall behind the coffin—a nice, homey touch, considering that they framed no accompanying window, just a poster of Hank Williams. I shimmied past the long box and yanked them shut before me. It was quite the tight squeeze. I've seen tax men with hearts more capacious than that miserable boxcar of a room, though I grant you perhaps the coffin did contribute to the general claustrophobia. The only way it would fit was wedged between one wall and a dingy, iron-stained sink. I knocked two big, ratty towels off the attached chrome drying rack as I wormed by.

No doubt my voice came somewhat muffled as I instructed Rubilene to replace the towels and get a move on. She crammed them back in place angrily and tried one last time to make me see reason. I remained adamant behind the draperies, refusing even to look at her. I assumed I had convinced her of my determination. I didn't hear her retreating footsteps, but I did hear the dressing room door slam, then silence.

One turns rather philosophical when all one has to stare at is a pattern of itsy-bitsy red-and-white checks. The wall felt cold against my back. It was pure cinder block, covered over with that yucky rubberized paint, except where Hank made it crinkly. I dared to part the curtains by a fingertip, just to have something *different* to stare at mindlessly. Thank Gawd we Branfords have always had the aristocrat's slender fingertips, because *that* moment and no other was when Cowboy Randy Russell and Whitney came in.

I froze in place rather than try to jerk back the offending digit.

No sense in catching mine enemy's eye with an inopportune flutter of the draperies, *à la* Polonius. We both know what became of *him*. Binks, you would have been proud of me, standing there like one of your Dad's best bird dogs on point. I was entirely rigid.

I wasn't the only one. Impressive. There was no mistaking it, either; not in those jeans. My Gawd, they never do cover that aspect of being a vampire in *Dracula*, though I confess to having an inkling. No woman I ever knew was willing to settle for a hickey. When Cowboy Randy Russell initially rose from the grave, I know which portion of his anatomy surfaced first, the swine. *Definitely* the undead.

Oh, the pain, Binks! To have to stand there, helpless, and watch my—I mean, *your*—Whitney's clothes drop faster than the Dow Jones. Cowboy Randy Russell was quite the quick-draw man himself. There was a brief vertical scrimmage, and then—I remember being idiotically smug about this and wishing Rubilene could see her words proved wrong—he *did* carry her to the coffin.

I don't know, Binks; does she ever get vocal when you and she—? Well, she never did with *me*, and I was asking out of strictly scientific curiosity. You know she's nothing to me now. Perhaps it was the fact that Cowboy Randy Russell was a singer. He even left that tacky white guitar of his propped up at the foot of the casket. The dear girl must have felt obliged to provide backup group accompaniment so he'd feel at home. Just one *ooooh-wah* after another.

My view of the proceedings was unimpeachably perfect. Lord, do we all look that ludicrous *in flagrante*? You won't catch *me* putting any mirrors on the bedroom ceiling. My palms grew slick with sweat as I gazed down upon them from behind the draperies. I felt like a guest at a funeral giving the dear departed one final goggle and discovering they'd laid out Uncle Randolph in a Chanel tea gown. You wouldn't believe where some people have dimples.

And then, just when I thought someone ought to adjust dear Whitney's treble, Cowboy Randy Russell raised himself on his elbows, opened his month—Yes, of *course* he had fangs, Binks; what did you think he was going to use on her? A Swiss Army knife corkscrew? Don't interrupt; you're *ruining* the climax—and said, "Now, sugarlips, you're gonna ride with me till God and Satan slap leather at high noon on a dirt street in Eternity."

Well, *that* tore it. I grabbed one of the towels, twisted it into the great grandfather of all locker-room rattails, and flicked it hard across the foul fiend's Country and Western buttocks.

Gallant? Noble? Heroic? No. I'd call it moronic, if anything. Anyone who saw that creature's blazing red eyes jerk up and fix themselves on me would agree. Homicide would be the least of it. Whitney tried to cast her arms around his neck and get his mind back on business, but *cui bono?* He shook her off like raindrops from a Burberry. He was enraged, and I was dogmeat.

His face contorted into a hellish grimace that I only peripherally recognized as a smile. "Now, why'd you want to go and do a fool thing like that for, son?,' he drawled, clambering out of the coffin with disturbing agility.

"It's your own fault," I temporized, still clutching the towel. "Whitney and I have—had—an understanding. Besides, we're Yale, and I cannot in good conscience allow her to form an alliance with one so uncultured as yourself. Did you actually *say,* 'till God and Satan slap leather'? What *have* you been reading?"

From the coffin, Whitney peeped, "He's *Cowboy* Randy Russell, Tripsy. Cowboys are *always* saying cute things like that."

"A cowboy from *Georgia?*" I countered. "Gawd, Whitney, it's bad enough you dumped me for a vampire, but a *poseur?* And you made such a fuss when Buffy got pinned by that Community College yahoo."

Whitney's immaculately French-manicured nails gripped the edge of the coffin. "You won't *tell* Buffs about this, will you, Tripsy? Even after I'm undead? That bitch would put just the wrong light on this. Randy and I wouldn't be able to go *anywhere* that mattered."

"I'll think about it," I said coolly. Such a treat to watch her beg.

It didn't last long. I heard a growl in the key of G, and felt a hand heavy with gold rings fall on my shoulder. "Son," said Cowboy Randy Russell, "onliest thing you're gonna have to think about is where we ship the body."

Which was approximately when the white guitar came smashing down atop his head. He and I both turned simultaneously to see Miss Rubilene Nash standing there holding the splintered neck of the instrument and screaming some pret-ty strong epi-thets at the vampire. I was too shocked by her Parris Island vocabulary to ask myself where she'd dropped from. I hadn't *heard* the door open, but I'd been a tad distracted, true.

Russell reeled, though more from her guttersnipe words than the blow. You know vampires: bullets won't stop them, so why should a whack upside the skull with a Fender? Now understand, the man was stark raving naked. We're none of us at our most self-possessed in that state. He *cringed*, poor soul, then snatched the towel from my hands and wrapped it around his middle.

"Young lady," he said, wagging a finger at her. "Young lady, this ain't none of your bidness."

"I'll say it is!" Rubilene countered. She cast a positively scoriac eye at Whitney's fair young bod in the coffin. How your darling wifey shrank beneath that glare! "Jesus, Randy," said Rubilene, "bad enough you're trying to murder this poor boy here, but social climbing, too? Think you can take up with Miss Hot Shit On Toast, and that'll make you any better than the backwoods trash you always been?" She shook her head. "Fine time you pick for sucking up to a Webster. I thought higher of you, boy."

Cowboy Randy Russell's avuncular air dropped by the wayside. He was miffed. His eyes went from bright scarlet to Harvard crimson—never a good sign. I tried to sidle away, but there was no space to permit free-lance sidling. Without bothering to look around, he grabbed me by the collar of my best Land's End polo.

I believe I remarked, "Ackh."

He was more voluble. "Time I need your goodwill's long past, Rubilene," he said. "Seems as you've taken a fancy to this candy-ass Yankee. Try telling *me* you're not just as hot to haul yourself up a rung now you got the chance!"

Rubilene lowered her eyes. It was then, for the first time, she murmured those three little words every man so longs to hear: "I love him." These to be swiftly followed by three more, viz: "Drop him, dickhead."

Cowboy Randy Russell only twisted my polo collar a few addi-tional points to starboard. "I'll drop him, honey, soon's he stops breathing."

Through blurring vision I caught the glimmer of his bared fangs. Rubilene hung back, still clutching the neckpiece of the broken guitar. Could you blame her? She owed her life to this monster's previous forbearance. She was his . . . *pal.* There had to be limits to how far one could push the privileges of such a social connection. I assumed she didn't wish to discover them just yet.

All of which spoke well for Rubilene's prudence, but wasn't doing jack shit to save my neck. Binks, you know I abhor violence, but when your own life's on the line, kicking ass seems like a *darned* good idea. No matter that I knew that a vampire possesses superhuman strength, I would not go gentle into that good night. I hauled back and gave him a right to the jaw.

I don't know which of us was the more shocked: he when that wild punch landed, or I when he shrieked in pain and dropped me. A nasty gash opened up on his cheek, deep and bloodless, but no less impressive. He staggered back, stumbling against the coffin. Whitney uttered a maternal whinny of distress and flung her arms about him, pleading to kiss the boo-boo and make it all better. It was the only favor that woman ever did me, and all unwitting. Her effusions kept him tied up just long enough for me to slip between him and the sink and make for freedom.

Well, almost freedom. He gave a roar and shrugged her aside, shouting, "You goddam sushi-suckin' sumbitch!" Before I could escape the room, he clamped onto my shoulders. I made a fruitless grab for Rubilene's hand, but the vampire spun me around to face him.

"I'm here for you, Trip," I heard her say softly. Her breath stirred the short hairs on my neck. Russell ignored her as unworthy of attention, all his rage focused on me.

"What in hell did you hit me with?" he demanded.

"A—my—the—," I stammered, my hands clenching and unclenching like onanistic starfish. Then I felt it, the thick metal band encircling the third finger of my right hand. You know how some things are always there, so you never really think about them. Like the family trust fund? Briarcliff girls? One's Yale ring? One's *sterling silver* Yale ring? I stared at the monster, and instantly every bit of B-movie lore about silver and its perfectly charming effect on creatures of darkness came flooding through the old brainpan. The scar on his cheek was smoldering. Surprise, surprise, all that silver-bullet bushwa was true.

"Well, *what*? he repeated. He was a most persistent fiend, and his breath—? *Mega* yuckorama.

"This," I retorted, and, raising the fist in question, I let him have another paste across the chops. He hit the floor on that one. Now I did seize Rubilene's free hand and yelped something thoroughly original, like: "Let's get out of here!"

She was yanked from my grasp so hard that she dropped the guitar neck. I watched in horror as Cowboy Randy Russell dragged her back toward the coffin. "Traitor," he growled. "We got ways of dealing with your kind." I might well have gotten away then, for all of him. Turning his back on me, he bent her over the crook of one arm, his fangs bared, heedless of Whitney's clamorous objections that he'd sworn to quit sipping around on her. "Now it's *really* all over," he said.

Which it was, but not for her. Never turn your back on a Yale man. I picked up the splintered guitar neck and thrust it home. Easier than I hoped, really. No trouble at all from little details like intervening ribs and spine. Either there's truth to what they say about the strength of desperation, or else that sorry creature had the *worst* case of osteoporosis you'd ever see. When it comes to a reliable source of calcium, Brie beats blood every time. His bones snapped like melba toast, and I skewered the heart on the first try. But it was messy. No free lunches, Binks. Whitney fainted.

We left her there. Her late paramour conveniently dwindled to a towel-wrapped pile of primal dust that looked like someone had been dipping snuff a whisker too enthusiastically. No *corpus*, no *habeas*. Whitney would have no trouble from the authorities over the singer's vanishment. The evanescent nature and gypsy habits of *show bidness* people are legendary. Anyway, Webster's Mills was hardly going to make a stereo stink about anything concerning the heir to the town's main industry. I could throw Whitney to the wolves with a clear conscience based on the tacit understanding that cannibalism is *not* a lupine trait. She'd survive. She did, didn't she?

As for Rubilene and myself we judged it wise to get while the getting was good. We eluded all backstage personnel and slipped unnoted onto the parking lot—empty by now. I followed her truck with the Beemer, assuming that we were heading back to town. I just wanted to put as much distance between my ass and Cowboy Randy Russell's earthly remains as possible.

It was well after midnight, most of the Melodrome lights were out, and the asphalt dribble of a state road was illumined only by our headlights. I was too undone by my recent ordeal to do my own navigation. I supposed that soon we would be back in the center of town, and then I could barf my guts up at leisure.

I was taken aback when she pulled the truck off into a roadside picnic grove halfway to Hades, turned off the headlights, and got out. I followed suit, thoroughly disoriented and confused. More so when she sat down at one of the wobbly tables, cradled her head in her arms, and began to cry.

I admit she had reason to. She had just aided and abetted the extinction of that rarest of endangered species, a vampire who knew all the lyrics to "If Jesus Drove a Semi." Too, she must have had some fond memories of the fiend, back in the days when she, and not Whitney, was his—I blush to say it—drinking buddy. My heart went out to her. To think she had done so much, risked everything, for me!

I sat beside her, patted her on the back, stroked her hair, threw a purely companionable arm around her shoulders, lifted her chin and kissed her a bit to cheer her up, loosened any constricting clothing to prevent a faint. She looked a fright, dark circles under her eyes, and they all red; from crying I concluded. At the time I was so preoccupied with cheering her up that I failed to wonder why I could *see* the color of her eyes when we were sitting in total, pitchy dark.

The occasional sob shook her as we kissed. One devolved into a modest burp. Poor child, she was *terribly* embarrassed. She told me that she'd been so caught up in saving my life that she'd missed her dinner entirely. How guilelessly her eyes shone when she said that; how incandescently they crimsoned.

I told her she'd feel better with something in the old tum. Seeing as how much we'd recently meant to one another, and always the sport, I offered to treat her to a bite.

No need. She helped herself.

You know, I *thought* one of those sweet young things in the 1950s photos of Cowboy Randy Russell looked familiar. Ditto in the sixties. And of course *everyone* looked alike in the seventies, even rhinestone carhops, but still. . . . Drinking buddy indeed. Back there in the dressing room, it was almost as if she'd plopped down from some perch among the rafters. *Traitor,* he'd called her. When someone calls you a traitor, it means you both must have played on the same team before. Suddenly all the pieces came together.

Which would have been just fine if Revelation had struck about ten minutes earlier. Fat lot of good it did me then, with Rubilene's fangs more firmly embedded in my throat than my dear Mums is foxholed into the D.A.R. My brilliant deductions were swept away in the tide of life-memories passing before my eyes. I lost consciousness just as I was weeing in the baptismal font at St. George's Episcopal.

I woke up the next night covered over with a layer of that good ol' Georgia red clay Rubilene hauled around in back of her pick-up for emergencies. I was thirsty; not, I assure you, for another *Cocola*. It was dark, but I was having no problem with night vision. Somewhere in the old mental file cabinet was the spanking new idea that Frequent Flyer had just taken on a whole fresh meaning. Then I saw her anxious face hovering above me.

"You're not mad at me, are you, sugar?" she asked demurely.

What could a gentleman say?

Binks, I married her. Didn't have much choice, did I? And she does love me. It's the crew buns that get 'em, every time, stroke, stroke, stroke. Most of my old crowd developed ingrown previous engagements when the wedding rolled around. They thought I was marrying beneath me, like your wifey's Daddy. Darling Buffy was the first to cut us dead. Ah, if she only knew. There's no saying how much I appreciated you and Whitney attending the ceremony, but I really thought it was in execrable taste for her to pick out that set of *silver* fish-forks as a wedding present. Meow, meow. It's not as if she doesn't know.

Now you do, too.

No, no, no, I won't *hear* of you putting off our date. Rubilene would be utterly crushed. She doesn't handle disappointment at all well. No more do I.

You'll be expecting us seven-ish, then? Good. Mix Bloodies. We'll be there. *A bientôt,* Binks. Hugs to the little woman.

Esther Friesner is the editor of *Blood Muse,* an anthology of vampire stories about the arts, and author of many novels, including *Blood Of Mary, Psalms of Herod, Druid's Blood, The Sherwood Game,* and others.

There are those who know what evils lurk in the night.
There are those who have sworn to guard and hold against the dark.

The Silver Coffin

BY ROBERT BARBOUR JOHNSON

areful, sir!" the old man warned me. "Tread cautiously, for these old stairs are worn away and slippery here. And the tunnel itself is very low and narrow. 'Tis better so, of course, for 'tis less conspicuous. Only a couple of the cemetery men know that it's down here at all, sir, below the other vaults. And neither of them knows where it leads to, nor what lies down here in the old crypt."

He lifted his lantern. I saw a vast stone chamber ahead, the walls dank with moisture and covered with strange lichens that were like a pale leprosy over everything. The silence of death was about us as we stood there.

"Here we are, sir," the old man said. "Here's the spot where I've kept vigil all these years. How've I stood it? 'Tis a question I've often asked myself, sir. But I guess what we must do we'll find the strength to do, hard though it be. And then, ye see, I'm what ye might call *bred* to the thing. 'Twas me father's task before me, and he did it well! It makes a sort of tradition in the family, ye see, legacy we daren't relinquish.

"There's my own son, sir. Paul (he's just turned twenty this year). He'll have to take me place down here in the crypt when I'm too old to carry on. He knows about it already, and he's resigned. But sometimes I can see the shadow of the future on his young face, and it troubles me, sir, troubles me more than I can say. But then he could be worse off, ye know. He'll have a sure job and good wages throughout his life, just as I've had, and all just for watchin' down here at night. In these evil times a man could be much worse off. The Holt trust fund takes care of the pay, guarantees it through all time. And as for a raise—why, bless ye, sir, I could ask for ten times the money I'm getting now, and there'd never be a question. Why don't I, then? Well, it's like I said, sir. I feel that this thing is a duty and not a job. Somehow even talking about more money for doing it seems—ye know, sir, I was about to say 'sacrilege'! Funny, isn't it? For the good Lord knows there's nothing sacred about this business. It savors more of the Other Place, if ye take my meaning!"

The shadows crawled like crippled rats about us.

"Ye see, sir," the croaking voice went on, "there must be always a guard down here. Someone has to watch, night after night, someone who had discretion and patience and courage, if I do say it meself as shouldn't! Those were me father's virtues before me, and I've copied them as best I could. And ye know, sir, a man just wouldn't *last* down here unless he was fairly steady! Ye get the strangest thoughts sometimes in the long hours before dawn, when there's no sound but the drip, drip of moisture from the old arches and that other sound that ye'll be hearing in just a moment, sir, that sound that hasn't ceased in half a century, and that may never cease until Judgment's trumpet sounds to end the horror along with all else.

"You understand, of course, that the Holts aren't just another family. They are the best, if ye know what I mean, sir. They're proud, and they've a right to be proud. They were nobility back in England, sir, and they've been noble folk here, too, since Virginia was still a royal fief. There was General Ebenezer Holt, who fought beside Washington all through the Revolution, and Abijah Holt, him as was with Perry on Lake Erie, and—oh, a lot of others just as distinguished. The Holts are a mighty line, sir. Stiff-necked, some call them, but 'tis their blood that makes them so.

"And so, of course, this stain has to be kept a secret, at all costs.

There's even some of the family that don't know; they have just heard that something queer was amiss. Only the 'Head' of each generation ever comes down in the vault, and then only on occasional inspection tours to be sure that all's well. Young Mr. Gerald Holt—though he's not so young by now, I reckon; time gets away from ye down here—Mr. Gerald had his hair turn gray at the temples the first time he saw the vault! So I guess I've naught to complain of, at that. I'm not touched personally by the thing, ye see. It's only objective horror to me, of course, just as 'twill be only objective to my son when I'm gone. But the horror that waits for each young Holt when he comes of age—why, it turns ye sick just thinking about it, sir!

"Of course, the whole secret has been well kept all these years. The Holts themselves own this cemetery. I'm supposed to be just one of the regular guards. I wear the uniform and I help out a bit at grave-digging and funerals now and then, so that there'll be no suspicion of me. 'Tis generally believed that I'm watching this place because of the silver casket. *That* would be a prize to robbers—now wouldn't it, Sir'?—although of course there's no danger of robbery now. 'Tis for quite a different purpose I watch down here from dusk till dawn, sir—not to keep something out, but to keep something *in*, if ye take my meaning!

◊◊◊

"Ye didn't know about the silver coffin? Why, yes sir! It's the only one ever made, so far's I know. The old man ordered it made himself, in his will. He'd great faith in it, they say. Ye see, silver has always figured strong in the legends about Them, sir. Silver bullets was the only things potent against their unholy lives. And this, sir—this was a silver bullet seven feet long, welded into a solid mass! I've never seen a sight so amazing as that coffin was. I used to raise the pall sometimes at night and look at it. It'd make me feel safer to see that gleaming surface between me and the Horror through long night watches. . . .

"They say, sir, 'twas old Andrew Holt himself who collected the silver that went into it. He was abroad for many years on his smuggling trips, and he picked up a lot of foreign stuff, candlesticks and vases and even silver crucifixes, they say, that he melted down into ingots. But thousands and thousands of silver dollars went into the ingots, too. They found a fortune in metal bricks in the old man's room when he died, hidden under a cloth. That's how they knew the curse was on him, you see—by that and by the will he left, providing for the making of the coffin and for the preparation of this crypt and for the trust fund for perpetual care—which is me now, sir, and which was my father—Old Andrew's butler he was in his youth, you see—and which will be my son who comes after me. And his son, too, I suppose, unless the blight be lifted by then. . . .

"'I shall rest quietly in a silver coffin,' my father told me Old Holt said in his will. 'There will be no need to fear, so long as there be no chink or rift in the metal. I have conned well the lore of these things, and I know. So it is my final prayer that no stake through the heart, no mutilation or ceremonial wounding shall desecrate my body after it be interred. So let my unnatural enduring go on until the taint that is in me shall perish through lack of nourishment for its unholy life. For without the blood there surely must be eventually a death even for the Undying!'

"The Holts carried out his wishes to the letter. They built his vault for him and set my father to watch over him in his silver casket. And the years went by without incident of any kind. Throughout my father's lifetime Old Andrew's grave was just another grave by day; though God alone knows what went on down here during the long night watches. My father's hair turned white long before his time. But he lived to be more than seventy, sir, and died at last peacefully in his bed. The Holts had him buried in their own plot, and put a headstone at his grave that reads: 'Well done, thou good and faithful servant!' I shall sleep there beside him when my turn comes to go, Mr. Gerald tells me, 'for the debt my family owes to you and yours,' he says, 'can never be repaid.'

"He was referring, of course, to that business of a few years ago, when the horror sort of boiled over, you know. And it was me alone that first found out about it. Of course that's my job to watch for just such things. That's why I'm down here in the night. But strangely enough, 'twas not by being on duty in the vault that I learned about it. 'Twas by reading local newspapers at my home uptown, during the day!

"I don't know yet why I should have been so interested in those children and their mysterious 'disease.' Just a presentiment, I suppose. All my life I'd been fearful that such a thing might happen, even though the coffin seemed a safeguard. And after all those long years of safety! But I realized at once the significance of that epidemic that broke out among the poor wretched little brats in the Minsport tenements scarcely a mile away from here. 'Pernicious anemia' the doctors insisted it was. Child after child sickened and wasted away, their little bodies growing each day more pallid and bloodless and wan until finally death ended their sufferings. One—two—three—a dozen of them all taken the same way in so many days, or rather nights, crying out to their parents of queer, wild dreams, complaining of pains in their little throats each morning on awakening from troubled sleep; but dying, sir, slowly dying despite everything that science could do to save them! Wasting away to little cold corpses that were dumped like sacks into the potter's field in this very cemetery.

"God know's how long it had been going on before it came to my notice. But when at last I knew, I went at once to Mr. Gerald with the story. 'It's come at last,' I told him, 'The horror that we've been dreading all these years.' I showed him the items in the papers. 'You recognize the symptoms, sir?' I asked.

"For a moment I thought he was going to faint. It's no joke, sir, seeing a healthy man's face go white as marble and his breath cut off by sheer, overwhelming shock.

"But—but,' he stammered at last, 'it can't be true! It can't be! You've been there watching every night! You would have seen—"

"I shook my head. 'You don't see Them if they will it otherwise, sir!' I told him. 'That's what all the books I've ever read agree on. They come and go like ghosts; only They aren't ghosts, but something far, far worse! The silver in that casket must have cracked, Mr. Gerald. Some flaw has come in it. You'll see!'

"He didn't want to believe me, of course. But I finally persuaded him to go and look at one of the poor little victims laid out for burial in the local morgue. And there could be no doubting the truth then. No doubt at all! Blind or mad the doctors must have been to prate of 'anemia' and to overlook those marks that were so plain on the dead babe's white throat; the swollen livid marks where needle-sharp teeth had pressed home to drain away the life-blood and leave the little form so wasted and thin that it might almost have been some grotesque rag doll that lay there before us on the slab.

"'Nosferatu!' the master muttered as he turned away. 'Nosferatu, the undying! Somehow I never really believed it until now. I've carried out Grandfather's wishes because it was his will that I do so. But my sanity always clung to the hope that it was all only madness of a childish old man, out of his head with the wild tales and superstitions he'd picked up in his Balkan wanderings. I read in his will of the Thing he said had bitten him in the night, had sucked his blood and made him into—well, into what he said he was! But I never really believed.'

"I shook my head sadly. 'Ye'd believe,' I told him, 'if ye could be down here in the vault with me at night, sir—if ye could hear what I've heard and see what I've seen. But until now I believed that no harm could come to anyone, that the casket was proof— but now, don't ye see, sir? We daren't trust it longer. We must act, at once. The Thing gains strength and cunning with each little life it takes. We must lay it once and for all. I know how it's done; I've read the olden rituals for laying them a thousand times over. And I've had all the needful things ready for just such an emergency.'

"But poor Mr. Gerald held back. 'No stake through the heart,' he quoted to me, 'no mutilation or ceremonial wounding shall desecrate my body after it be interred. Our pledge to poor Grandfather has been carried out all these years. Your family as well as mine has served in it. Must all our efforts go for nothing now, just because of one little rift in the coffin? Surely we can find that crack, seal it up—'

"But in time there'd be another, sir,' I reminded him. 'And another. Even the silver is not strong enough to hold against the eternal struggling of that which never dies, which never ceases in its blind efforts to escape and find its unholy nourishment!'

"And then suddenly Mr. Gerald's face lit up. 'Strength!' he gasped. 'That's it! More strength! The silver's potency is unimpaired. All it needs is support, the reinforcement of something harder. Man alive, there are other metals harder than silver nowadays! We've the resources of modern science to pit against this horror out of the past. I tell you, we may yet be able to seal it up for all eternity. Wait and see!'

"The very next day the workmen came, sir, from Bessemer—came with their weird apparatus and their scaffoldings and blow-torches. For days this old vault was lit with hissing blue flame like a spot in Hell, sir, and resounded with such hammering and pounding as quite to drown out—well, whatever other sounds there might have been. And when the men had done their job and gone away again—look, Sir! That's what they left behind!"

He held the lantern high. What was that vast black shape its ray's lit lambently at the vault's far end?—that monstrous gleaming shape on stone trestles? A coffin? But surely it was larger than any coffin ever shaped by the hand of man.

"They tell me it's a new alloy they use for battleships, Sir!" the old man said proudly. "An outer casting of stainless steel welded solidly to the silver coffin itself. Soldered, the outer and the inner layers, so that the magic power of the white metal, whatever queer potency it has to hold evil at bay, will be eternally supported by the strongest steel on earth! I doubt that a bolt of lightning could so much as dent that shining surface, sir. Seamless and airtight, it'll endure a thousand years, even with what still struggled inside it.

"Yes, sir! I heard it too, sir. Of course I heard it. 'Tis no novelty to me, ye know. All these long dragging years I've been hearing it, down here in the night's hush. But I was wondering when *you'd* first notice it, sir. 'Tis plain enough when your attention is called to it, for all 'tis so muffled it might be coming from miles off. But it's right here in the crypt with us, that sound, only filtered through the silver and the steel.

"There's really nothing at all human about it, is there, sir? It might be the howling of a wolf, or almost anything savage and bestial. And yet sometimes there's such a note of human misery and despair in it as to fair bring tears to your eyes, sir. Only tonight there's more of menace in it somehow, sir, more than I've, ever heard in all these years. You know, sir, I'm wondering if—good God, sir! Look! Look there!

"The coffin! It moved! I know ye think me mad—that thing weighs a score of tons. Your strength and mine united could not as much as tip it. And yet I saw it move a bit. There! Again! Ye see, sir? 'Tis not just the wavering of the lantern light. Can't ye feel the vibrations of it in the very walls about us, in the stones about us as it shakes? Oh God, sir! It's all my fault. I should never fetched ye down here. I never thought—it's your blood, of course, that maddens him—the smell of your blood! He's used to mine, from all these years familiarity. But you, young and strong—he'd burst himself to bits to get at you, sir. All these long years he's had no slaking for his hideous thirst. He's dying, sir, of a starvation so slow and so hideous it don't bear even thinking about. And now, fresh blood . . . your blood. . . .

"No, sir, we daren't flee from him. There's no running from things quicker than light, swifter than an adder's pounce. We must fight him, sir! Here, take this. I know 'tis but an aspen stake, well sharpened, but a better weapon ye'll find it than any gun against what no gun could ever hit, sir! And here! Wind this string of garlic about your throat. Now stand, sir, and we'll defy him together. We'll fight all Hell, if need be. . . . Oh heavens, sir! how that coffin does shake! How it rocks and lurches on its stone trestles! All those tons of weight quivering like a jelly—I tell you, sir, I never saw the like of it before. The blind fury and malignity—can he break out? Oh, God, sir! I don't know! I don't know! I never saw him like this before. We can only pray. . . .

"Crash! And that awful sound of rocks splintering to powder, those clouds of dust arising to choke us—that was the coffin falling, sir. I saw it teetering just at the very edge of the trestles. Then it toppled—but now you can't see anything, sir, not even your hand before your eyes! And this dust gets in a man's nostrils, cuts off his breath. And all the while that howling and screeching rises to a very devil's paean of triumph in our ears. Stand firm, sir! Pray to whatever God ye believe in, and be ready. We've our stakes here, and we'll strike with them at the heart of anything we see in the dust-cloud—the evil heart that only an aspen stake can pierce; that an aspen stake should have pierced long ago. We'll defy him together. D'ye hear. Hell-thing that was once old Andrew Holt! *We defy ye.* . . .

"Take it easy, sir. Don't try to get up yet. Just rest there for a moment. I guess ye must have fainted, sir. I caught ye as ye fell!

"Ye must forgive an old man's nerves, sir! It's these long years of solitude and long night vigils. I'm not the man I was once, and the shock of the thing—but of course there never was any actual *danger!* How could there he? Did I not say that nothing could possibly damage that coffin, sir? See, there it lies, still there on the floor's cracked old slabs, safe and sound, for all its battering; though the Lord knows how we'll ever get it back on those trestles, sir. It may be that it will have to stay always half propped like that, for I doubt that twenty men could lift it. Sure, the struggle with it exhausted even him, sir. There's been no sound from him, no movement since that last frenzied effort. I wonder, sir. . . . Of course there must be natural laws governing these things, just as governs ourselves, sir. And too much effort may be—well, fatal to them, as to us!

"Perhaps ye've seen the last dying struggle of That which should never have lived at all, sir. Perhaps ye've seen peace come at last to the soul of old Andrew Holt!

"And if not now, surely it must come at last, sir, mayhap not in my time, or even in my son's time. But in the end—steady, sir. We'll go this way."

He helped me stagger toward the old stairs, through the leprous dark.

Robert Barbour Johnson wrote a handful of memorable stories for *Weird Tales* in the 1930s and 1940s.

What happens when a modern vampire decides to challenge the
grandfather of all vampires himself—Dracula?

Like a Pilgrim to the Shrine

BY BRIAN HODGE

he end of the road took him to central Florida. Flat
lands, this state, like one vast sandbar. Where Kraeken
would, ironically enough, find his mountain.

He had spent the past weeks in leisurely travel, for if there was
anything he possessed, it was time. And mountains stood until
time immemorial, did they not? No rush to reach St. Petersburg,
then. He'd known this when the journey was but a flicker in his
mind.

His swath through the states of the southlands had been bold
and rich. Beneath heavy moon and humid mists, those most
ephemeral of cloaks, Kraeken indulged appetites great and small.
Forever the outsider, he stood alone like something the locals of
every town feared would arrive someday, inevitably. Generations
of suspicion given someone to dread, one glimpse of him ample
incentive, even the blind could tell he was alien.

Not from around *here,* are you, boy?

They had *no* idea. He rarely bothered to answer. The sight of
him alone was evidence enough.

This evening burned as only a Gulf Coast night could, mid-summer dreams on the wind slapping the fronds of palms. Hot gusts drew first sweat, the taste of salt in the air. A night to be felt in every singing nerve, every inch of skin, wonderfully sticky to the touch. In every corpuscle taken from another and given fresh vitality in his own veins.

Booted foot heavy on the gas, Florida two-lane as level as an outback highway, simmering asphalt, shimmer in the night. Lesser creatures skulked at roadside, twin red flickers of eyes jailed by weeds, snared by headlights for a moment's spell, then turning tail for safer ground. Four-legged wisdom was always true.

These weeks on the road, Kraeken had dined neatly for too long. Heavy sport beckoned, an eager compulsion. With St. Pete dead ahead, a few more miles, it was about time.

He wheeled in at the first buzz of cheap neon. Some bar, the name irrelevant, dusty beer lights in the window, glass tubes humming red and blue, orange and green, yellow. Fishermen would drink here while the catch of the day rotted in the backs of their trucks. Weekend sailors would come here to mourn boats repossessed by their banks. If Hemingway had made it only this far, instead of to Key West, he would have killed himself years earlier.

Kraeken liked it fine. Entered, and heads turned. He could always count on that.

Six-six, but the boots added more. Leather slacks, black, like a second skin he had yet to shed. For summer in the south, a simple T-shirt, gray, sleeves gone. Glossy dark hair, long now, sometimes in a ponytail other times drawn back from his heavy forehead into a topknot. Skull occasionally shaved, when the mood struck. He moved with the resolve of a barbarian prince, and was every bit as solid.

The bar stool groaned with his weight, and Kraeken leaned on one elbow. Read the permanent graffiti etched into the bar's wood, scars left over the ages by random metal musings. Knives, forks, and fishhooks, leaving behind names and initials, declarations of love and futility. Small, sad efforts at immortality. There were no more caves, nor pyramids, just these dark temples of cirrhosis, and supplicants who offered their own organs in sacrifice.

"What'll you have?" asked the bartender. Wary eyes, one hand beneath the bar, and Kraeken figured—not without amusement—that the hidden hand gripped a shotgun. He frequently had that effect on strangers, particularly at night.

"Jack Daniels."

Three shots down while the bartender was still there, then a twenty slapped faceup enticed him to leave the bottle, and Kraeken nursed. Spun slowly around, long legs extended as he stopped, braced, watched a couple games of pool underway. Furtive faces along the sidelines, less than half the booths occupied.

Ten minutes, no more; after the livelier of the games ended, boot heels thudded toward the bar. Southern fried redneck, resident badass, local since the day of his birth; every bar was home to at least one. Kraeken had already guessed which muddy truck in the lot was his.

He idled in near Kraeken, closer than he needed to be while getting his next beer. Smelled of sweat and wasted days, not blinking, looking Kraeken over with bored distaste, and he was a sizable lad himself.

The redneck cocked one eye down at Kraeken's right thumb. The nail was cultivated an inch and a half beyond the tip.

"That's real cute, sweetheart. You paint that thing?" He had the smirk down perfect, years of practice with few who rose to the challenge, fewer still who walked away with dignity and teeth intact.

"No." Kraeken didn't even bother looking at him. Not yet. Not yet. "That's not what it's for."

"Then how's about you telling me what it is for." Grinning.

"It's to hear questions from people whose brains are tinier than their balls." And Kraeken smiled.

The redneck blinked, then bristled. Feral temperament, each impulse near the surface at every hour of the day. He slid his tongue between upper teeth and gumline, sucked his teeth a moment, then grinned cold and hard. "We gonna tango out in that lot, looks like, ain't we?"

"I've got some drinking to do first."

The redneck considered this, and with the better part of a longneck in his fist, apparently decided the notion had merit. Not that he was forgetting an insult, though, hell no.

Oh, Kraeken could have explained about his thumb, but what

would have been the use? This hyperpituitary lout would appreciate no culture which did not include Merle Haggard. Kraeken could have told him that, in Northern Australia, there was a tribe called the Tiwi, whose men grew long thumbnails on their dominant hand. Filed them sharp, honed them as tough and thick as a bear claw, and used them as weapons, and tools. The Tiwi needed to carry no knives to gut their fish, ever.

Kraeken could have expanded his mind in so many ways. But . . . pearls before swine. For one who possessed so very much time, he was oddly reticent about wasting it.

This nameless foe eventually thudded back toward a short, angled hallway. Bottle of Jack Daniels in one fist, Kraeken watched his back until he disappeared around the corner. By now, they were no longer the focus of even peripheral attention, dismissed as a pair of drunken blowhards, bolstered enough to make threats aplenty and too far gone to put them to the test. Kraeken had to admit that, as drama, they had grown quite boring.

He set the bottle on the bar. Gave the redneck ten more seconds, then followed his path to the bathrooms, which sat side by side with adjacent doors, the men's peeling strips of paint.

Kraeken passed the men's room, shoved open the door to the women's. The hook-and-eye lock bent and popped like lead, as the sole occupant turned her head toward him in surprise, then a finely contained fury. Brassy and overpainted, she had the hard look of a career waitress someplace where tips came too few, too small, too far between. She opened her mouth to verbally lash him, tongue and temper sharpened by years of experience with clods of every kind—

She suddenly paled, and shut her mouth. He frequently had that effect, too.

"Leave," said Kraeken, his whisper as harsh as a cancerous throat. She hoisted her panties and did so without so much as a peep of argument.

Kraeken stood before the wall shared with the men's room. Focused upon it, within it, beyond it. Senses assailed, as tender and receptive as flayed nerves. Scenting the odor of sweat through the wall, and urine, while Kraeken shut his eyes, found his center—

And drove one arm through the wall, following with the other a moment later, like tree limbs hurled into a house by hurricane winds. His fingers sprang open on the other side, grappling to enclose redneck head and redneck shoulders, yanking back again. The wall between his arms imploded with an avalanche of mildewed plaster; wide-eyed redneck face newly materializing, sputtering dirty white dust and sudden sweat.

Kraeken hauled him through another foot, dragging his chest atop the urinal, one hand clamped around his throat to choke off feeble cries. Then turned him, wedged in the hole like a stillborn breach-birth, until he stared at the ceiling, while on the other side of the wall his legs kicked in empty air.

As the redneck gaped, tried to cough, Kraeken raised his right fist, as if offering a thumbs-up of enthusiasm. Turning thumb down then, slowly, an emperor of pagan Rome dispensing the worst of all news in the arena.

Jabbing down with his thumbnail, into jugular and carotid. Freeing his thumb, he held back a moment while a few frenzied heartbeats sent crimson up onto the wall. Redneck indeed. Such aesthetic severity to arterial spray, like an abstract painting. He had found that no two were ever quite the same.

Kraeken lowered, drank his fill in great gulping draughts, and soon there was no need to hold the man in place. Going limp, boneless in the gap, balanced on the ruined wall between male and female until he was empty of everything but potential decay.

Kraeken left him there, pale and still. Such decadent luxury after these past weeks, so many hasty burials at roadsides, in backyards, on quiet hillsides with no traffic for miles, only the moon and its patient grave watch.

Now, finally, he could start leaving a trail.

He shut the ladies' room door behind him, covered the barroom floor in unhurried strides. Out the door and to his car. Following the call back to the highway, the whiplash of tires and gasoline like a mainlined drug.

Kraeken popped a new tape into the player and turned it for maximum decibels. He loved Spike Jones. Such madcap absurdity.

Such apt commentary on his life.

He left them in his wake through St. Petersburg, left them as they died in that moment when they surrendered their veins and arteries for the enrichment of his own. Left them in poses of languid grace, or the aftermath of ignoble frenzy. In their homes, or darkened alleys, or cars on midnight lots where new lovers became acquainted.

Left them empty. It quickly became, of course, a matter of public concern.

After nearly a week in town he staged his most exhilarating tableau yet. Her name was Emily, of sun-drenched hair and a scent of cocoa butter lingering from earlier beach worship. They had talked, they had danced, she had found him reeking of danger and, therefore, irresistible. She told all. Wine was not even needed for such honesty, though she had poured it liberally nonetheless.

Walking downtown, then, later than late, while she clung to Kraeken's hard arm, it came off her in waves: the secret fear she masked so well with flippancy, unseen by all but the most observant; a fear not of what this giant stranger might do to her tonight, but of whether he would still be in her life tomorrow. Kraeken could smell it, deciphering every impulse of neuron and synapse. It was not pity he felt, precisely more an aching sorrow for her fragile secrets. And perhaps pride in his being the instrument of her deliverance.

They embraced in the shadows of downtown's tallest building, Emily enfolded by his arms, and she gave only the tiniest cry of surprise when they began to rise. He, now weightless, she borne aloft by minimal effort. One moment concrete under her feet, the next air, soft night Gulf winds whipping around their bodies as downtown shrank beneath them. Kraeken kept his eyes shut the entire time—he found it easier this way. Levitation was all very Zen-like, a calm picture in the mind, no questioning, merely a deep resolve to simply accept, and be weightless, and let his breed's defiance of natural law do the rest.

They lit upon the office tower's roof as she clung to him with a trembling mixture of anticipations, the delight and the dread;

never had she been so aware of her mortality, and never would it seem more miraculous. St. Petersburg spread before them like a promised land . . . boulevards leading toward clusters of lights, lives he might one day pilfer; palms that once towered now reduced to twigs. Seductively beautiful by night, as those daytime kingdoms must have appeared to a tempted Christ atop the mountain. *All these will I give to you if you but fall down and worship me.* He could give them to her, and in that final moment when she knew what he was, Kraeken knew Emily would accept, and gladly.

But no, not tonight.

He took her quickly, wholly, and kept her sufferings to a minimum. He never hated them. Except for the obnoxious ones, like the redneck a few miles north of the city several nights ago, his kind chosen more for their irritation value, and a desire for cat-and-mouse torments. And perhaps a twisted sense of benevolence; maybe Kraeken was doing the rest of humanity a favor by weeding these from their numbers.

Kraeken lifted his lips from Emily's punctured throat. Popped his thumb into his mouth to cleanse it, nail and all. Kneeling beneath a sky of rolling clouds, so black, so gray, so deeply purple it felt like a night of royalty. How very appropriate that was. For what was this episode all about, if not a final call into the night, the greatest summons he had yet issued. To royalty.

A summons at last answered.

One moment Kraeken was alone with the still body, the next he was not. Feeling the arrival but not the approach. Rising, turning with a faint smile on lips still salty.

Should he have felt a sense of awe, gazing for the first time upon this forefather of sorts? It wasn't there, though neither was there animosity. The name of Dracula was, in most circles, not without enormous respect. Among Kraeken's generation, though, it sometimes came with a measure of disdain. He remained undecided.

"Ah *hah*," said Kraeken, appraising. "The mountain has come to Mohammed."

The sight of him was humble enough, which was heartening and disappointing by turns. Tall and thin, with white hair in wisps, longish and unkempt. When a breeze flipped it clear of his forehead, Kraeken saw that the old scar had reappeared, inflicted by a bludgeoning shovel a century ago while Dracula had lain in a box of earth, the sleep of the dead.

The Count blended well down here. He might have been any vaguely aristocratic retiree in good health, come to spend his final days beside an ocean and guaranteed of warm weather.

"You've been extending invitations to me all week, haven't you?" Dracula said. "Leaving signs that I had company come to town."

Kraeken smiled, spread arms wide, a stage bow. "Anybody can knock on a fucking door."

Dracula strolled closer, looking as if he should occupy an office in this building rather than tread across its roof. A lightweight gray suit, silk tie. He knelt beside the last of Emily, took hold of her limp jaw, tilting her head one way, then another. Gazing down on her pale lovely repose.

"Mercy, you showed to this one. How unlike you, if the news accounts are to be believed." He stood. "You're crude. You're ill-mannered. You have the subtle finesse of a bull elephant."

"To mine own self be true," and Kraeken winked.

Dracula rose, nudged the dead girl aside with one foot. Left her forgotten. "What is it you want?"

"Why, I'm on a pilgrimage. To visit my elder," Kraeken said simply. Walking toward roof's edge while Dracula followed, never closer, merely equidistant. "St. Petersburg," and Kraeken laughed into the night, in the face of the city. "Who'd've thought you'd end up here? This city's been called 'God's waiting room,' but I suppose you've heard that one."

"I have. But know this: I never *end up* anyplace. I make it my own for a time, and I move on."

Kraeken was still laughing. "Not long ago St. Pete won an award for per capita prune consumption. Now there's something to be proud of, isn't there?"

"I enjoy the change of pace. You would do well to pace yourself."

Kraeken shrugged, still feeling this mystifying surprise, learning that rumors were true. While their kind were frequently territorial, and therefore never truly trusting of those not known, they were also a bunch of incorrigible gossips. Blame it on their numbers, so small when compared to those of the herd through which they walked and on whom they fed, like some elite clique of eternal life. Gossip seemed almost beneath them, but from more that one source Kraeken had heard rumors that this Count of legend was now spending his days in St. Petersburg, in quiet solitude. That fact alone, but never the why.

Kraeken had finally decided to see for himself.

"I'll ask you again: What do you want?"

Kraeken ignored it, closing the gap between them. Dracula? He looked like an old man, and this he was, certainly, though he had easy means to conceal it. For the blood was the life, and he had but to partake to turn back the effects of clock and calendar.

"How long's it been since you fed?" Kraeken asked.

"Three years."

"Unbelievable." Kraeken shook his head. "What do I want? I'd think that's obvious."

Dracula leaned forward, old man's testy snarl beneath his downturned white mustache: "Enlighten me."

Kraeken spun away for a moment, found a ventilation duct and hopped atop it, boots connecting with a resounding gong of sheet metal. A burst of pigeons showered into the night, panicked from sleep, wings like the snap of tiny sails, and he squatted as if before a fire.

"You were a dark prince, once," Kraeken said. "You sat on a throne like none other. If the legends and stories from those days are even half true, one mention of your name and entire villages would slam their doors and shutters closed and drop to their knees in prayer. Your presence could poison entire communities." Rising, then with one sweep of his arm: St. Petersburg, behold. With a look of puzzled disappointment on his face. "Prunes?"

Dracula said nothing.

"Once a prince," Kraeken went on, "now a king, I'd think. A king yet to be crowned. Our kind? We're not isolated from each other anymore, like some say we used to be. We can cross the world in a day. Not like when you were spending weeks dragging boxes of earth across Europe. We meet often now, our paths cross

Like a Pilgrim to the Shrine

all the time . . after a year, two, five, ten. But we need a king, some think. Not to rule us. More like . . . a figurehead."

"And how many of our kind are there, across the globe? Seven thousand, eight?"

"About that."

Dracula spat upon the roof. So many seasons since feeding, it was amazing he had the moisture. "As a mortal I was the boyar of a warrior nation. Armies under my command, tens of thousands, the scourge of eastern Europe. Of what use to me is the kingship of a nation with such paltry numbers? A nation without even a land to call its own."

"You're forgetting something: That each of us is a king among mortals." Kraeken hopped down from the duct housing. "They might claim to hate us, or fear us, if they're even aware of us at all . . . but we've cheated death. And because of that, they envy the hell out of us. Whether they like it or not, in their eyes that makes us kings. Every last one of us. And you, then . . ."

"A king of kings." Dracula scowled. "It's been done."

Kraeken shrugged easily, conceding the point. "But a couple thousand years ago. And a *very* different kingdom."

Anachronism or not, what savage joy it would have been to have hunted with the Count in his prime, centuries past. In a simpler world, where the fulfillment of superstition could give birth to timeless legend. Where reigns of terror long ended would yet live on through the ages, passed down among generations of survivors. To have inspired such whispered tales of dread would have been sport at its grandest, and Kraeken lamented that such an era was past, to be forever denied him. For there was more than one manner of immortality.

Dracula smiled, stroking his mustache. "I was born of an age when kingdoms were meant to be taken. So why not you? You're brash enough, you have ambition enough. Why not take this throne for your own?"

Kraeken grinned. It was a cold, cold sight that sent mortals backing away a step or two. Here, though, he was an equal; it was a refreshing change, actually.

"Fight you for it," Kraeken said.

"It's not something I desire. I have no use for it."

"Our legend, then. Our heritage. Who do *those* belong to? Look at it that way." Kraeken walked over to the edge of the roof, swept an arm the width of horizons. Encompassing the lights of this city, those of Tampa, miles distant across the bay. "You and I, we're the same, but we're so different, too. You know? Like any predator, our kind has evolved just so we'll have an easier time surviving, and blending in. Garlic sends you running. Me? I love the stuff. The power of the cross still holds you, but to my generation its symbolism is impotent. You have to hide your fangs; we don't even have them. So we improvise." He held up his thumb. "And you. You can't even eat normal food and drink just for the pleasure of it. We can." He smiled, thinking of an earlier trip south. "Once I spent a week in New Orleans with this little roving pack. Three of them; they tool around in a black van like it's a twenty-four hour party. And they're beautiful . . . the most hedonistic, gluttonous little fuckers you can imagine. *They love this life.* Because they didn't have to give up a thing. They have it all now."

How was Dracula feeling, hearing that, Kraeken wondered. Did he feel the patriarch's pride? Or the sting of time's arrows, shot while he wasn't looking and sunk deep while world-weariness had him down already?

The sweep of Kraeken's arm, again: the night, the city, the world beyond. "So let me put it to you this way. Who does it all belong to now? To the living past? Or to the present?"

"So, this fight of yours, it's a battle of ideals, then, is it not?" Dracula smiled, thin and cunning. Fox and wolf. "Make sure you understand what you're involving yourself with. I was playing chess with lives centuries before your grandparents were even born. I have tricks you've never dreamed of."

"Who needs dreams when you live the real thing?" Kraeken winked. "Besides, I'm not interested in fighting you physically. I want to fight your soul."

Dracula drew back in mild surprise. "Then here it is, these are my terms: Three nights from now we'll again meet here. In the time between then and now, each of us will enact within this city a tableau he feels best exemplifies the extreme of his aesthetic. Whoever creates the greater public outcry, he is the victor."

"That's it?"

Dracula raised a hand, one finger pointing. *"Without* the taking of a single life. You say anyone can knock on a door? I say anyone can butcher. I know your skill there, but this is not about the amassing of the bigger pile of corpses."

Kraeken nodded. Reached beneath his T-shirt and pulled out a cross, dangling from the end of a chain. Held it out toward his elder and watched him take a reflexive step back, with furrowed eyebrows and clenched jaw. *"Boo!"* said Kraeken, and laughed.

◊◊◊

Kraeken was still an adolescent, really, early into the teen years since that night of his rebirth from mortal into something beyond. His first birth by womb had been in the mid-fifties, far west of here; he had grown up in everyday sight of the Rockies.

Second birth in New York City, another world away. Early 1978 and he had months before wandered east, where culture would not stultify. Days and nights of recreational haze gone hardcore, much more of this needlework and he would become an addict. Kraeken and his shell of leather and black jeans, CBGB's for music, relying on the kindness of strangers he called friends for a bed or floor or sofa on which to spend the night. Swimming the currents of the underbelly, with others of similar mind and similar clothes, like uniforms of sullen despair. Bones were prominent through skin and clothing; none of them ate well. None of them planned on surviving to twenty-five, anyway, so what was the use. . . .

And then arrived the night when he thought he was going to make the grand departure with a two year margin. Heroin in his veins and a mouth at his throat; he remembered her little knives more clearly than her face; remembered her flowing wrist at his own lips rather than her name. She had a room at the Chelsea Hotel, where months later, Sid Vicious would stab Nancy Spungeon, his soul mate in damnation. And there Kraeken was left behind while his dark angel winged elsewhere with her bloody mouth. Kraeken, spent and abandoned, a near-empty shell curled on the bathroom floor.

Metamorphosing.

February 2, 1978. Forever frozen at the age of twenty-three. And while there were worse fates than had befallen him in a landmark hotel gone to seed, none could have fostered any greater shift of outlook. The nihilist marches resolutely forward into oblivion, and Kraeken had spent many a mortal night contemplating his exit from life; the sweet release when brain waves flattened.

Darkness? Oh, this he knew on first thirsty realization of what he had become. Not because of its predator's ethic, but because, for the very first time, the true concept of time without end had opened up before him. A tunnel with no light whatsoever at its end, and too late to turn back. It was a nihilist's worst nightmare, or greatest salvation. Because it forced one to uncover the meaning of his existence. Or to invent one before he went mad.

Time could do that to you.

◊◊◊

Had to give the old Count his due, and Kraeken was glad to do it. By the next morning, St. Petersburg was abuzz within ever-growing circles. Word of mouth at first, such scandal, and Kraeken had no doubt at all but that this was the handiwork of Dracula.

As Kraeken understood it, a parishioner entered a Catholic sanctuary for afternoon confession. The desecration she found was carnal, and ongoing. Middle-aged priest and a trio of nuns, though their office could not be told by appearance. Robes and collar and habits had been cast aside, along with celibate inhibitions. They lay tangled together in eroto-geometric configuration at the base of the pulpit, coupling enthusiastically, though oddly devoid of passion, as if under some sort of mind control. . . .

While the censer spewed jasmine smoke.

Nice touch. Bravo, bravo.

Try as it might, even the power of the Roman Catholic Church could not keep such a scandal hushed. Polite society was eager to be appalled, and had its chance within hours. Rumor and innuendo spread quickly. As Kraeken watched the abbreviated, PG-13 coverage on a local news station in his hotel room, he smiled broadly, applauded, and toasted the television with a bottle of claret.

Dracula had done well. Repercussions of this would no doubt ripple for months, perhaps all the way to Rome. Catholics took this sort of thing very seriously. A pity that neither of them would be privy to the Church's investigation to come. Well done.

Of course, the city had seen nothing yet.

◊◊◊

On the southeastern rim of St. Petersburg, directly on the edge of Tampa Bay, sits the Salvador Dali Museum. A clean white building, like a warehouse renovated into upscale status. Kraeken had visited there shortly after his arrival in St. Pete, days before Dracula had answered his late-night summons. Had spent hours wandering its main gallery, home to more than a hundred of the surrealist master's originals. Paintings, sculptures, sketches, even a revolving hologram of Alice Cooper holding a sectioned Venus.

Now *here* was a refuge he could truly appreciate. Dali had raised absurdity to the level of genius. Kraeken had known he would return here from the moment Dracula had spoken his terms. This museum called to him like no other corner of the city.

At the far end of the main gallery, the floor receded into what was called the Master's Pit, home to five of Dali's seventeen masterworks. One end was dominated by a piece of epic scale, oil on canvas sized thirteen feet by nine-and-a-half. It went by two names, but Kraeken preferred *The Dream of Christopher Columbus*. A flowing, two-story collage of imagery to commemorate the discovery of a New World, redolent with trappings of the holy sanctity of the voyage. Sailing ship and pontiff and celestial figures, and pious monks hoisting crosses and halberds. An amazing number of crosses scaling the heights of the canvas and the dream.

Kraeken was truly inspired.

And here he was found when the museum opened for visitors his second morning after having met the Count, here for all to see. Kraeken's was a tableau of surrealism that even the master painter might have appreciated. The night's guards stripped naked, then curled beneath the painting wearing only loose cloth about their waists, pudgy, like old depraved cherubs. They had been bled unconscious from neck wounds, though not to the point of death; while Dracula had said no killing, he had never prohibited feeding.

Kraeken floated above the guards in the still, eerie silence of levitation, naked but for a loincloth, arms stretched wide in cruciform pose scant centimeters from the tallest crosses on the canvas. Long barbaric hair loose about his shoulders as his head slumped toward chest. Crowned not with thorns, but a laurel woven of dollar bills.

Here he stayed, motionless, without so much as a breath to betray his sentience, while the gallery swelled with ranks of the horrified, the fascinated, the official. Hung in the air while the night guards were wheeled away on gurneys, while day guards and police and museum officials conferred on what was to be done about that last one up there, and what was holding him up, anyway?

Kraeken waited until, through slitted eyes, he spied the ladder brought in by custodians. He raised his eyes skyward, then, to the renewed ripple of conversation in the gallery. And gently, so very gently, drifted on a diagonal path down to the floor in grand descension. Trying not to laugh, looking no one in the eye while he calmly walked past uniforms and suits, while, indeed, they parted to make a path for him on his way out the doors to disappear into the bay.

He knew no one would dare get in his way.

The demonic and the divine were remarkably similar, at least in that respect.

◊◊◊

They met again, a rooftop union under the cover of moonlight. Beings who could walk by day but felt far more at home by night. A city sprawled beneath them, aflame in the hearts of its residents, from bayside to gulfside, no two with quite the same view of the absolute *strangeness* of these past days. Murders and madness, and above all, visions. Mortal reactions ran the gamut below; if Kraeken listened very, very closely, he could hear the prayers born of abject terror, as well as those of rapture. It all depended on perspective.

Such fuss.

Kraeken watched as Dracula folded his hands together over his jacket, gazing east. The thoughts of his centuries locked away with no hope of pilfering, his mind a strongbox; what an enigma the Count was. Venerated by history as a devil, delicious and despicable by turns, yet a devil whose time had all but passed him by.

"Do you realize," Dracula said, "that for this same vantage point, three hundred years ago, we would have stood atop a church? A century and a half ago, a capitol building? Now, tonight, look where we are." His eyes, gazing downward, upon this tower of commerce. "They always build tallest what they value most."

To look into his eyes was to see a petulant pride, held quiet by the dignity of ages. Dracula knew he had been bested, knew that Kraeken understood as well. There was no need for concession of defeat, and this Kraeken preferred over maudlin admission, by far.

The years of Dracula's retreat from the ways of predators had been but a few ticks of the clock to one who would live forever; a moment's pause for reflection before resuming old ways. But no more, Kraeken sensed; their encounter had changed everything.

Dracula had been mired in Victorian thinking; perhaps, now, truly realizing it for the first time. Oh, his corruption of the brother and sisters of the Church had been total, and it had been grand entertainment. But in a world where faith had shifted so far afield to other things—the domes of State, the towers of commerce—too few viewed his act of corruption with sensibilities truly aghast. It was more fodder for amusement.

As public outcry went, Kraeken had won hands down. The drinker of blood as savior, coming down from his painted cross in a temple where art and commerce had become indivisible. The pride within was total, because Kraeken had been ambiguous enough to make sure witnesses had ample room for silly interpretations. Because no one knew precisely just what they had seen.

The aftermath of Dracula's scenario might well reach Rome . . . but Kraeken bet he himself could return to St. Pete, six months from now, and find cults had sprung up in his honor.

Although by then they would have remade him over in whatever image they liked best.

Maybe he would oblige them. Then again, maybe not.

"I suppose I should confess," said Kraeken. "Me, tooling down here looking for you?" He shook his head. "I was never looking for a king. It was never about looking for a figurehead."

"You think I don't know that? Maybe certain things *do* hold a power over me that have no effect on you . . . but foolishness is not one of them." Dracula turned from the edge of the roof and paced toward the center, as Kraeken followed. "Although I was unable to fathom your true motives."

Kraeken turned his palms up—simplicity. "They're not that complicated."

"Then out with them. You travel down here like an upstart brat; you cause more turmoil here in one week than I have caused in three years. . . . You owe me an explanation, at the very least."

Kraeken supposed he did. He had never been conscious of withholding the truth for its own sake. He'd thought his lies were designed to light a fire under the Count, but now wasn't so sure. Perhaps, all along, he had simply wished to avoid the appearance of weakness.

"I just wanted to know," said Kraeken, looking at the city— God's waiting room— "if *this* was all I had to look forward to in a few hundred years. I . . . just had to know."

"And did you expect me to actually answer that?"

"No. Not you. But I expected something to."

Dracula reached up to smooth the thick mustache; his eyes, under white brows, were piercing. "Answer me something. I know what the younger of our kind frequently say of me. Those I have never met, those I never will, those who know of me only through rumor and legend. I *know* how they think of me, and of those older than I. They despise me for the Achilles' heels that afflict me but have no effect on them. They think me frozen in time. They picture me in drab European fashion from a century past, and think I still dress that way, and the very notion makes them sick. So answer me this: Why not you? You look the part of impudence as extreme as any of them. Why did you come seeking answers, instead of contenting yourself with derision from afar?"

"Twelve, thirteen years ago, that *was* how I felt. I'd've been tempted to tear into *your* throat, just to see if I could." Kraeken reached down to the roof, picked up a fraying palm frond, blown here and left to rot. He began stripping it to the stalk. "But it was just a phase. I outgrew it. I've outgrown others. Mostly because . . . I wondered how our kind will evolve by the time I've been around as long as you have now. And how the young ones will see me. If they'll even know my name. Or, worse, if they will . . . and have no use for me at all."

The palm frond was in strips of litter, and he pitched the stalk aside. "I just want to know what to expect."

But when he turned from momentary reverie, Dracula was gone. Kraeken hadn't even felt him leave. Seconds later, though, the Count stepped from the shadows of a utility stairwell doorway. Something held in his hands, like a folded flag.

"Our heritage, you spoke of? Our legacy?" said Dracula. "By our terms, this is yours. You won it. So take it."

Kraeken unfolded the gift, found it to be an exquisite silken cape, black, with lining of vermilion. It smelled of decades; not unpleasant.

He pushed it back. "I can't wear this. I'd look like an idiot."

Dracula would not accept its return. "Nor have I worn it since I can remember. Who says *you* have to? You won it by terms to which you agreed. Now have at least the honor to take it."

So Kraeken did. Folded it once more, draped it over one arm. What he would do with the thing he had no idea. What it represented he had but the barest inkling, some benign link to an age he had never known, never would know.

"There are no answers, are there?" Kraeken said, finally

"No answers. None that I've found. Only our existence." Absently, Dracula ran the tip of his thumb over his teeth. Sharp, with the elongated canines on either side. No wonder he spoke so stiff of jaw: age-old habit of trying to conceal his teeth. "Just as mortals build tallest what they value highest, I've found that societies have the most names for what is most important to them. The Penan tribe of Borneo has forty words for the sago palm. Eskimos have nearly that for ice. Are *we* a society, too,

Kraeken? Our kind? I don't know, anymore. Because, still, we have only one word for blood."

And with a clumsy warmth Kraeken would never have believed could have resided within the Count, he lay a tentative hand upon Kraeken's shoulder. A cold touch, like ice on this midsummer Florida night; there, then lifted.

Without another word, Dracula walked to the edge of the building . . . and did not stop. There one instant, the next on a silent plummet. Kraeken followed his path, stood at the edge, looking after him. The sheer wall of glass and steel planed down like the vanishing point of a desert highway. Late night traffic, so far below, and pedestrians, everything so tiny . . . and wholly undisturbed.

Kraeken turned away. Alone.

He decided to take the stairs down to the street, for once.

A half hour later he was in his car, having vacated his hotel in the middle of the night. These were prime driving hours, not to be wasted. So few cars on the road to get in his way, and the stereo always sounded clearer after midnight.

South out of St. Pete. Surely he could make the Everglades in time for sunrise.

He grudgingly paid his toll to get onto the Skyway Bridge, ten miles of spired architectural marvel that curved southeast back to the mainland. Somewhere in the middle, Kraeken cocked one arm out of the car to send the musty old cape fluttering over the side, to waft down to the sea. Was it Gulf? Or was it Bay?

He pondered this while plucking Spike Jones from the tape player and opting for something new. An old standard, "I Did It My Way."

Not the Sinatra version, though. He found the remake infinitely preferable

Sid Vicious, naturally.

Brian Hodge is the author of six novels, including *The Darker Saints*, *Nightlife*, and *Prototype*, and two collections of his short stories, *The Convulsion Factory* and *Falling Idols*.

There are some dangers that transcend all prejudices,
all lines—both North and South.

The Cursed Damozel

BY MANLY WADE WELLMAN

asn't Shiloh supposed to be named after an angel or a devil? Angels and devils were both there, sorting the two armies through for who should live and who die, who go to heaven and who go to hell. We Southerners won the first day and part of the second, even after they'd killed General Albert Sidney Johnston. When I say he was about as great as General Lee, I expect to be believed. When we fell back, Bedford Forrest sent some of us to save a field piece that Bragg's artillery left behind. But the Yankees got there fustest with the mostest men. They carried off the gun, and two or three of us Tennessee cavalry with it.

They were bivouacking on the field—sundown, April 7,1862. I was marched far back. Passing a headquarters, I saw a fateful little man with a big cigar—General Grant. With him was a taller, red-whiskered man, who was crying. Someone said he was Sherman, but Sherman never seemed to me like a man who would cry over any sorrow, his own or another's.

This introduction is jumbled. So was my mind at the time. I must have looked forlorn, a skinny grayclad trooper plundered of saber, carbine and horse. One of the big blue cavalrymen who escorted the prisoners, leaned down from his saddle and rubbed the heel of his hand on my feebly fuzzy cheek.

"Little Johnny Reb's growing some nice black whiskers to surprise his sweetheart," he said, laughing.

"I haven't got a sweetheart," I snapped, trying to sound like a big soldier. But he laughed the louder.

"Hear that, boys?" he hailed the others of the escort. "This little feller never had a sweetheart." They mingled their cackles with his, and I wished I'd not spoken. They repeated my words again and again, tagging on sneers and merriments. I frowned, and tried not to cry. This was at dusk, the saddest time of day. We'd been marched back for miles, to some sort of reserve concentration in a tiny town.

"We've robbed the cradle for sure," the big blue cavalryman was saying to friends he met. "This little shaver—no sweetheart, he says!"

A new gale of laughter from towering captors all around me. It hushed suddenly at a stern voice:

"Bring that prisoner to me."

He rolled out from between two sheds, as heavily and smoothly as a gunlimber. He was a short, thick man in a dragoon jacket and one of those little peaked Yankee caps. There was just enough light to show me his big beard and the sergeant's stripes on his sleeve.

"Bring him along," he ordered again. "March the others to the stockade."

A moment later, he and I stood alone in the gloom. "What's your name?" he asked.

"High Private Cole Wickett," I replied. A prisoner could say that much. If he asked about my regiment, or the conditions of the army—But he didn't. His next question was—"How old are you?"

"Fifteen next birthday." Again no reason to lie, though I'd told the recruiting sergeant eighteen.

"Fourteen years, and some months," the big man figured it out. "Come with me."

He put a hand the size of a hayfork on my shoulder, and steered me into a back yard full of soldiers playing cards by firelight. He paused, and scolded them for gambling. Any sergeant in Forrest's command who had tried that would have been hooted at, maybe struck at—we Confederates respected God and General Johnston and Bedford Forrest, and scorned everyone else. But these men put away the cards and said, "Yes sir" as if he had been an officer. He marched me on into the house beyond the yard, and sat me in a chair in what had been the kitchen.

There he left me. I could hear him talking to someone in the next room, There was a window through which I might have climbed. But it was dark, and I was tired, hungry, sick, and not yet fifteen. I couldn't have fought my way back through Grant, Sherman and the rest of the Yankees. I waited where I was until the sergeant opened the door and said, "Come in here, Wickett."

The front room was lighted by one candle, stuck in its own grease on a table. There sat a tall, gray officer with a chaplain's cross for insignia. He was eating supper—bread, bacon and coffee. My eyes must have been wolfish, for he asked if I'd have some. I took enough to make a sandwich, and thanked him kindly. Then the chaplain said, "My boy, is it true what Sergeant Jaeger heard? That you're only a child, and never had a sweetheart?"

I stuck my chin out and stood up straight. The Yankees must be worse than all our Southern editors and speech-makers claimed, if even a preacher among them made jokes about such things. "Sir," I said, keeping my voice deep in my chest, "it's none of your business."

"But it is my business," he replied solemnly, "and the business of many people. Upon your answer, Cole, depends an effort to help some folk out of awful trouble—northern and southern both—and to right a terrible wrong. Now will you reply?"

"I don't know what you mean," I returned, "but I never even thought much about girls. What's wrong with that?"

"Nothing's wrong with it," answered the big sergeant named Jaeger. "You should be proud to say that thing, Wickett, if it's really true."

"Sergeant," I sputtered, "I'm a southern gentleman. If you and I were alone, with horses and sabers, I'd teach you to respect my word."

His face grew as dark as his beard, and he said, "Respect your elders and betters, youngster. So says the Bible."

"The catechism, not the Bible, Sergeant," corrected the chaplain. "Cole, it's only that we must be dead sure." He pushed a black-bound book across the table toward me. "This is the Bible. Do you believe in the sanctity of an oath?"

"My word's good, sir, sworn on the Bible or not," I told him, but I put my hand on the book. "Must I swear something?"

"Only that you told the truth about never having a sweetheart," he said, and I did so. The chaplain put away the book, and looked at Sergeant Jaeger.

"Something tells me that we have the help we needed, and couldn't be sure of in our own forces," he said. "Take care of this boy, for we're lost without him."

He went out. Sergeant Jaeger faced me. He was no taller than I, even then, but about twice as broad.

"Since you're a man of your word, will you give your parole?" he asked.

I swallowed the last bite of bacon, and shook my head. "I'll escape," I announced, "as soon as there's light enough."

"Will you give me your parole until sunrise?" he almost pleaded.

Wondering, I gave it. He put his hand on my shoulder again, steered me to a narrow stairway and up to a little room the size of a pantry. There was a cot with a gray blanket, Union army issue, on it.

"Sleep here," he said. "No, no questions—I won't answer them. Be ready for orders at an hour before dawn."

He left me. I took off my tunic and boots, and stretched out on the cot. Still puzzling over things, I went to sleep.

I woke to the touch of a hand, cold as a washrag, on my brow. Somehow there was light enough to see a woman standing there. She wore a frosty white dress and veil, like a bride's. Her face was still whiter.

I saw a straight, narrow-cut nose, a mouth that must be very red to be so darkly alive, and eyes that glowed green. Perhaps the eyes gave the light. I sat up, embarrassed.

"I was told to sleep here, ma'am," I said, "Is this your house?"

"Yes," she whispered, "it is my house." She sat on the edge of the cot. Her hand moved from my face to my shoulder. Her grip was as strong as Sergeant Jaeger's. "Your name is Cole Wickett.

You are a brave soldier, but you never had a sweetheart.

I was tired of hearing about it. I said nothing, and she went on. "I will be your sweetheart." And she put her arms around me.

She was beautiful, more than anyone I had ever seen. But when she came that close I felt a horrible sick fear. Perhaps it was the smell of deadness, as of a week-old battlefield. Or all of them.

I wriggled loose and jumped off the cot. She laughed, a little gurgle like water in a cave.

"Do not be afraid, Cole. Stand where you are."

She, too, rose. She was taller than I. Her eyes fixed mine, and I could not move. If you want to know how I felt, stare for a while at some spot on the wall or floor. After a moment, you'll have trouble looking away. It's called hypnotism, or something. She came near again, and this time I did not shrink when she put her hands on my shoulders.

"Now," she said.

Then Sergeant Jaeger opened the door, took one look, and began to say something, very rapidly and roughly. It sounded like Bible verses: "In the beginning was the Word, and the Word was with God—"

The woman shrieked, high and ear-tingling, like a bat. She let go of me.

She was gone. It was like a light being blown out, or a magic-lantern image switched from a screen.

I stared stupidly, like a country idiot. Jaeger cleared his throat, and tugged his beard. "That was close," he said.

"Who was she?" I asked, and the words had a hard time forming in my throat.

"Somebody whose call we'll return," he put me off gruffly. "She thought she'd destroy the one power we're counting on. It's time to strike back."

I followed him outside. The night was black, but the early-morning stars had reeled up into heaven. We passed two different sentried, and came through the sloping street of the little town to a church, either ruined or shell-smashed. Beyond was a burying ground, grown up in weeds and walled around with stone. At the broken-down gate stood the chaplain. He held the bridle of a chunky black stallion colt, not quite full grown.

"I can vouch for the beast," he greeted Sergeant Jaeger. "It is sad that we watch our animals so much more carefully than our own children."

"This night I almost failed in my own duty of watching," replied Jaeger in a sad voice. To me he said, "Crawl out of those clothes. Don't stare. Do as I say."

By this time there had been so much strangeness and mystery that I did not care. I shucked my uniform, and the pre-dawn air was cold on my bare skin. The chaplain motioned for me to mount. I did, and he led the colt into the burying ground.

There were wreathes and wrappings of mist. Through them I saw pale, worn-out tombstones. We tramped over them. It wasn't polite nor decent, but I saw that the chaplain and the sergeant—he came behind, carrying some shovels and a mattock—meant business. I kept my mouth closed. Riding the colt, I was steered across that burying ground, and across again.

In the middle of the second crossing, the colt planted his hoofs and balked.

Jaeger, bringing up the rear, struck with the handle of a shovel. The colt stood firm. The chaplain tugged in front, Jaeger flogged behind. The colt trembled and snorted, but he did not move.

The chaplain pointed. A grave-mound, a little naked wen of dirt among the weeds, showed just in front of the planted hoofs.

"Your book tells the truth," he said, strangely cheerful. "Here is a tomb he will not cross."

"Get down, Wickett," commanded Jaeger. "Dress, and help dig."

I hurried to the gate, threw on my clothes anyhow, and returned. The chaplain was scraping with a shovel. Jaeger swung a mattock. I grabbed another spade and joined in.

As the first moment of gray dawn was upon us, we struck a coffin lid. Jaeger scraped earth from it. "Get back!" he grunted, and I did so; but not before he heaved up the lid with his mattock.

Inside lay the woman who had come to my cot, in her bridal dress.

"The stake," said the chaplain, and passed down a sharp stick like a picket pin. I judged it was of hawthorn, cut from a hedge somewhere. "Strike to the heart," went on the chaplain, "while I strike at the throat."

He suited action to word, driving down the blade of his shovel. At the same moment Jaeger made a strong digging thrust with the stick. I heard again the bat-squeaking; and then, was made faint by a horrid stink of rottenness.

Jaeger slammed down the lid—I heard it fall—and scrambled out of the grave. He and the chaplain began tumbling clods into the hole.

Jaeger looked at me over his shoulder, haggard but triumphant.

"I give you back your parole," he panted. "Jump on that colt and clear out. To the west there'll be none of our troops. If you ever tell what was done here, nobody will believe you!"

I needed no second permission.

Manly Wade Wellman (1903-1986) is one of the best-known fantasy authors of southern regionalism. He is the author of the collections *Who Fears the Devil?*, *Valley So Low*, *Lonely Vigils*, and *Worse Things Waiting*, as well as many novels for adults and children.

John's life was dull and lackluster, every day the same as the rest.
How was it that a vampire *could be more alive than he?*

The Scent of Magnolias

BY LAWRENCE SCHIMEL AND BILLIE SUE MOSIMAN

The bells on the door tinkled so softly I thought at first it was the dawn wind, but something made me look up from my homework to find her there: solitary, beautiful. She had brought with her the lush, heavy smell of magnolias, and for a moment I saw her greeting me at the wide oak doors of a mansion that stood like a temple amid the black fertile land where cotton fields lay like snow carpets; the archways dripped with purple wisteria as she strolled at my side along a path lined with camellias and azaleas on a shadowy cool afternoon. All around us was exhibited the lushness of nature, the fecundity that springs from the earth.

I don't know what about her made me think this; she was dressed simply, as any woman might be, in a loose cotton print that draped long to cover her ankles. She wore a wide-brimmed white sun hat, even though the sun had yet to rise. But something about the way she held herself bespoke grandeur, and awoke in me a strange desire, a hungering for the sensual pleasures of richness and excess that were part of a life I had never and would never lead.

In her presence, the furnishings of the motel seemed so irrevocably squalid: the yellow, plastic-covered couches loomed like a herd of cattle grazing on the worn blue rug. This motel, in this wasted, empty Alabama city, was too harsh for anyone not already damned to it.

She drifted towards me, moving so lightly, as if she were ethereal, a phantasm of the morning mist that had strayed indoors by mistake.

It was only as she neared that I realized that there was no mistake; a chill ran down my spine and I knew, deep in my gut, that she was not a lady who had lost her way, but someone who really did belong here. She intended to be well-hid before the first cockcrow as had others who had come here. I'd never met one anything like her before, though I knew the room she wanted and where the key was kept.

I gave her the price per night—or per day as in this case. She stared through me, as if her energy was drained too low to argue or she had no other options, coming in so late. She brought out a wallet and as she pulled out two hundreds and placed them on the counter, I glanced curiously, even jealously, at the man's photo on the ID.

"The money's good she said. Her voice: a deep timbre, like drum signals sounding from deep in a native forest.

"The town is off limits," I said. "House rules."

"My husband," she said, indicating the ID.

"Lucky stiff." I almost winked, but froze where I stood when I saw the fierce glint in her eye. She would not be teased or mocked—though that's not what I had meant to do. It was a case of nerves, pure and simple. She both frightened and mesmerized me. I feared her and at the same time felt an almost blind crazy urge to slip my arm across the counter and touch her on the cheek as a gesture of adoration. Her skin was alabaster, emphasizing the black silk of her eyes and lashes and hair. If she was not a goddess, then I would never know one.

"If you'll take me to my room now," she said, turning aside and looking down the dreary hall. "I'm very tired."

She looked tired, yes, but she also looked . . . hungry. Had she fed, in that wild black night she had emerged from?

I trembled, stumbling on the edge of the rug as I came from behind the counter to escort her down the hallway. I heard her behind me, her footsteps softly following, sounding like nothing more than wind swirling dead leaves along the floor. I came to the door and halted. I unlocked it. I pushed it open and stepped back to allow her entrance. She moved in front of me and stood a moment. No windows. The dim light from the hallway lamps cast our shadows, twin grotesqueries, against the row of coffins stacked against the far wall.

"Take your pick," I said. "I'll see you in the evening."

◊◊◊

"I see a key is missing, but someone didn't register. How many times have I told you to make sure they register?"

I was rattled from my lazy nap by this inquiry from my mother. "Hmm, I guess I forgot." I sat up in the big yellow chair in the lobby and stretched my arms over my head. It must be noon, I thought, squinting at the white sunlight streaming through the front windows. I could use some breakfast.

"You forgot? Well, who was it? Did you get cash?"

"Yes. Cash. It was one of *them*." I stood and moved to the cold drink machine. Sometimes it worked without eating my quarters. I could kill for a Dr. Pepper right then.

My mother must have moved from behind the counter as the can rolled its way down into the bottom of the tray, for she had crept up behind me and her voice caused me to flinch. "You were supposed to stay awake and keep an eye on the hall! What if he came out and caught you sleeping? I can't watch this place every hour of every day and night."

"It's a she."

"Hmm, odd. I don't think we've ever had a lone female before. You should've charged her more."

"Good god, Mother, that's the silliest thing I ever heard in my life. We already get good money for those coffins overnight. We don't have to be so damn mercenary, do we?"

"I'll tell you when we have to be mercenary, young man. When they come here because they have no place else to go, that's when we can be *mercenary*. We can charge what we please and they have to pay it because, by glory's gates, it is a bad strain on my heart to let them come at all. I think you could have at least asked for two-fifty."

I sighed to hear her go on so. If I'd had the money to support myself through school, I wouldn't have stayed. Her heart put a strain on *me*. She used her frail condition to bludgeon me to her will.

"Will she stay another night?" Mother asked.

"I don't know. She didn't say. She looks . . . wan. Not well. Rather . . . starved."

"Oh mercy." I watched Mother's hand flutter to her bosom. She pretended to be afraid of our special guests, but she had been serving them her own brand of Southern hospitality since before I was born.

"You've never once been bitten, Mother. In all these years. I wish you wouldn't act like this one weary guest is going to come out as dark falls and rip your head from your torso."

"John!"

"I'm sorry." And I was contrite for all of a few seconds. There was no point in my being so blunt. Mother was mother. She had her ways. I had no call to push her around and give her lip just because sometimes her playacting made me lose patience. "I'm sorry. I take it back."

"You know I don't like violence, even the *mention* of it." She trundled to the counter and lifted the gate. She returned to counting the night's receipts.

I knew what she did like: money. Had it not been for the coffin room, we would have been destitute and on the street long before. One tended to overlook the violence of others when survival hung in the balance. But I could not say that. A team of wild horses pulling me into quarters could not make me say that.

"I think I'll go make myself some scrambled eggs and grits," I said, aiming for the hall and our apartment we shared at the end of it.

"After sucking down that Dr. Pepper, I think that's a wise decision," she said, never lifting her gaze from the bills stacked in her hand.

◊◊◊

Mother had shopping to do after I returned from my two o'clock at the state college. I sat in the lobby trying to read Voltaire and failing. My mind kept wandering, down the hallway to the coffin room. How cool and dark it must be inside the white satin-lined caskets, I thought. How utterly peaceful and sublime. To be near her, cuddled in her sleeping arms, breathing the scent of her, feeling her breasts pressed next to me, my face buried in that silken raven hair . . .

Casey Burton swept through the door, which banged shut with the creak of doom. Only those down on their luck stayed with us, and Casey must have been born luckless. He owed two weeks back rent for his room and promised to pay every day when he came in reeking from a stint at the Lone Rooster Bar. Sure he would pay. When we knocked him to the floor and rifled his pockets, that's when he would pay.

"Casey," I said in greeting. I didn't have the energy to badger him for the rent today.

"I want to meet that woman," he said, sauntering over to take one of the yellow sofas for himself. He spread out across it like a big leggy dog. He didn't look half bad for a guy on the skids. He kept himself shaved and his jaw was firm, his eyes clear even after hours with the bottle. If he'd been blessed with more brain, or had gone to school a few more years to make up for a lack of one, there's no telling what he might have made of himself.

"What woman?" I knew, of course. There was but one female guest.

"That one came in too goddamn early this morning. Woke me up, y'all talking did. I could hear you gabbing all the way down to my room. Hey, you know these walls ain't made of granite."

"You saw her." Not a question. He must have peeked out, him in his soiled undershirt and shorts, lusting after that woman.

I had lusted too. She carried a sexual aura around her person like a royal mantle.

"I saw her," Casey was saying, "and I want to meet her. I want you to introduce me."

The Scent of Magnolias   85

"Can't do that. Against policy."

"What policy? This dump got policies? I don't think so."

"Yeah, we have policies. Like paying your rent on time or you're out on your ass. My mother's losing it and by Friday, she's going to blow sky high. You wait and see."

"I'll introduce myself," Casey said, ignoring the threat of imminent eviction.

"No, you won't." I was sitting spine-straight now, Voltaire having been put aside on the rickety end table. I had moved into a ready position as if to rise and fling myself on him. Even my voice was beyond my control. I sounded, even to my own ears, like a man who had been told someone was going to put a move on my wife.

I had no wife. I had no woman. The woman in the coffin room was not mine, and I doubted if she had ever been anyone's, certainly not the man whose ID was in her wallet.

I had to look away from Casey and loosen my fists. I spread out my hands along the arms of the chair. "She's got a husband. I don't think she wants to be bothered."

"Why don't you let me find that out for myself?"

I watched Casey pull his lanky frame up from the sofa, steady himself on his feet, and wander down the hall.

I sat back and rolled my shoulders, loosening the muscles there that had begun to cramp. I unclenched my teeth. I took a breath, then another.

My gaze wandered from the hall to the front window where the sun sat lower in the western sky. Soon it would be behind the mountains and gone, sunset. She would wake and she would prowl. She might leave and never come back. It didn't matter what Casey thought he would do, trying to get near her. She might be out of both our lives before morning came. Vanished.

At least I would see her once more before she left. At least once more.

I shut my eyes and rested my head back on the chair. I thought I could smell magnolia and hear water rushing in the distance, a waterfalls. I thought I held her hand in mine as we walked deeper into the emerald gloom, thought I could hear her deep musical voice addressing me, like Naomi to Ruth, "Whither thou goeth, I wilst go."

And I knew it was all a dream. All a fantasy, however pleasant. She was vampire.

And I was not.

◊◊◊

I waited for her as the sun dipped toward the horizon, wondering if she would stay another night or move on to wherever she was headed. I didn't think she was planning on going to the husband she laid claim to him via that wallet. I had a feeling he was no longer numbered among the living.

Was it her danger that attracted me so much? None of our other special guests had charmed me, not in all these years. I had been witness to hundreds of the undead who took advantage of the coffin room and not one had made me fall in love. And was this love?

The notion was too startling. I longed for her, as if I were already bitten and slave to her every whim. If it wasn't love, it was a facsimile, and strong enough to make me understand how lost people are who fall for one another.

She came into my thoughts again, a vision, and immediately I imagined her beside me, walking along the footpaths surrounding a large plantation house. I could only think of that word: love, as we sat on a bench beneath the azaleas and I melted into her embrace.

I waited for her to rise, to walk, to come into my presence so that I could fantasize in a waking dream with her before me.

Had she overslept? I worried. She had seemed exhausted when she arrived. Perhaps she'd stayed out too long, caught a bit of reflected sunlight that debilitated her powers to rejuvenate.

Could she have left via some other exit? Transformed herself into some winged beast, perhaps, and flown out a window? At least she'd paid cash and in advance. I wondered if her wallet would be left in the coffin if she had indeed escaped into the lowering twilight.

I started, a few times, to go to her room and see if she were still there. I could always have used the pretense of needing to clean the place, although I'm sure she'd recognize it for the lie it was.

If I know anything about the night creatures, I know this: They understand more than we wish of the human mind. And it was not as if we had much call for that particular room. We might have one, two visitors a month to take up residence. Since Dad's truck flipped over six years back and I'd taken over the night shift for mother, our business had dwindled for the coffins. I didn't know if they were moving away from our small town or if they'd found a new route in their wanderings across country. But we had fewer of them than when Dad was alive.

Her voice brought me back from my daydreaming. I blinked away the phantom plantation, the small intrusive memories of my father, the smell of the magnolia that overlaid it all, and sat up, waiting for her to appear down the hallway. Then I heard Casey, and realized she must have been talking to someone for me to have heard her. I raced for the hallway, hoping he wasn't giving her too much trouble.

I heard a door close, and thought with relief that she must've shut him out. I could imagine him knocking on all the doors until he'd found hers. Although he probably could tell where she was staying from looking at the board and seeing which key was missing. If he'd had the wits to think of it. Given that he was smitten by that early-morning sight of her, he might've been devious enough, especially since even in my daydreams I should've heard if he'd been making a nuisance of himself, knocking on all the doorways in search of her.

And what had he said when she'd opened the door? I'd been too far away to hear any of it.

I turned the corner to where her room was, still running. The hallway was empty. Casey must've gone back to his own room. He was close enough to hers, which I guess was how he'd spied her that morning, as I was checking her in. I walked to her door and listened for any sounds that betrayed she was inside. Would she think I was Casey again, come to pester her still, lurking outside her door like some sleazy Peeping Tom? At the thought, I couldn't help suddenly imagining her: lying naked in the coffin, her breasts full, her skin so pale and smooth . . .

I walked away, embarrassed at myself and my uncontrollable thoughts. But were they really any different than anything I'd thought all day long, just because I had them while standing outside her doorway?

I heard her voice again, and paused, listening. Who was she talking to? Could it be . . . ?

I walked to Casey's door, and unmistakably I could hear her voice inside, cooing to him, telling him how she liked it when he touched her there.

I felt a hundred different emotions tearing me apart: jealousy and outrage and a desire to burst in there to stop them, stop this charade, stop it!

At first I thought I had wanted to protect her from Casey. But shouldn't I be trying to protect Casey from her? I knew there was more than just sex involved; she would drink his blood. But I couldn't help wishing I was in his place.

The town was off limits, I kept thinking to myself, house rules, and that included customers right here in our own place! What kind of hospitality could we offer if we let our own guests be killed by one another? Nor would her kind come here if it became haunted by investigators and policemen trying to solve vile murders.

And Casey did still owe us two weeks back rent.

But I couldn't move. Not to protect either of them, or even myself. I couldn't even walk away from them and spare myself the agony of hearing Casey's grunts as the bed began to squeak and jiggle, or give them the decency to have sex in private. I listened to them, bumping and grinding away on the other side of the door. I couldn't help thinking how smooth and white the skin of her thighs must be. I wanted to know what it would sound like when she began to drink his blood. Would I hear a difference? Could I hear Casey's life slipping away, pint by pint?

I realized suddenly that Casey was in many ways acting like a vampire, leeching off of us without paying his bill. This was only what he deserved, really.

Did anyone really deserve to be killed, simply because they couldn't, or wouldn't, pay their debts?

I didn't think so. But it would be a mercy to have Casey gone, although Mother would take it out on me for not getting the two weeks back rent from him.

The Scent of Magnolias

And what about the body? We'd have to do something with it. Oh, I wished she wouldn't do this. . . . I wished Casey hadn't intruded on her and brought this about. I wished she'd wanted me. Their sounds caused my mind to roar with lust; I pressed to the door, wanting her more than my own life.

There was silence at last inside the room. Had she drunk his blood already? She might open the door and find me there. I waited a moment, listening, then turned and walked awkwardly away. I didn't go to the front counter but back toward my room. I couldn't bear to see her again now, and hoped she'd leave tonight. I wanted her gone.

Yet still I ached and I imagined her, beside me.

I halted before my own door, my hand on the doorknob, knowing I couldn't ignore what had just taken place in Casey's room. I dreaded going inside where they had coupled, but I knew it had to be done, eventually, and better it was me than Mother, who might not be able to handle it if anything happened.

I began to sweat and smelled myself drenched suddenly with the stink of fear. I knew he was dead, he must be dead. I walked down the hallway again and passed by his door without pausing, walked straight into the lobby where the lamplight pooled over the stains and the scuffed wood around the carpet's edges. I paced, the lust having receded from both mind and body, and tried to work my courage up to the point I could enter Casey's room to see the truth for myself.

After ten minutes of a building tension, circling endlessly around the yellow sofa and chairs, I headed again for the hall and his door. I had to know. I had to make arrangements if Casey lay dead and drained. I didn't knock. I turned the doorknob and pushed open the door, moving forward into the room like a relentless wind, and stopped.

Frozen in place. Staring unbelieving at her handiwork.

Casey lay in the iron full-size bed on the disheveled sheets. He was naked, on his back, his legs spread and crooked, his penis lying to one side in the turf of dark hair. He was white as cloud and *shrunken*. In the darkened room, the shades drawn and the curtains closed, his body stood out like a talisman amid the gloom.

She was gone from here. I turned and looked over my shoulder, thinking she might be there at my back, ready to swoop toward me, but the hall stood empty. She had returned to her room while I was in the lobby. Leaving Casey here for the flies.

I went closer to study Casey's still face. He had died with a grimace and it now held his features in thrall, a mask of last pain. His neck was a ruin. No small puncture marks here. A great open gash that caused my stomach to turn and my throat to close. His neck was meat now, not flesh, torn and ragged. Yet not more than a few sprinkles of blood had escaped that open wound to stain the pillow or sheets beneath his lolling head. His bier was neat, though his neck was wrecked.

I backed away slowly, sickened and overcome by a grotesque urge to reach my hands down into his neck cavity and rip out the remaining connections that kept his head attached to his shoulders.

I hated him for many things. For being who he was, for making a move on our guest, for taking her sex the way he might take a whore, and then for dying so untidily that I would have to do something to cover up his passing. If only he'd stayed away!

Impulsively, I was drawn away from the bed and the dead thing there, into the hallway and to her door. If she were still here she'd be fast asleep again.

I didn't know what I was expecting when I went in there. Perhaps I should kill her, I thought, drive a stake through her heart, banish her from both life and my dreams, once and for all. She wasn't like me. She could never love me. She gave herself to the scum of the earth, like Casey, and lived on through centuries of time without someone to adore her the way I adored her. She would be better off if she ceased to exist.

I lifted the lid on a coffin. It was empty, its white-satin walls reflecting shinily in the room's single bulb.

Where was she? I let the lid drop and began opening the nearby coffins, nearly choking in a sense of sacrilege and of longing mixed with fear, feeling like I were looting and despoiling some burial ground. But these graves had been looted before me: every coffin was empty.

Until one.

My eyes roved up the body of the woman who had occupied all

my thoughts these past many hours. Her hands folded across her gently rising and falling chest as she breathed in deep sleep, the silky white skin of her throat, her peaceful face that only minutes before had ravished a man and torn out his larynx.

I leaned over the satin bed, reaching out one hand, rested it on the side of her cold marble face and caressed her cheek. It was foolish, contrary to all sound judgment, but I was entranced and unable to stop. My hand slipped down the column of her throat to the small hollow made by the breastbone, and down to the soft flesh rounding.

Suddenly, as if coming to myself, I took away my hand. The imprint of her remained in my palm. I stood helpless beside the coffin, fighting off the urge to climb into it with her and force my way inside her.

I shook my head to clear it. I could not kill her, never. I could not blame her or be repulsed by her affliction as a creature of the night, living on the dregs of society's underbelly. I slowly lowered the coffin lid, then backed from the room, my heart beating like a wild thing, swamped by a love so strong it bound me forever. I would do anything for her, and everything. I would probably even die for her. Yes, I would die for her, if necessary.

I went again to Casey's room and wrapped him in his sheet, like a mummy. I hauled him up and over my shoulder and carried him quietly down the hall to the back of the building and the exit there to the alleyway where I kept my car parked. I put him in the trunk and drove his body to the outskirts of town, through the early dark, toward his last resting place. I knew exactly where to go. I'd spent many summer days with friends of mine, diving into the icy cold cobalt waters. It was a lake created by limestone blasting and removal. After the company had dragged out the last of the limestone and the operation grew too expensive, they left the vast hole in the ground, surrounded by cliffs of rock that glittered in the sun. A hundred rains had filled the basin and it became a popular summer swimming hole for the brave and intrepid.

I took Casey there, down a dirt road, through thick stands of pine and cedar. No one was around, thankfully, though often teenagers came here to drink and smoke and have sex. I took him from the trunk and dropped him like a heavy sack near the cliff edge, then rolled him with my foot until his weight carried him over. The splash roused drowsing birds, that screeched and flew like a horde of bats around the top of the water before scattering back into the woods and cover.

Casey sank like stone, but he would float again in a while. And if no one found him, he'd sink once more and lie in the mud, eaten by minnows until only his bones were left behind.

Back at the motel, I sat alone in the lobby with Voltaire open on my knee, waiting, I knew not for what, and listened to Mother complain.

"Maybe she'll stay another day," she said from behind the counter. "We need the money. And speaking of money, have you seen that good-for-nothing, Casey, today? Have you asked him when he's going to pay up?"

I turned my head toward her and said, softly, "Casey skipped."

"He what?"

"I checked his room earlier. All his things are gone. He's out of here."

"Without paying what he owed?"

"Don't worry, Mother. We've had guests like him before and we will again. I'm glad he's gone. I never liked him from the beginning."

She sighed and turned her mind to the books. We would eat our sparse dinner together in the apartment and then she would take her favorite recliner and watch television until she dozed while I commanded the front desk.

Our days together as mother and son followed a routine that was life-draining. It was dull, lackluster, dusty as an attic where light never ventured. I often wondered what her life was worth, what it meant. Then I wondered about my own life, where it might be heading. Mother didn't really care for me, to be truthful. And she'd not much cared for my father when he'd been alive. She cared for money, only that. She cared for the motel, as decrepit as it had become, because it brought her money. She loved her television programs, and her coffee cup with the red robin on it that she drank from while she sat in the recliner deep into the night, drifting off and sometimes still there when I came in the morning to wake her.

I once asked her about the special guests, how that had come to be, and she'd waved off my questions with, "I don't know how they knew I'd make a safe haven, unless they can read minds. I try not to think about them or those . . . those coffins. That room. I just take them in and it keeps us alive, that's all you need to know. As long as they don't break house policy, I don't care who they are or what they are."

That was the problem, at least for me now, sitting and waiting for her to rise, having disposed of a body to protect her, having touched her, and fallen in love.

The problem was Mother didn't care.

Voltaire fell from my knee and landed with a loud plop on the floor. I bent over to retrieve the book and when I sat up again, she was there, the beautiful vampire, the plantation beauty of my dreams, standing no more than two feet from me. Her eyes, I realized, were violet, the hue of the woodland flower. The pupil was large and reflective, black as the back of a cave. I looked up into her serene face and whispered, "Where will you go now?"

"I felt your touch in my sleep," she replied, not accusatory, just statement. "I know the fantasies that fill your head." I swallowed, feeling the skin stretched tight across my throat as if eager to feel the pierce of her fangs. "Do you know what it means to walk at my side?"

I thought of Casey's corpse, the way his neck looked, the weight of his body as I lugged it toward the lake. I thought of how it would feel to have her by my side for all eternity, and what I was willing to give up or do to achieve that. I had so little to lose—a second-class education, a motel for the dead and for bums, a life marred by futility, suffering, and loss.

When her lips met mine, my fate was sealed. A flurry of memories washed over me, images, not all from my own life, scattered moments of intense emotion: pain and fear and bliss. I didn't try and understand any of it, just drank in the sensations, the images, feeling them, cowering beneath their force, reveling in them. I saw again every vampire image I'd ever seen or thought, including the imagined lovemaking between her and Casey, flashing almost simultaneously in my mind.

I had no idea how long our lips touched. We broke apart from our kiss and my lips still burned with sensation. I leaned my head to the side, baring my vulnerable neck. She softly laughed. "You don't know the least of it." She walked to the doorway and I was as transfixed as I watched her go, unable to believe she was leaving me behind, rejecting me, abandoning me. The bells on the door tinkled softly as she passed through and was gone, into the night.

I ran after her, a cry welling up deep within my chest and throat, but even as it reverberated through the empty street I knew she was gone from there. I bit down at my own lip to draw the blood she'd refused. I ran back into the motel and to our apartment, determined to find a knife and slit my throat if she wouldn't. But even as I held the steel, ignoring Mother's questioning voice from the living room, I knew that killing myself wasn't the answer. No, I had to prove myself to her. I had to become a vampire—somehow, convince one of her kindred to transform me, induct me into their immortal ranks, and then I would find her and take her and we would walk side-by-side, as equals, forever.

I would find her, wherever she went, I felt certain of it. I wanted desperately to follow her immediately, while the trail was freshest, but I knew I could not. She would not accept me as I was. I knew, too, that I could not stay here any longer, even though it would be the easiest place for me to meet another of her kind, whose path had drawn them to our hospitality. If I were ever to go, it must be now. And once I left there would be no turning back. They would blame me for Casey's death, once he was found, this I knew. That alone would keep me from ever coming back.

There was still one thing for me to take care of before I left. I lifted the knife, bared my teeth at my reflection in the blade's silver; this would be my fangs until I was ready.

She was in her recliner, sipping from her red robin mug. I was tidy and neat and fast. I smelled the tempting magnolia blooms and felt the embrace of white thighs and I lusted, even as I killed. Her stuttered cries went unheard. When it was done, life having fled that old tired face, I turned off the television and patted Mother's hand where it lay on the arm rest.

I then turned to my future and my heart rallied as I walked for the last time down the hall, across the moonlit lobby, and past the empty counter, out into the promising good night.

Lawrence Schimel is the editor of The American Vampire Series, in addition to more than a dozen other anthologies, including *Tarot Fantastic* and *The Fortune Teller.* Billie Sue Mosiman is the author of eight suspense novels, including *Pure And Uncut, Widow, Stiletto,* and *Nightcruise.*

Like a moth to the flame. . . .
There's something very intense about the power of attraction.
And flames can attract more than just moths.

The Flame

BY FRED CHAPPELL

any women are wonderfully attractive to men. Beautiful or unbeautiful, witty or dull, rich or penurious, they draw males to them and keep them about them the way the greater planets in our system capture and keep at arm's length rings of disappointed asteroids. But some women are attractive only to certain kinds of men. The leggy freckled blonde probably has an athlete or two awaiting her leisure, while the tweedy and precise brunette has gathered scholars to her like homely footnotes cuddling a dissertation. A cheerful mother once described her daughter as "working on her fourth banker." But for Andrea Greenleaf the situation was not so happy. Andrea attracted vampires—a half dozen or so at a time.

At first she had no idea that they were vampires, only that wherever she went at night—to films, to concerts, to the productions of the Gatesboro Opera Company, to restaurants—she always spotted two or three or even four pallid and slender men in dark suits who stared at her with fever-cold eyes. And then at midnight she would hear on the steep slate roof of the old house she had inherited from her Aunt Embry the muffled beat of pads and click of claws, and slitherings and shiftings unidentifiable but certainly unpleasant. As her house was situated on the outskirts of Gatesboro with no close neighbors, Andrea suffered a ragged nocturnal restlessness.

It was her friend Moon Crescent who enlightened her. "That man?" she asked, looking across the clattering restaurant to the gloomy thin man who sat at the bar, devoting all his disconcerting attention to Andrea. "He's a vampire, my dear. He calls himself Count Estragu, though of course that's not what his mother named him, any more than mine named me Crescent. He's quite well known in Gatesboro—in some circles I mean." She patted Andrea's hand in a rather patronizing manner and added: "Not in yours."

Though she couldn't help feeling a small seethe of impatience, Andrea would have to admit that her friend was correct. She didn't run with the same crowd as Crescent, having no interest in reincarnation, pyramids, Atlantis, crystals, or apocalypse. She pronounced the name of Edgar Cayce as if it rhymed with "second base." She couldn't decide whether she believed in ghosts or not. But she was not pleased at having drawn the notice of a vampire, especially of one with such an intense gaze. It would not be inaccurate, she thought, to describe that gaze as *hungry*. "What does he want?" she asked her friend. "Is he going to hurt me? He could have injured me long ago if that was his plan. Why is he following me?"

"Well," Crescent said, "why don't we go ask him?" She completed her nibble of spinach salad and began to push her chair from the table.

"Oh no." Andrea blushed to the roots of her amber-colored hair.

"Why not?"

"I'm scared. And I feel silly. What if you're wrong? What if he's not a vampire?"

"That part I'll guarantee," Crescent replied. She rose and laid her crumpled napkin in her chair. "I'll go find out what else is happening."

This sort of embarrassment was more than Andrea was accustomed to endure. In fact, she rarely had occasion to be embarrassed. But now she tried to avert her eyes from the colloquy taking place at the bar. Crescent was expostulating, making jerky elbow movements in her black leotard top. What if people guessed that this animated conversation concerned her? She realized afresh that one of the reasons she liked Crescent was because she admired her brash courage. Who else would have the nerve to walk up to a vampire and confront him face to face?

When her friend returned to the table Andrea asked, "Is he really a vampire?"

Crescent looked at her as if taking her in for the first time. Andrea was not a gorgeous woman, nor even a pretty one, in the ordinary way of magazine photographs. She was by no means obese, but her body was too ample entirely. Her hair spilled over her plumpish shoulders in a tangle of dark fire, her mouth was large and as luscious-looking as an overripe peach, her brown eyes were both active and melting at once. She was simply too much. Her words flew from her like little startled flocks of gold finches. Crescent became aware of a desire to press her face between Andrea's opulent breasts in the forest-green sweater and giggle like a schoolgirl with a naughty secret.

But she only answered half carelessly: "He's a vampire, all right. That was never in question, Flame."

"Flame? Why do you call me that?"

"That's what he calls you. What they call you. The Flame." She leaned across and took Andrea's plump, strong hands in her slender, cool fingers. "They're dead, you know. Where vampires are it is black and cold and lonely. I can't express how lonely it must be in the place where they are. And they're always there. Even when we see them now, right here in the Open Gate Cafe, they are also in the other place."

Andrea's sympathies were easy. "Oh, that sounds dreadful." She sneaked a glance at the Count but he had turned away to stare into the unresponsive bar mirror.

"Don't look at him," Crescent told her. "He's shy. He doesn't want you to look at him while I explain. He's a little ashamed."

"Will he hurt me? What are they going to do?"

"They call you Flame, he says, because you are so full of life. You are very rare that way. Everybody sees that, even if you don't.

And vampires see it more quickly because they need it more."

"I don't understand what it is."

"Oh, you know—life force. There are some people who make the rest of us seem like shadows. They are like natural springs while we are like tap water. We are like smoldering matchstems while they are like—well, flame. Just as the vampires say. Hearth fires."

"I don't believe I'm that way." Andrea's judgment was firm.

"If you could believe it, you wouldn't be," Crescent answered. "Your lack of egoism is one of the reasons you're the way you are."

"It is very confusing," Andrea said. She had always thought of vampires as inimical creatures who did harm to God's other creatures out of sheer malicious perversity. She had not thought about them as abandoned animals condemned to fare lonesome through the dark and freezing nights and forbidden the light of the warming sun. They were dangerous, she knew that, but abandoned animals are likely to become feral, if they don't die beforehand. Vampires, it seemed, died first and then became feral. She had imagined a vampire sinking venomous fangs into her, tearing away painful gobbets of flesh, beating his coarse-haired chest and howling at the blood-red moon. But now she thought the situation would be different, more like finding another stray cat beneath her viburnum, the dull-eyed animal frightened and shivering with sickness and too anxious to defend itself. "I really don't understand," she concluded.

"That's why I've invited the Count to visit you," Crescent said. "He will explain everything better than I ever could. And he's promised to show you how to fix up your house so you'll feel safe. They're not going to harm you, but they know you don't *feel* safe."

"You invited him to my house? When?"

"Thursday evening," Crescent replied. "You and I were going to the movies then anyhow. So now we'll do this instead."

"I don't know. It's pretty scary."

"I'll be there with you. And, believe me, he's not—*they're* not— going to hurt you. If you treat him as an envoy, as a sort of ambassador from the Vampire Nation, everything will work out fine."

"Really?"

"Oh, come on, Andrea," Crescent said. "You've never turned down a request in your life. From anyone. About anything."

It was true. Andrea's body was generous, her mind was generous, her heart was as generous as a Kansas wheat harvest.

◊◊◊

Thursday evening chez Andrea was not a great success. Things started badly when Crescent teased the nervous guest about his chosen name. "He's Romanian, all right, but he doesn't belong to the nobility. He was actually Just a troublesome peasant two centuries ago. He gave himself a title when he came to America. Isn't that so, *Count* Estrago?"

He admitted the fact readily enough, but his demeanor changed. Unused to social company, he was extravagantly shy. Of course, Andrea gave her all to make him feel at home, but just when he had begun to unbend Crescent had made her remarks about his title. After that he became sullen as well as withdrawn. It was easy to see that he did not blame his hostess for this gaucherie, easy to see that he adored and even worshiped her and would like to remain in her company. But Crescent put him off with her impertinence, she violated his sense of propriety. Andrea had observed that her friend affected many others in the same way, and the situation was worse with this vampire because of his painful diffidence.

After the faux pas he became all business and toured Andrea around her own house—with which he showed an unsettling familiarity. He had the air of a contractor planning to replumb as he took her from room to room, showing where she might place ropes of garlic, basins of holy water, silver crucifixes, and so forth. When Crescent observed that it was like installing burglar alarms, he ignored her. When he had entered the house, he had spoken in an almost normal tone of voice, but after Crescent's first sally he muttered his sentences in a quick but broken fashion. Now that she made her lame joke about burglar alarms, his voice subsided to a whisper when he said to Andrea, "I'm telling you these things because you ask. These precautions you do not need.

Neither I nor any of my . . . confreres would ever do you any harm. You must believe me."

She reassured him warmly. "Oh I do, I do believe you," she said. "It's only that—well, I expect to get married someday and have children. Messy hordes of children. Dozens. And I want them to be safe and not frightened. That's when I'll take advantage of this information you've been so kind about imparting. I'm sure you won't mind when that happens."

The Count was slow to reply, and before he did he exchanged a long and darkly knowing look with Crescent. A recognition passed between them that Andrea could not guess at. Then he whispered, putting his words together with exquisite care: "If you have children, we shall never harm or frighten them. We shall go away from this house and not return. In fact, we will do so now if you request us to."

His earnest and wistful tone quite overcame her. "Oh no," she said. "You mustn't leave. . . . But if you might keep just a little more distance. All those noises on the roof at night." She essayed a cheerful little confession. "I enjoy my sleep just terribly much. I really do."

He looked for the first time into her eyes and his yearning was so boundless that her heart quaked and her knees trembled. "I know you do," he said. And then, as if he'd given himself too much away, turned to his demonstrations again. But now he was cursory and in haste and though the women tried to insist he took leave of them in so brusque a manner he was almost rude.

◊◊◊

After his departure Crescent asked her hostess for a glass of scotch and Andrea was surprised. Her mystic friend usually eschewed hard liquor because it disordered her aura or astral body or karma or something.

"I have some white wine in the fridge," Andrea said.

"It will have to do," Crescent replied and strode purposefully to the kitchen where she helped herself.

Andrea followed. "I wish he hadn't left so soon," she said. "I had lots of questions I wanted to ask."

"About what?" Crescent drained her glass of chardonnay too quickly and poured another.

"About being a vampire. What it's like and—"

"—And how you can help?"

"Well, no. Not exactly."

"Yes. Exactly. That's you. You want to help. But I know that bunch better than you do. You don't want to get too involved, let me tell you."

"Why not?"

"You just don't."

"All right. But what was that about between you two?"

"What was what about?"

"I saw the look you gave each other. When I said I wanted lots of children."

"Nothing. It was nothing."

"Crescent."

"Well—" Her body slumped, then straightened as she made up her mind. She looked directly into Andrea's eyes. "They're right, you know, to call you The Flame. That's what you are. The flame of life. You're just too much, Andrea. You are too much."

And now she had the sorrowful experience of watching as Andrea began to understand, as her blooming complexion drained white and her warm brown eyes welled hot with tears. The flame she was could warm the dead and cheer them for an hour or two of their black eternity. But a living man could not withstand it; he would be consumed utterly.

Fred Chappell has been blurring boundaries drawn between mainstream and genre fiction in his many novels and collections of stories and poems, but almost always from the stance of a southern writer.

How do you overcome a vampire who doesn't believe in God?

God–Less Men

BY JAMES KISNER

ast Texas:

The people of Shannonbaugh, a dirtball little town on the outskirts of nowhere, had a problem.

Somebody was killing their young women in an unusual way—draining them of their blood through holes in their necks.

Like in the movies. Like when vampires did it.

Sheriff Lucas McIntyre didn't buy that vampire bullshit, but he did know one thing: people didn't keep running after they got hit with two or maybe three .357 Magnum slugs.

Not regular people anyhow. But the guy Lucas saw running away from the car with the dead young woman in it took the shots he fired at him—Lucas saw him jerk with the impact—but didn't stop for a second.

Lucas had tried to follow the trail of blood the guy left, but it went only a few feet then suddenly disappeared. As if the guy himself had somehow disappeared.

It didn't make a damn bit of sense.

◊◊◊

Lucas had to tell the preacher, Reverend John Satchel, about the dead woman personally. She was the preacher's daughter.

Reverend Satchel was in his late fifties, a medium-sized man who generally wore a wide-brimmed black felt hat, a plaid shirt, and jeans when he wasn't in the pulpit. His face was craggy and weatherbeaten, the face of a man who had seen too much—even before this tragedy.

Rumor was that before he replaced the late Reverend Paige, Satchel was involved with snake-handling cults and other renegade Christian sects. He'd neither confirm nor deny the rumors. But his visage bore the stamp of having seen hellfire up close and personal, like no other preacher.

His son had been in trouble with the law a couple of times, mostly because of drinking and driving, and his daughter had been his only solace in life. She was a good Christian girl who made her father proud—who would've made her mother proud, too, if Lona Satchel hadn't passed on ten years before.

Satchel turned from the dead girl on the table in the clinic, trembling and nodding his bald head.

"A God-less man did this," he muttered, wiping his brow with an orange bandanna. "God-less man took my Beth."

"This is number six," Lucas said quietly. "It's more than I can handle, Reverend. We need the Feds now, for sure. I should've called them in sooner—before this. . . ."

"I know of a man," Satchel said, turning his bloodshot eyes in Lucas' direction, his bushy eyebrows dripping from the heat, "a man who is a specialist in these matters."

"What in hell you mean, Reverend?"

"A tracker. A *real* detective who's dealt with this kind of evil before. The *federals* will not take it seriously and they will not catch our man."

"But, Reverend, don't you think we should . . ."

Satchel stood firm, staring up in Lucas' eyes with a determination that scared the young man. "I know what's right, by God. I'm a preacher." He lowered his gravelly voice an octave. "And it takes a God-less man to catch another one."

"I don't understand."

"You shot him. He kept on going. You're not dealing with a normal man. Maybe not even a *mortal* man. Maybe some kind of monster. Whatever he or it is, is certainly not something of God."

Lucas realized Satchel was buying into the vampire theory, though he didn't come right out and say it. What kind of preacher would believe in vampires? And what was this heavy talk about "God-less" men?

Lucas tried to argue, but the preacher wouldn't budge. So the sheriff agreed to call in the specialist, the vampire hunter.

How could he deny Satchel when his *daughter* had been slain?

◊◊◊

It was another hot day that July when the diminutive, bronze-skinned man appeared in Lucas' small office, but the man didn't remove his straw hat or wipe his brow, despite the lack of air conditioning. He wasn't even sweating.

Lucas, thirty-five, with thinning blond hair and azure blue eyes, remained behind his desk, staring up at the short Indian with ill-concealed disdain. His own shirt was soaked, and the fan buzzing in the corner offered little respite from the humidity.

"You don't look like a detective, Cochise," he said. He leaned back in his chair a bit to give his guest a look at his lanky, tall body and the gun at his side. He always greeted strangers in more a physical than a verbal way, figuring it was best to intimidate anyone who might cause trouble before they even thought about it.

"I'm not a detective. I just get paid for what I do, White Eyes." The man evidently wasn't impressed by Lucas' body language. "And my name is not 'Cochise.'"

Lucas relaxed a little. He'd had dealings with Indians before and knew some of them were hardheaded and easily offended. This one, though small, had an air of confidence about him, a no-bullshit stance that Lucas had to admire.

"Sit down, Mr. . . . ?"

"Sundance. Joe Sundance."

"Right, Sundance." He watched as Sundance sat down rather stiffly in the folding chair at the corner of his desk. The Indian wore a denim shirt and jeans, with snakeskin boots. He made eye contact with Lucas without flinching, another admirable trait in the sheriff's book of reckoning.

"What's your problem?" Sundance asked.

Lucas looked away, out the window at the cracked pavement running through the center of town. Across the street he saw a rich local climbing into a red Cadillac after leaving the hardware store. A kid rode past on a small bicycle. Then a big red dog ambled by in the opposite direction, his nose to the ground, following some odd scent. Lucas suddenly felt foolish; Shannonbaugh was a small, *normal* town. Weird things just did not happen here. Six girls didn't get killed savagely. By a monster.

Yet he had invited a man who was known as a vampire hunter to come help him. As if that were normal police procedure. He hadn't anticipated how ridiculous and foolish he would feel when the time came to deal with the man.

Sundance waited patiently.

Damn him, Lucas thought, wishing he'd go away. Finally, he said, "Well, we've had a slew of killings lately, and the evidence points to something—well, maybe—I don't know—something unusual." He wondered how Satchel even *knew* about people like this Sundance guy. Maybe the old man had handled more than snakes in his time.

"You don't believe in Changers, do you?"

Lucas was caught off guard both by the question and the Indian's unaffected manner of speaking. "What the hell do you mean?"

"Changers. Vampires."

"Oh. Hell, no, I don't. Why should I?"

"Because that is what is killing women here, and that is what will continue to kill them until it is stopped."

"I think it's just some sick bastard."

"Could be. Some people like to think they are Changers, just like some people like to think they are God, or trees."

"Why would anyone like to think he was a damn tree?"

"Why would anyone like to think he was a damn vampire?"

"I don't know."

"Me, neither." Sundance almost smiled, but his rugged face wasn't built for handling that expression. His long black hair was streaked with gray, and Lucas guessed he was fifty or so, though it was hard to tell with Indians. He might be a hundred.

"Let's cut through all the crap, Sundance," Lucas bristled. "I was against calling you here, but you're here now, so maybe you can help me. I don't have but one deputy and he's part-time and dumber than owl shit to boot. You're probably a good tracker if nothing else, so, whether this character is a vampire or not, you're hired."

"Fine with me. You don't have to believe if you don't want to."

"So what do you normally do first?"

"I want to see his latest victim—if you haven't buried her yet."

"No problem. She's in cold storage over at the clinic, which serves as funeral home and morgue in this town."

"Let's go. We need to do much before nightfall."

"Why's that?"

"He will strike again tonight. I feel it."

Lucas said nothing. He realized he was going to be weirded out by the Indian no matter what he said or did and decided, grudgingly, to accept it. He grabbed his hat, motioned to the door, and followed Sundance out into the hot sun.

◊◊◊

She was about nineteen, and even with most of the blood gone from her body, it was evident Beth was attractive, especially with that long blonde hair. It was a damn shame the killer was picking out the best local specimens of womanhood to prey on.

Why couldn't he attack nasty fat old women with bitchy attitudes that not many people would miss?

Lucas considered asking Sundance that, but the little man was busy studying the holes on Beth's neck.

"Judging from the space between the holes, I'd say this Changer is an adult."

"I could've told you that. I shot the son of a bitch."

"I know. Preacher Satchel told me. I was stating the fact for the record."

Lucas started to ask "What record?" but decided against it.

"So what else?"

"If a chemist took some blood from the wounds, he would find a substance there such as vampire bats secrete when they feed on animals—something in their saliva that keeps the blood from coagulating."

"Should I get someone to examine it?"

"If you want. Makes no difference now. Woman is dead."

"But that'd prove something, wouldn't it?"

"Proves your killer is a Changer and not a madman who only *thinks* he's one. But woman still is dead, and so will the next one be. Do what you want. Now take me to where she was found."

About two miles outside of town was a Lover's Lane, on an old gravel road that led up to a ridge overlooking a forest, where the preacher's daughter had been found in her car.

"Now Beth was a good girl," Lucas told Sundance, "but she wasn't perfect. The preacher knew she went out occasionally, though I doubt she let anyone go all the way with her. So I figure she was making out with the guy, then be kills her. The damnedest thing about it is there are no signs of struggle. How in hell could he do that to her without her fighting back?"

"Magic eyes."

"Say what?"

"Hypnotism. Changers are like snakes who hypnotize birds. The woman submitted without fighting. As I suspect the other victims apparently did."

"That's right," Lucas admitted.

"Bad sign."

"Why?"

"A lunatic may think he's a vampire, but he usually has to kill, then drink. Only a true Changer has the magic eyes to drink while the victim lives."

"Maybe not. Maybe he . . ." Lucas had no "maybe" to apply now that he thought about it.

Sundance asked to see where the man had run to and Lucas showed him. There were still dark brown spots on the ground where the blood had leaked.

"And it stops here."

"Bad sign." Sundance was down on his haunches, dipping his finger in the browned dirt. He wet his finger so dirt would stick to it, then brought it up to his nose to sniff. "Bad sign."

"Now what?"

"Two possibilities, both bad. One is Changer has special blood that coagulates almost instantly. Ordinary bullets may make hole, but not for long. By now, he's probably healed."

"Bullshit."

"The universe is full of bullshit, Sheriff."

"What's the other possibility?"

"He took off like an eagle. Some Changers can become different animals, depending on the necessity of the moment."

"Now you *are* bullshitting me, Sherlock." Lucas removed his hat and wiped his forehead, marveling again at how the Indian didn't sweat.

"I don't make the rules," Sundance replied. "I only report the facts." A cool breeze came out of nowhere, and he shivered. "Tonight will be a good time for the Changer. It will rain. It will be hard to find him in time. He will not expect us."

"How the hell will we know where to look? He's killed in several different places."

"I have an idea where he will *come* from."

Lucas scratched his head in amazement. "How in blazes could you have an idea? We don't have a goddamn clue."

"There are no atheists in foxholes, Sheriff. Remember that when the time comes."

Lucas' mouth dropped open at the apparent non-sequitur. Was Sundance being inscrutable to irritate him, or did his words really mean something?

Or was it all a bunch of crap, a show for the gullible White Man resented by all Indians?

Lucas decided to wait and see. But if Sundance was jerking him around, he'd kick his ass from here to Houston.

◊◊◊

An hour before sunset, after a quick dinner at Belle's Cafe and Service Station, Joe Sundance and Sheriff Lucas McIntyre went together to gather what Sundance called his "trapping apparatus," which he kept in a cloth bag behind the beach seat in the ancient Chevy pickup truck he drove.

Sundance struggled to unwedge the heavy bag from its hiding

place. When he finally pulled it loose and set it on the ground, Lucas saw it was three feet long, about a foot and a half high, and another foot or so deep. A beaded figure was sewn on one side of the bag—some kind of bird as far as Lucas could make it out—and on the other side was a representation of a crucifix, not in beads, but in embroidery.

Lucas had to ask, "You a Christian?"

"I am a God-fearing man."

"But are you a Christian?"

"No. I worship my gods."

"Then why the cross on the suitcase?"

"You never see a vampire movie?"

"Now, Sundance, don't try to tell me that even half the horsecrap in a movie is . . ."

". . . more than half is based on some legend which some people believe somewhere. In every part of the world there have been Changers, some say since the beginning of time. So every part of the world has a way of dealing with them. Myself, I am a pragmatist."

"A what?"

"A practical man. I don't have to believe in Jesus for Him—or in this case His symbol—to have power. I've got Holy Water, garlic, ten-inch spikes, a wooden stake and mallet, among other things in my bag, as well as a well-honed *kukri*—in short, my friend, all the necessities for killing Changers, vampires, or even mortal men."

"What the hell is a 'coo-kree'?"

Sundance almost smiled as a child might who wanted to show off his toys, then knelt, unzipped the bag, and pulled out a knife with a curved blade that was at least a foot long.

"This is a *kukri*, Sheriff. Ask a Vietnam vet. This weapon can behead a man with a single motion." Sundance demonstrated by slicing the air, and Lucas shuddered.

"Put that goddamn sickle away. I'm not going to let you go around chopping people's heads off."

"You may want me to when the time comes. Chop off Changer's head, destroy it, or stuff mouth with garlic, bury— Changer dead for good."

"You're a sick fuck," Lucas said solemnly. "I've half a mind to send you packing."

"Wait till after tonight, Sheriff. After I do my job."

Lucas watched Sundance drop the knife in the bag, then take out a small brass crucifix before zipping it shut. He tucked it in one of his shirt pockets and stood.

"All right, Sundance," Lucas said, "you get one chance."

"One is all I need." He cast his eyes to the sky. The temperature had dropped ten degrees and dark clouds were forming overhead. "Here comes the rain. And night soon, too." He hefted the bag over his shoulder by its strap. "Come, it's time to go after the Changer. He should be stirring soon."

"But where the hell are we going?"

Sundance got into the sheriff's car, tossing the bag in the back seat and closing the door on the passenger side. "You're driving."

Lucas got in and slammed his door shut. "Where, for God's sake?"

"The good preacher's house—drive there."

"Now, wait a minute.

"We have no time for argument, Sheriff. Besides, what have you got to lose?"

"Just my badge."

"Better than losing your ass, Sheriff. Take it from one who knows."

Lucas grumbled, then started the engine as the first big drops of rain pelted the windshield. He switched on the wipers, put the car in drive, then drove slowly to the edge of town, while Sundance sat and watched quietly.

By the time they reached Satchel's home, the rain was a dense sheet before them, and the sky had darkened.

It was night at last, and Sundance finally showed some fear. The little man was sweating like a pig as Lucas turned off the engine. Lucas rested his hand casually on his .357, determined to be ready for something, even if he wasn't sure what it was.

They sat and watched and waited while the rain fell and it grew darker and darker.

◊◊◊

The reverend's house was a small old frame structure, one story high, with a pointed roof. There was a porch out front on which sat a rusty swing glider, which the wind was causing to sway back and forth, making it emit tiny shrieks.

"Somebody ought to oil that thing," Lucas whispered.

Sundance said nothing. They were parked off the road on the edge of the woods that circled part of the town. They could see both the front and back door of the house. Sundance watched intently, barely breathing it seemed to Lucas, as if he were a cat and not a man.

After an hour of sitting in the rain, listening to the porch glider squeak and seeing nothing, Lucas spoke up.

"Why are we here?"

"You will see."

"You know, Reverend Satchel recommended you, though I don't know how the hell he would know about a guy like you."

"People who need me find me," Sundance said simply. "What I'm getting at—well, if Satchel called you, why are we watching him?" Lucas cast an uneasy glance at Sundance. "Damn, you don't think *he's* the killer?"

"No, I don't."

"Then who . . . ?"

Sundance stared out into the rain. It seemed a couple of minutes before he answered.

"He has a son, doesn't he?"

Lucas didn't know what to say. Maybe Sundance was the lunatic in this situation. Maybe Satchel himself. Maybe Satchel was crazy enough to think his son would kill his own baby sister. Which would make Jeremy Satchel crazy, too.

Hell, maybe *he'd* be screwy before this was over.

◊◊◊

Lucas awoke with a start, then realized he had been jabbed in the ribs and yelped.

"What the hell?"

"He preys." Sundance pointed toward the back of the house, where a figure draped in a dark plastic rain poncho was departing.

"That's Jeremy . . ."

". . . the reverend's son," Sundance finished. "Follow him. Slowly. At a distance. But do not lose him."

Lucas started the car and edged out on the road. "Why doesn't he take the old man's Buick?"

"It would raise suspicion. He doesn't need it, anyhow. He is fleet of foot. See how he moves. Like a wraith. Like a low cloud."

Lucas watched and had to confirm what Sundance observed. Jeremy Satchel seemed almost to float along the shoulder of the road as he headed into town. "I'll be damned."

The rain had slackened somewhat, so visibility was much improved and they could follow Jeremy at a safe distance and still see him clearly enough not to lose him.

"You have any idea where he's going?"

Sundance shook his head. "This is your town, Sheriff. Who is close by?"

Lucas thought a moment. "Two possibilities. A couple of blocks down, Linda Stumpf. Twentyish. Works at the restaurant. What the hell time is it?"

"After midnight."

"She'd be home then on a weeknight."

"And the other?"

"A nurse. Thirty or so. Lives in the trailer park. The only single woman there."

"Which is closer?"

"About the same from here, depending on whether you go north or east."

"He turns east."

"Linda."

"Hurry, Sheriff. We need to get there ahead of him if we can."

"I can go in from the back."

"Do it!"

They parked in the alley behind a small duplex in one half of which Linda Stumpf lived. Sundance dragged the bag from the back seat and they approached cautiously.

The rain was coming down hard again by the time they reached the back door.

"I hope you're right," Lucas said, rapping on the door. "A hungry man goes for the quickest meal. He has not fed since the preacher's daughter. He is no doubt famished and crazy with the great thirst that drives his kind."

"Quit that vampire talk for a while, Sundance. It's getting on my nerves. We have to *prove* Jeremy's the killer, you know. We can't just assume . . ."

The door opened and an attractive brunette woman with a full bosom, barely covered by a robe, greeted them.

"Why, Sheriff, what y'all doin' at my door this time of night?"

"Saving your life, I hope."

Linda blanched. "You mean. . . ?"

"We think he's picked you next."

"Come on in out of the rain, then, Lucas." She ushered the sheriff and Sundance into her kitchen, "Who's this?"

"Special deputy," Lucas said quickly. Then he glared at Sundance. "Well, hot shot, what now?"

"Turn out the light. Lady, go back in your bed."

"Whatever for? I was going to make some coffee for you and . . ."

"Do it," Lucas said. "No time to explain anything." Linda nodded nervously and switched off the kitchen light. She led the sheriff and Sundance down a hall which was dimly lit by a night light in an outlet near the bedroom. "I leave that on in case I have to go tinkle in the middle of the night," Linda said. "Y'all know what I mean?"

"Hurry," Sundance whispered.

Linda hesitated at her bedroom door. "Are you coming in my bedroom, too?"

"Yes," Sundance said. "We'll hide by the bed."

"Can I trust this Indian?"

"Yeah, sure. He won't molest you. Just get in the bed and pretend you're asleep."

"I don't know if I can."

"Hurry. He comes!" Sundance pushed her toward the bed, which was barely illuminated by a street lamp shining in through the curtained windows, then pulled Lucas down with him as he dropped to the floor.

"How do you know. . . ?"

"Listen."

Lucas heard the sound of rain hitting something soft. "What is it?"

"The poncho. He may walk in silence like the night, but the rain cannot be hushed as it hits his cloak."

As the sheriff and Sundance huddled on the floor next to the bed, Linda drew the covers up around her neck.

"Keep your eyes shut," Sundance ordered. "He must not suspect."

The sound of wood resisting pressure squeaked in the room. There was a shadow at the window of a man trying to pull it open.

"That window won't open," Linda whispered. "Painted shut."

"Shush!"

"He'll give up," Lucas said.

"No" Sundance muttered. He unzipped the bag. Lucas could hear him pulling something out.

The shadow stopped tugging on the window abruptly.

"Damn!" Lucas said.

"Oh, my God, I peed my pants!" Linda gasped.

"No time . . ." Sundance said.

Then there was an explosion of glass and splintered wood as the shadow hurled itself through the window, hit the floor with a roll, and sprang up on the bed, immediately pinning Linda's arms down.

She screamed.

Lucas stood up and drew his pistol.

The shadow hissed.

Sundance turned a bright flashlight on the shadow, revealing the snarling features of Jeremy Satchel, whose mouth was gaping open. Sharp fangs jutted from his teeth. His eyes were yellowish and bloodshot, his brown hair matted to his head from rain and sweat. He looked much older than his twenty-five years—*much*, much older.

"Stop, Jeremy!" Lucas yelled.

"He will not," Sundance said.

"Do something," Linda said, beginning to thrash under Jeremy.

Jeremy let go of one of her wrists and swung at Lucas. When he connected, the sheriff was jolted half way across the room.

Then Jeremy grabbed Linda's wrist again and started to press down on her, his lips quivering as he sought her neck.

He had apparently forgotten about Sundance.

Sundance had the small crucifix in his hand now. He thrust it under Jeremy's face.

Jeremy growled and swatted the offensive symbol away.

"So you do not believe in this God," Sundance said.

A *God-less* man, Lucas thought.

Jeremy paused to laugh. "If there is a God, why would he allow *things*—creatures—like me to exist?"

Lucas had recovered enough to throw on the overhead light. Somehow he had managed to hold on to his pistol, so he lifted it and aimed for Jeremy's shoulder.

"I'll stop him!" He pulled the trigger and part of Jeremy peeled off and splattered both Sundance and the girl. Linda screamed louder than ever when the blood hit her face. Jeremy shuddered but quickly regained his hold on the woman and resumed his attack.

Sundance tossed the crucifix on the floor, then ducked down to get something else from the bag.

"If you do not believe in one God," he said, rising with the.curved knife in one hand and something wooden in the other, "other gods will find you. *My* Gods will do." He brandished a carved eagle in Jeremy's direction and the young man found himself unable to move; "This God condemns you! This God that I believe in!"

"No!" Jeremy squealed, obviously shocked by the eagle's effect on him—so much so that he let go of the woman to cover his face.

Sundance took advantage of Jeremy's reaction quickly. He wielded the knife and with a single swift motion neatly lopped off the vampire's head and the hands covering the face.

The beheaded body, gushing dark blood from the neck, pitched forward on Linda, who emitted sounds that might have caused earthquakes in less sturdy surroundings.

Jeremy's head bounced across the floor, landing at Lucas' feet; the eyes seemed to be staring in amazement. The two severed hands flew into the corner.

Lucas' stomach heaved. He thought the eyes blinked. Reflexively, he shot the head, blowing a good third of it away.

"Good," Sundance said. "You have saved me having to destroy it." He pushed the body away from Linda, and tried to calm her. "It is over."

It was many hours before she calmed down, and many more hours before Lucas was able to explain what happened without choking on his own words.

Sundance remained inscrutable throughout it all.

◊◊◊

The next day, Sundance was waiting for Lucas in his office when he finally arrived, around noon.

Lucas' face was ashen and there were dark circles under his eyes. "It was the damnedest thing," he said quietly to Sundance as he sat behind his desk. "The reverend didn't get that upset. He even insisted I tell him every detail of what happened. The only thing he wanted was for me not to mention anything about the vampire part. As if I would."

"It is to be expected."

"He even seemed relieved."

"That, too, is to be expected."

"I don't get it," Lucas said. "None of it. Why *Jeremy?*"

"He didn't believe in God. Someone—some *thing*—another Changer, perhaps, took advantage of that to make him into one of their kind."

"But surely he didn't believe in the eagle thing you had."

"But I did, my friend. That is why there are no atheists in fox-holes. Every soldier believes in a god, and the enemy that doesn't is easier to overcome."

"It's too simple."

"Not simple at all. I make it simple so I don't have to talk about it for three hours."

"But Satchel—he said you were a 'God-less' man."

Sundance nodded gravely. "To him, yes. To him there's but one God. No sweat. My faith is as strong as his. We both end up in paradise or. . ." He paused and his eyes almost twinkled. ". . . in hell."

"You're a strange bird, Sundance."

Sundance nodded imperceptibly, then started toward the door.

"My work here is finished. My bill will go to the reverend—by his request. I am tired and the journey back home is long."

"Wait a minute. Since you know everything, maybe you can tell me why Satchel wasn't so upset today."

"Another simple thing. He summoned me. He *knew.*"

"He *wanted* you to destroy his son?"

"It is always a loved one who calls to put them out of their misery. The preacher's son was suffering torments I hope neither you nor I will ever endure. And the preacher was suffering too, knowing his son had forsaken *his* God. He tried to live with it, the horror of his son, but when Jeremy killed his sister, Satchel could no longer protect him."

"So you suspected him from the beginning."

"Yes."

"Then why go through all the rigmarole of inspecting the body and staking out the place?"

"I had to be sure. It was possible the preacher was mistaken, too."

"Sounds reasonable and damned logical. I guess I underestimated you."

"People often do." Sundance pulled the door open.

Lucas stood. "I'll walk you out."

Outside, before Sundance got into his truck, he stopped and confronted Lucas.

"Tell me, Sheriff, do you believe in vampires now?" Lucas' brow wrinkled as he considered all he had seen in the last twenty-four hours.

"I'm damned if I know," he said finally. "Cutting anybody's head off is going to stop them."

"Sounds reasonable," Sundance replied. He shook hands with Lucas and climbed up into the truck. "Good knowing you, Sheriff."

"What now, Chief?" Lucas asked.

"People who need me find me," he said, starting the engine. "You'd be surprised how much business I get."

James Kisner has written stories that appeared in *Masques 2, 3,* and *4,* as well as *Stalkers, Cold Blood,* and *Scare Care.*

An orphan forced to live with distant cousins—
cousins with some very odd habits—learns just how far family can go. . . .

Blood Kin

BY DELIA SHERMAN

At ten o'clock of a spring night in New Orleans, Clarisse Delmondé circled the front parlor of a fine pillared house on Washington Street, anxiously waiting for her cousins to arrive.

They were late. Clarisse felt she'd been waiting for hours. She'd read a fairy tale and looked at old photographs through her father's stereoscope. She'd made faces at herself in the mirror over the mantel. She'd tried to brush the ashes off the skirt of her black sailor dress. At the moment, she was weaving and circling her way along the rosy garlands of the parlor carpet.

One swoop took her from the fireplace to the bookcase. On the third shelf, between a medical book and an atlas, was a gap large enough for a two-pipe rack and a box of matches. Her father's nephew on Prytania Street had taken the pipes and the rack as keepsakes just after Dr. Delmondé's sudden death. Clarisse darted out her hand and tipped the atlas to bridge the gap. If her cousin smoked, he could just keep his pipes somewhere else.

Turning her back on the bookcase, she set out along a new garland, little quick steps from rose to rose, first to the long window opening onto the garden, then to the settee, where the book of fairy tales reproached her from its broken-backed sprawl. Guiltily, she picked it up and closed it. Mé-mère had been particular about things like taking care of books.

She stamped her foot and demanded of the clock, "Oh, where *are* they?" It ticked on, indifferent.

"Oh, pooh," she said, and marched to the ottoman straight across the garlands. It had been a silly game anyway.

There'd been a picture of the cousins among the stereoscope slides. Clarisse knelt by the ottoman and rummaged until she found the one labeled "Cazeaus and self—1875" in her mother's neat hand. When she turned it over, three tiny figures stared out of two nearly identical photographs printed side by side. Clarisse fitted the slide into the stereoscope and looked through the eye-piece. The figures sprang into sepia-tinted solidity.

A strange young woman wearing a small straw bonnet sat awk-wardly on the ground. She was plump and timid-looking, with a rosebud mouth and a round face. A strange young man stood behind, clutching the edge of his waistcoat and scowling at the photographer. Despite the scowl, he had a nice face, Clarisse thought, and a fine black mustache, almost as fine as Papa's. And there was Mé-mère, seated on a bench between them, very young and odd in old-fashioned clothes, but recognizably Mé-mère. Out of the stereoscope she looked back at her daughter with cool serenity, her chin lifted and her fingers laced in her lap. There were white roses pinned in her dark hair.

Clarisse leaned her forehead against the stereoscope and sobbed.

A portly black woman in a white head-cloth and apron looked in the parlor door and clucked her tongue. "It do beat all, Mam'selle Clarisse, how you manage to ruck your collar up to one side like that. Come here and let me pin it straight."

Clarisse rubbed her nose over her sleeve and obeyed.

Lanie took a handkerchief from her apron, spat on it impas-sively, and began to scrub at Clarisse's cheeks.

"This'll bring out your color, child, and Lord knows you need it. M'sieu and Mam'selle Cazeau'll be here directly, and you so peaky-lookin' anybody'd think you was expectin' monsters instead of your own blood kin. There." Lanie pulled at the bow perched like a shiny black butterfly on the top of Clarisse's head.

"*Voyez*, I've picked a bud for your sash, and another for Mam'selle Cazeau *comme bienvenue.*"

Clarisse took the two tightly furled buds, then burrowed her face into the starched white scarf folded across Lanie's bosom. "I don't want to give Mam'selle Cazeau a rosebud. Why should I give Mam'selle Cazeau one of Mé-mère's rosebuds?"

"You want to listen to me, Child." Lanie's hands were warm on Clarisse's shoulders. "M'sieu and Mam'selle Cazeau're your ma's kinfolk. She and your pa, they thought they were fit to raise you. You studyin' to set yourself up as smarter than your pa?" She gave Clarisse a gentle shake, then took one of the rosebuds—a white one—and tucked it into her sash. "No more foolishness, hear? That's the door. If you want Madame Delmondé to look down from heaven and be proud of you, you mind your manners."

Clarisse had heard this argument so often in the last few months that it had pretty well lost its effect. But she smoothed her skirt anyway and decided it wouldn't hurt to be polite. They'd looked nice enough in the photograph.

The door opened, and a tall lady in black serge came into the room, rushed up to her, and saluted her cheek with a wet, smacking kiss.

"Poor *petite*," bayed Mam'selle Cazeau. "Poor orphaned lamb. I declare, Jaspar, when I think of poor, dear Chloë leavin' this sweet child without a mother, I could just lie down and howl."

Clarisse had not seen Monsieur Cazeau enter, but when she turned around, there was a thin man in black sitting on the settee. He was reading fairy tales as if he'd been there all day. Without looking up, he said, "There, there, Juno. Don't take on so. Tragic affair, tragic. But you're upsettin' the child."

"But no," said Mam'selle Cazeau. She held Clarisse out to arm's length and looked at her with sad brown eyes. "I'm not upsettin' you, am I, *chérie?*"

Clarisse felt a little prickle of anger. "Yes, ma'am," she said. Her cousin's high forehead creased in distress. Remembering that she'd decided to be polite, Clarisse held out the scarlet rosebud to her and said, "I am very pleased to welcome you to your new home."

Mam'selle Cazeau looked unhappier than ever. "Did Chloë never tell you, *chérie,* that I am a martyr to rose fever? Of course not, why should she? You must take it away at once, but I thank you for the sweet little thought. You will call me Cousin Juno."

I don't like her, Clarisse thought, taking in Mam'selle Cazeau's thin-lipped mouth and long, lined face. Her cousin looked older than she'd expected, not at all like the plump, timid girl in the photograph.

As if she'd read her young cousin's mind, Mam'selle Cazeau grinned unpleasantly, displaying a set of unnaturally long, white teeth. "Go greet your Cousin Jaspar now, *chérie.* You have no roses for him? *Ah, bon.*"

Monsieur Cazeau was so absorbed in the fairy tales that he didn't notice Clarisse standing awkwardly in front of him. Despite the warmth of the evening, he wore a large shawl that hung over both arms like woolen wings and a pair of darkly smoked spectacles that hid his eyes. His skin was waxy, his lips were pale; in fact, the healthiest thing about him was his horseshoe mustache, which was black and very luxuriant. Clarisse shifted uneasily from one foot to the other. He'd looked bigger in the photograph, but maybe his sickness, whatever it was, had made him shrivel up. He, too, was older than she'd thought he'd be.

Monsieur Cazeau turned a page. If he didn't look up soon, Clarisse thought, she'd just walk right out of the room and let Lanie scold her if she was minded to. She decided she didn't like Cousin Jaspar Cazeau any more than she liked his sister.

"Jaspar. The child," Mam'selle Cazeau barked.

"Ah, yes." Monsieur Cazeau laid down the book, pushed his smoked spectacles farther up his nose, and held out two fingers for Clarisse to shake. The spectacles gave him a blind look, and his fingers were cold and limp against her palm.

"*Enchanté,*" he said. The glossy wings of his mustache lifted and twitched. "Tragic thing. Blood kin, y'know. Terrible waste. Terrible."

Staring fascinated at the mustache, Clarisse said, "Yes, M'sieu. Thank you, M'sieu."

Mam'selle Cazeau gathered up the stereoscope and the slides and installed herself at Madame Delmondé's writing desk with them. "Oh, Jaspar," she cried. "See what a lovely picture of Chloë! Who's that handsome couple she's with?"

Clarisse, surprised, turned to stare at her. "But Mam'selle . . . Cousin Juno. That's you!"

"Why, so it is." Mam'selle Cazeau squinted shortsightedly at the slide. "I declare, I hardly recognize myself under all that puppy fat. We were ridiculously young, weren't we, Jaspar?"

Monsieur Cazeau shrugged, rose, and wandered over to the bookcase, where he straightened the atlas. Clarisse wrinkled her upper lip at him in a way that would surely have earned her a scolding if he'd noticed. But he didn't. Boldly, she stuck her tongue right out at him and made for the door.

When she opened it, a housemaid was standing on the other side with a tray of sandwiches.

Mam'selle Cazeau sniffed loudly. "Thoughtful child!" she exclaimed. "How'd you know I was perishin' with hunger? And I purely love sliced beef."

Clarisse felt put-upon, but passed the sandwiches anyway. Mam'selle Cazeau took two. Monsieur Cazeau declined.

"Meat's so bad for his digestion," said his sister. "He eats almost nothin'—you might almost think he lives on air. Now, *chérie*, it's high time you were in bed. M'sieu Cazeau and I, we have a deal of unpackin' to do." She rose and, to Clarisse's dismay, hugged her to her black serge bosom. "Oh, I just know we're goin' to be such good friends, *chérie*, just like your poor ma and me."

"Guardians, y'know," added Monsieur Cazeau, patting her cheek with his cold, damp hand. "Mother's kin. Your own flesh and blood."

◊◊◊

Up in her own room, Clarisse let herself go at last. "She wasn't Mé-mère's friend. She couldn't have been," she wailed as Lanie undid her buttons. "I can't believe Cousin Juno is even *related* to Mé-mère. She's so . . . awful."

Lanie pulled the black dress over her head and hung it in the armoire. "Hush yourself now, child; that's no way to talk."

"But she gulps, and sniffs, and squints, and she'd talk the

whiskers off a pig. And she said she had rose fever, and wouldn't take the rose, and didn't seem to care anythin' about me. Mé-mère would have taken the rose."

"Shame on you," said Lanie severely. "You got any smart sass 'bout M'sieu Cazeau?"

Clarisse thought a minute. "I don't know. He's not like Papa."

"Course he ain't. He's sickly, poor gentleman." Lanie waited for Clarisse to climb into the tall mahogany bed, then pulled down the mosquito bar. "You want your ma to be proud, you study to please him, and Mam'selle Cazeau too, and don't trouble your head over whether they please you. With kin, it ain't likin' or not likin' that counts. It's blood that counts, and don't you forget it."

◊◊◊

Clarisse came down to breakfast in the morning to find Cousin Juno there before her. At first Clarisse thought she was the first one up, seeing as the dining-room curtains were drawn shut. But when she went to let in the sun, Cousin Juno's brisk voice addressed her out of the gloom.

"My goodness, *petite*, don't open the curtains. I just know it's comin' on a scorcher, and on a hot day, there's nothin' cooler than a dark house, don't you think? I've told the servants to keep the curtains and shutters closed until nightfall."

"Mé-mère never did that," Clarisse objected.

"But I do," said Cousin Juno.

And that was that.

Clarisse soon learned that normal definitions of supper and breakfast, night and day, meant nothing to her cousins. No matter how early she got up in the morning, Mam'selle Cazeau was eating a steak in the breakfast room. Monsieur Cazeau, on the other hand, stayed up at night, slept during the day, and took his meals alone in his room. Monsieur Cazeau, Cousin Juno explained, had delicate nerves that couldn't endure the brightness and bustle of daylight.

"It's a *family* disorder," she told Clarisse. "Didn't poor Chloë . . . ? No, I don't suppose she did. It's been in the family for generations, I believe, since before the Cazeaus came over from France. The cold hands, the weak eyes, the exquisite sensitivity to noise and light—it's all part of your inheritance, *chérie*."

She made it sound like a treat, but Clarisse was not impressed. "If you say so, Cousin Juno," she said sullenly.

"If I say so? *Ma foi!* It's clear Chloë has taught you nothing of family feeling! What will I do with you?" She gazed at Clarisse mournfully, then brightened. "I know. Your cousin Jasper likes to be read to. You shall read to him. You may begin this evening, after supper."

Clarisse said that she hated reading aloud, that she always stuttered. Cousin Juno said a little practice would do her good. This argument led inevitably to an argument with Lanie, which led inevitably to Clarisse's standing in front of the library, sullen but resigned to her fate.

She knocked. Monsieur Cazeau called *"Entrez,"* and she pushed open the door. Except for an unseasonable fire and a heavily shaded oil lamp, the library was unlit and looked empty. A low, rasping voice spoke from behind Dr. Delmondé's big desk.

"You must call me Cousin," said Monsieur Cazeau.

Clarisse peered into the gloom. Coal-red circles winked back at her, and she bit her lip to keep from gasping. It was just the firelight reflecting off Cousin Jasper's spectacles, after all.

"Bon enfant," he said encouragingly. Apart from the spectacles, he was just another shadow on her father's books, formless as smoke. The smoke stirred. Then a hand, a perfectly ordinary hand, help out a book and shook it impatiently. "This is what I wish you to read," said Cousin Jaspar. "Must I bring it to you?"

Clarisse blushed, took the book, and sat down by the lamp. The book was fat, with fat, creamy pages crowded with black type. It looked depressingly like sermons. She opened it. The title page read: *"Collected Tales.* Edgar Allan Poe."

"Begin," said Cousin Jaspar, "with 'The Tell-Tale Heart.'"

Clarisse opened to the story and glanced at the first line: "True!—nervous—very, very dreadfully nervous I had been and am; but why *will* you say that I am mad?" Did nervous gentlemen like to read about themselves? she wondered. But Monsieur Cazeau—cousin Jaspar—wasn't mad. Was he?

"What are you waiting for? Begin!"

So Clarisse read aloud about the nervous gentleman and his acute hearing and how he loved a good old man but hated his filmy blue eye, and so smothered him and cut him into pieces and hid him under the floor. Police came to investigate the screams. While they were questioning the nervous gentleman, he began to hear a sound, a low, dull, quick sound, the sound of the murdered man's heart beating under the floorboards, beating louder and louder until he could stand no more.

"'Villians!' I shriek, 'dissemble no more! I admit the deed!—tear up the planks!—here, here!—it is the beating of his hideous heart!'"

It was very quiet in the library when Clarisse finished. She put a hand to her cheek, which felt hot and flushed, and looked toward the desk.

Cousin Jaspar was sitting in shadow, but Clarisse could just make out his white hands folded around something dark: his spectacles she thought—the upper part of his face seemed lighter than usual. She'd been going to exclaim about the story, how horrible, how strange and frightening it was, but something drained her exclamations away into silence.

"Did you like it?" he asked her.

Clarisse had to think what he was asking her about. "Well," she said at last, "it scared me, with the eye and the heart and everythin'. But it was kind of excitin'. Wasn't it?"

"Yes," he said. "Excitin'. Just so. Tomorrow," he said, "you shall read another."

Over the next evenings, Clarisse read many others, most of them as strange, horrible, and exciting as "The Tell-Tale Heart." She would emerge from reading them as from cold water: shivering, her bones prickling, hardly able to remember what she'd read, except in nightmares. The excitement soon wore away, and she began to dread the moment every night when Cousin Juno looked up and said, "It's gone eight. You don't want to keep your cousin waitin'."

◊◊◊

It wasn't only the stories. It was the close, earthy smell the library was beginning to take on, and the way she must sit with her book in a pool of light while her cousin sat hidden in the shadows, watching her as she read. Sometimes she was so conscious of his naked eyes upon her that she couldn't go on, but sat blushing and staring silently at the book until he requested her sharply to continue.

After two weeks of this, Clarisse was ready to rebel. She couldn't think why she didn't. Once or twice, she did tell Cousin Juno that she wouldn't go to the library tonight, but somehow she ended up there all the same, reading about madness and death under Cousin Jaspar's shadowed gaze.

Trying to explain this to herself, Clarisse decided that she preferred the library, gloomy as it was, to the horror Mé-mère's parlor had become. Cousin Juno had crated up Madame Delmondé's pretty ornaments and pictures and gilded mirrors and stacked them in the attic, along with Dr. Delmondé's medical instruments, his magic lantern, the stereoscope, and the photographs. She left the walls bare. She covered the rose-brocade chairs with cheap muslin and the mantels and tables with animal skulls. It was as if she were determined to sweep Clarisse's parents out of the house on Washington Street, memories and all.

The only place Cousin Juno didn't seem interested in clearing out was the garden.

It wasn't a very big garden, but Madame Delmondé had managed to fit a trellis into it, numerous flower beds, brick paths, and even a small, round, white gaze-beau tucked down at the far end under a live oak. The trellis supported a creamy yellow rambler, the beds were fragrant with jessamine and violets, and dozens of roses bloomed in bright profusion against the wrought-iron fence. Red-striped "Papa Goutier" and snowy "Mme. Hardy," crimson "La France" and pale lilac "Marie-Louise," had been Madame Delmondé's greatest joy. After she died, Clarisse had shunned the garden until the need to escape the gloomy house drove her outside again. Now, most afternoons found her wandering among the rose beds.

One day a month or so after her cousins' arrival, Clarisse tied on her sunbonnet as usual and slipped out into the parterre. The sun was very hot, and after the dark mustiness of the house, the full color and scent of the roses poured over her like a bright waterfall. Clarisse twirled joyfully, her face lifted to the sun. It was a day for playing hopscotch down the brick paths, she decided. She was running to the gaze-beau for a piece of chalk when she tripped over an uprooted rosebush.

It was very new, very rare, Madame Delmondé's pride and joy: golden "Mme. Caroline Testout." Something—a dog, perhaps—had scrabbled around its roots, torn it out of its deep, soft bed, and left it on the hot brick to wither and die.

Horrified, Clarisse spun on her heel and ran inside calling furiously for the housemaids, for Lanie, for Cousin Juno. When no one answered, she ran without thinking up the long curved staircase and banged on Cousin Jaspar's bedroom door.

"Someone's dug up 'Mme. Caroline Testout,'" she called. "You must get up and do somethin'!"

Silence. Clarisse knocked again, but still there was silence: Utter silence.

A nervous gentleman, she thought, would have woken up by now. "Cousin Jaspar!" she shouted, pounding until her knuckles tingled. "Cousin Jaspar! Are you well, Cousin Jaspar? Oh, do please answer me!"

All at once, Cousin Juno was standing at the stair head, looking very fierce. "What do you reckon you're doing, girl?"

"Oh, Cousin Juno," sobbed Clarisse. "It's 'Mme. Caroline Testout'—Mé-mère's pet rose. It's been ripped right out, and I thought Cousin Jaspar should know, but he won't wake up, and oh, Cousin Juno—what if he is ill, or dead?"

"Dead? Nonsense! *Vaurienne!* Have I not told you again and again that my brother must not be disturbed?"

"But—" Clarisse began. Cousin Juno lunged at her, teeth bared. Clarisse ducked away from her hands, sped down th hall to her own room, wedged herself between the armoire and the wallstand, and broke into a tempest of weeping. It was so *unfair!* Mé-mère's rose had been wantonly destroyed. Someone should *do* something about it. Oh, how she hated Cousin Juno! How she hated them both.

Some time later, the gong rang for dinner. Clarisse did not answer. Footsteps approached her door, stopped; a hand knocked heavily. Clarisse curled herself more tightly into her corner. Maybe if she made herself small enough, Cousin Juno wouldn't find her. Faint hope. Cousin Juno always found her when she hid inside.

The door opened. "Child?" Lanie's voice was sharp. "Mam'selle Clarisse? What's wrong with you, hidin' in the dark like that?"

Giddy with relief, Clarisse scrambled up and ran to her. "Too much sun, I guess. Nothin's wrong, Lanie. It's just . . . I'm not hungry."

"Not hungry! Go along with you; you got to eat your supper. I reckon you'd eat it fast enough if Madame Delmondé was alive."

"If Mé-mère was alive," said Clarisse sullenly, "I'd be hungry."

Lanie shook her head. "What am I goin' to do with you, Mam'selle Clarisse? They're your kin, child. Everybody's kin got odd ways. You just got to put up with them."

Put up with being haunted by ghouls? Put up with being growled at? Lanie just didn't understand, and for the first time in her life, Clarisse felt too tired to argue. Dully, she removed the crumpled sunbonnet, washed her hands and face, and went downstairs. But her stomach was tight with betrayal, and she ate almost nothing.

"Do eat somethin', child," begged Cousin Juno, setting down a well-gnawed drumstick. "I declare, your appetite's gettin' as bad as Jaspar's."

◊◊◊

A few days later, Cousin Juno dismissed the yard boy, the cook, and the housemaids, and would have dismissed Lanie, too, except that Lanie wouldn't go. Clarisse wasn't quite sure whether Lanie was on her side or theirs, but she was still glad not to be left entirely alone with her cousins and her nightmares. When she woke sweating from a dream of pushing against a coffin lid that would not open, it comforted her a little to know that Lanie was asleep behind the kitchen, just under her room. Sometimes she'd creep down the back stairs, curl up by Lanie's door, and listen to her low snoring until dawn. Later, she'd go to sleep in the gaze-beau. Her dreams never followed her there.

One night after Cousin Jaspar had released her from the library, Clarisse was especially wide-awake and restless. She'd slept among the roses most of the day, and now she felt she never wanted to sleep again, or sit still, or read another word. She paced from room to empty room, listening for a rustling of shrouds and scrabbling of fingers against coffin lids. Beds hulked dark as biers in the lamplight; armoires gaped like upended coffins.

Clarisse ran into her own room, pulled back the draperies, and threw wide the shutters to the warm, living night.

A full moon hung over the live oak, bright enough to throw shadows. The garden was all silver and black, and a scent so strong it was almost another color—the perfume of a thousand roses, sweet and sharp at once, like Mé-mère.

Clarisse propped her elbows on the windowsill and sighed. As long as she had Lanie and the garden, she could bear her cousins and the dreams, she thought.

A figure—no, two figures, a man and a dog—stepped out of the parlor door and into the moonlight. Quick and awkward as a spider, the man scuttled away from the house; the dog—a tall, dark hound—paced gracefully beside him. Clarisse gave a strangled scream of anger and the man gaped up at her. Moonlight flashed from his spectacles and his long teeth and lost itself in the shadow of his monstrous mustache. Grabbing the silver hairbrush from her dresser, Clarisse threw it at him with all her strength.

The hound barked and the man flickered aside.

"Go away!" shrieked Clarisse. "It's *my* garden!"

Laughing, Cousin Jaspar spread his shawl like black wings, and was gone.

◊◊◊

It was morning when Clarisse awoke. The window was closed and the curtains drawn as usual, and she thought she must have dreamed the hound and Cousin Jaspar's gleaming teeth. But her hairbrush was gone and she didn't go out into the garden for fear of seeing footprints in the soft earth of the flower bed.

Clarisse went to the library that night with her heart beating hard and thick.

"I won't read you any more of Mr. Poe's horrid stories," she announced as soon as she was in the door. "I won't read any more at all."

"Very well," Cousin Jaspar said, his mustache fluttering weakly. "No more Poe. You shall read Mr. Stoker instead."

Clarisse had meant to leave after her declaration, and was astonished to find herself, a moment later, sitting under the lamp as usual, a book open on her lap.

"'Dracula,'" she heard herself say. "'Jonathan Harker's Journal. 3 May. Bistritz.—Left Munich at 8:35 P.M. on 1st May.'"

What followed was very dull, more a travel book about the quaint customs of Transylvania than a story. Clarisse's voice was clear. When she came to the bottom of a page, her hand reached steadily for the next leaf. But Clarisse herself, imprisoned in this calm shell, was shaking with fear. She didn't want to read, but she heard herself reading anyway, word after word after word, as though she'd never stop. And Cousin Jaspar wasn't sitting quietly behind Papa's big desk the way he usually did. Cousin Jaspar was making little clicking noises with his tongue, and muttering "Fool!" and *"Imbécile!"* at intervals. Soon he got up and began to pace around the room so briskly that his shawl fluttered behind him. By the time she'd come to the end of the chapter, he was clearly nervous—very, very dreadfully nervous.

"Enough, enough!" he cried, and plucked the book out of Clarisse's steady hands. "It's time for my dinner. You must go away now."

◊◊◊

The next night, Clarisse found Cousin Jaspar occupying her usual chair by the oil lamp. He was calm again, but very pale, a poor invalid cocooned in a black shawl. He twitched his mustache pleasantly when he saw her and pointed to the Turkey-work stool at his feet.

"Tonight, little cousin, we shall read together," he said.

After the previous night, the last place Clarisse wanted to sit was at Cousin Jaspar's feet. Yet somehow she was not surprised to find herself sitting down on the stool, taking the book from him, and leaning against his shawled knees as she read as though they were the best friends in the world.

Cousin Jaspar touched her hair lightly, a spider touch. She trembled and fell silent. "Continue," he said. And willy-nilly, while Cousin Jaspar stroked her hair with his icy hand, Clarisse read on, growing colder and colder with each sentence, both inside and out. She hardly knew what she read, except that it was no longer dull, no longer a travelogue. It had wolves and bats in it, and three women who thirsted for blood. Her fingers grew numb; she fumbled at the page. Cousin Jaspar bent over her, took her hands and chafed them gently, then lifted her up with irresistible strength to perch on his bony knees.

"Have no fear," he murmured as he lapped her in black, woolen wings. "The cold bites, I know. Warm soon. Warm as blood." He lifted her hand to his mouth; Clarisse felt the stiff brush of his mustache against her skin. "Little cousin. Own flesh and blood."

◊◊◊

Once Clarisse began to read *Dracula* with Cousin Jaspar, *Dracula* haunted her, sleeping and waking. Day or night, whenever she closed her eyes, she saw a pale figure bending over her, the hairy wings of his mustache clotted with blood. She felt bats fluttering upon her chest and heard wolves howling from the shadows. Often she walked in her sleep and woke in odd places, or dreamed of waking. Once she thought she saw a hound in the parlor, sitting up on the settee as prim as you please, daintily eating a sandwich. Another time she thought Lanie was holding her on her lap and rocking her in the garden. When she woke to dead, musty darkness, she wept.

One night she dreamed and knew she was dreaming. She was lying on her back in a coffin, her limbs cold and very heavy. Gentle hands laid her there; a gentle voice whispered a promise. "Soon you shall be my companion and my helper," said the voice. "Flesh of my flesh; blood of my blood; kin of my kin."

Clarisse opened her eyes on a dark transparency. The room was unlit, but she could clearly see a silk-lined tester above her head, and the four massive bedposts that held it there. Surrounding her were polished wooden planks. She smelled old blood and bones, like a butcher shop, and something else as well, something that reminded her of crawling under the gaze-beau when she was little. Damp earth, that was it.

Very calmly, Clarisse sat up, drew her knees to her chin, and considered. This was her parents bedroom—Cousin Jaspar's bedroom now. What was a coffin doing in Cousin Jaspar's bedroom? And why was she sleeping in it? Had her cousins thought she was dead? Cousin Jaspar, at least, should know better. Cousin Jaspar knew all about deathlike trances, just as he knew about madmen and ghouls and ghosts and vampires. And vampires.

As if the word had released her, Clarisse sprang from the coffin, scattering black dirt over the white-lace counterpane. She ran to the door and twisted the doorknob. But the door was stuck or locked.

"Lanie!" she sobbed. "Lanie!" She seized the knob with both hands and pulled at it with all her strength. "Lanie, I need you!"

"By gracious, child! What ails you?" Lanie sat up in bed and gaped at her. Clarisse gaped back. She was downstairs in Lanie's bedroom. which was lit by the same dark radiance as her parents'—Cousin Jaspar's—room. She didn't remember opening the door or coming down the stairs, and yet here she was, like magic, and there was Lanie with her hair all in tiny plaits, fumbling to light the oil lamp. Clarisse squinted in the sudden glare.

"You had a bad dream or somethin'? Lanie'll warm you some milk, child, and set with you while—"

"It wasn't a dream." Clarisse knew she could never explain, so she grabbed Lanie's hand and dragged her out of bed.

"I'm not a sack of meal, child," Lanie complained, but she took up the lamp and let Clarisse lead her through the dark and empty halls to the master bedroom, where her eyes moved from the door, which was sagging on its hinges, to the coffin resting on the high mahogany bed.

"*Sacré Dieu!*" she whispered. "I never seen such a thing."

"It's a vampire's coffin," said Clarisse. She felt better now. Lanie was here.

"What's that you say?"

It was hard to imagine that Lanie didn't know all about it, but then Lanie had never read *Dracula*. Patiently as she could, Clarisse explained. "Vampires drink blood and sleep in coffins. Sunlight kills them. Cousin Jaspar is a vampire, and this is his bed. If we empty all the dirt out of it, come dawn, Cousin Jaspar'll have nowhere to go."

Lanie turned to Clarisse, opened her mouth, and helplessly closed it again. Clarisse sighed. "I read about it in *Dracula*. Just you wait. He'll dry up and blow away."

◊◊◊

Lanie looked doubtful. "What about that Mam'selle Cazeau? I seen her out in the daylight, and she never dried up and blew away, more's the pity."

"No, Cousin Juno's not a vampire." Clarisse remembered the hound in the garden. "I guess she does for Cousin Jaspar durin' the day and turns into a hound at night. I don't know how it works—there's nothin' like her in Poe. She's just a dumb hound, Lanie—she's not important. *He'll* be back by dawn."

"By dawn." Lanie clutched her shawl around her and gave a mighty shudder. "Never did take to them, kin or not," she said. "They're no fit guardians for a young girl. I reckon they're not Cazeaus at all."

Dawn was no more than a hour or two away—Clarisse could feel its nearness in her blood. "It's not *important*, Lanie. We got to hurry."

"Where're we goin' to put this here grave dirt, Mam'selle Clarisse? If we pile it up somewhere, he might could burrow down in it."

Clarisse thought for a moment. "It's good rich earth. We'll spread it on Mé-mère's roses."

◊◊◊

The business of emptying the coffin was eerily ordinary. Lanie found two buckets and a spade in the shed. She shoveled dirt out of the coffin into one bucket while Clarisse trotted downstairs with the other and spread its contents over the flower beds. After a while, Lanie begged her to slow down, but Clarisse shook her head and trotted faster. She felt quite well for the first time in weeks. She also felt increasingly angry.

It wasn't fair. The Cazeaus had wormed themselves into Mé-mère's house—*her* house—and picked her life into a thousand pieces. She was sure, somehow, that they *were* Cazeaus, although certainly not the same Cazeaus in the photograph with Mé-mère, not the same Cazeaus Papa and Mé-mère had trusted to raise her. Cousin Juno wasn't so bad, once you realized she was nothing but a stupid hound, stupidly obeying her master's commands. No, it was Cousin Jaspar Clarisse hated. Cousin Jaspar had made her read things that gave her nightmares; Cousin Jaspar had drunk her blood. Well, she'd fix Cousin Jaspar. She'd fix him good.

By the time Clarisse had patted the last bucket of dirt around the roots of the rambler on the trellis, she was in a cold rage. She ran upstairs where Lanie was sitting on the daybed, staring at the fine rosewood coffin.

"Hurry, Lanie," she begged. "It's almost dawn." But Lanie only looked at her wearily, so Clarisse tore the curtains from their rings and jerked the shutters half off their hinges.

"Child, child, we done enough," said Lanie.

"No! Tain't enough. There're still a dozen places he could hide from the sun. He could creep into the armoire, or pull the coffin lid over him." Snatching the spade from Lanie's hand, Clarisse shattered the armoire door, splintered the coffin lid, and finally attacked the coffin itself, gouging great wounds in the wood with the edge of the shade. A terrible cry from the door stopped her in mid stroke.

"Little cousin!"

Clarisse spun around to see Cousin Jaspar clutching the door frame with white fingers. He was without his spectacles for once, and his naked eyes blazed red as his lips that snarled and writhed beneath his mustache.

He lurched into the room and seized Clarisse's shoulders with his cold, cold hands. "Where is my bed?" he whispered hoarse as the wind. "What have you done with my grave?"

Clarisse was frightened, but with a delicious, thrilling fear that fizzed in her blood. She laughed. "It's on the rose beds, Cousin Jaspar, Mé-mère's rose beds, that Cousin Juno's been diggin' up."

Cousin Jaspar ran for the window. Clarisse was a little surprised that he didn't leap out of it and swoop down into the garden on his woolen wings. Instead, he scuttled down the side of the house head first like a great lizard, and crept among the rosebushes desperately scraping at the soil.

A black hound leaped over the wrought-iron fence, barked, and bounded over to Cousin Jaspar, who spurned her with his foot. She whimpered, then sniffed the air and barked again.

"Dig, Juno," he ordered her.

The hound took a corner of his jacket and shawl in her great jaws and tugged. He tore away from her, gathered a little more dirt into his pitiful pile. She dropped the shawl and seized his foot. He kicked her. The hound sat down and howled a lost, despairing sound.

"Look, child," said Lanie. "Sun's comin'."

But Clarisse was too intent on the vampire's attempts to remake his bed to care that the sky was turning from black to gray to pale gold. A bird trilled from the live oak. Cousin Jaspar reared up on his knees and screamed like an enraged rat. The light grew brighter. He threw himself down on the pile he'd made. The sun broke over the live oak and shone, full and clean and dazzling, into the little garden and the bedroom window.

The dark hound pawed at the vampire's limp arm, lifted her muzzle to the sun, and howled again. In the bedroom, Clarisse sighed and folded onto the floor. When she did not move, Lanie gathered her up and rocked her to her breast.

"Ma fille, ma fille," she mourned.

In the garden, the dark hound howled again.

Lanie looked down at Clarisse, lying in her arms deathly pale and still. Half-moons of white showed below her lashes, and at the base of her neck were two oozing puckers like half-healed wounds. A breeze, laden with rose scent and sunlight, stirred her hair, and under Lanie's eyes, the wounds slowly dried and closed to two pink thorn scratches on the young girl's throat.

Clarisse sighed and opened her eyes. "Have I walked in my sleep again?" she asked.

"Maybe you was at first, child, but that last part wasn't no dream. He's gone, and he ain't never comin' back."

Clarisse blinked and snuggled into Lanie's arms. She was tempted just to lie there until the sunlight baked even the memory of Cousin Jaspar's numbing chill from her bones. A cloud passed over the sun. Clarisse shivered.

"I want to look, Lanie. I want to see for myself."

Gently, Lanie helped her to her knees so she could look out into the garden. Cousin Jaspar's black suit lay spread-eagled under the white sprays of a wild rose. Cousin Juno lay across him with her muzzle cradled on her outstretched paws. She might have been dead or only asleep. Clarisse was too tired to care.

"We can leave here, can't we, Lanie?"

"Yes, child."

"And never come back again?"

Lanie hesitated. "I don't know about that, Mam'selle Clarisse. This here's your home, when all's said and done, and you got a duty to Madame Delmondé and the doctor to look out after it."

Clarisse frowned. "Seems to me I *been* lookin' out after it, Lanie."

"That's right, child. I reckon you have. Your ma'd be proud of you."

"We'll stay," said Clarisse after a moment. "I want to stay." She pulled herself to her feet, looked around at the bed, the shattered coffin, the curtains tumbled on the dirty floor. "We'll clear all this up, Lanie, and rehire the yard boy and the cook and the housemaids. We'll put the pictures and the mirrors back. When the house looks like home again, I want to fill it with roses."

Delia Sherman is the author of two novels, *The Porcelain Dove* and *Through a Brazen Mirror*, and numerous short stories.

What if a vampire didn't have to take blood from its victim to feed?
What if a vampire could feed on pure emotion?

Carrion Comfort

DAN SIMMONS

ina was going to take credit for the death of the Beatle, John. I thought that was in very bad taste. She had her scrapbook laid out on my mahogany coffee table, newspaper clippings neatly arranged in chronological order, the bald statements of death recording all of her Feedings. Nina Drayton's smile was radiant, but her pale-blue eyes showed no hint of warmth.

"We should wait for Will," I said.

"Of course, Melanie. You're right, as always. How silly of me. I know the rules." Nina stood and began walking around the room, idly touching the furnishings or exclaiming softly over a ceramic statuette or piece of needlepoint. This part of the house had once been the conservatory, but now I used it as my sewing room. Green plants still caught the morning light. The light made it a warm, cozy place in the daytime, but now that winter had come the room was too chilly to use at night. Nor did I like the sense of darkness closing in against all those panes of glass.

"I love this house," said Nina.

She turned and smiled at me. "I can't tell you how much I look forward to coming back to Charleston. We should hold all of our reunions here."

I knew how much Nina loathed this city and this house.

"Willi would be hurt," I said. "You know how he likes to show off his place in Beverly Hills—and his new girlfriends."

"And boyfriends," Nina said, laughing. Of all the changes and darkenings in Nina, her laugh has been least affected. It was still the husky but childish laugh that I had first heard so long ago. It had drawn me to her then—one lonely, adolescent girl responding to the warmth of another as a moth to a flame. Now it served only to chill me and put me even more on guard. Enough moths had been drawn to Nina's flame over the many decades.

"I'll send for tea," I said.

Mr. Thorne brought the tea in my best Wedgwood china. Nina and I sat in the slowly moving squares of sunlight and spoke softly of nothing important: mutually ignorant comments on the economy, references to books that the other had not gotten around to reading, and sympathetic murmurs about the low class of persons one meets while flying these days. Someone peering in from the garden might have thought he was seeing an aging but attractive niece visiting her favorite aunt. (I drew the line at suggesting that anyone would mistake us for mother and daughter.) People usually consider me a well-dressed if not stylish person. Heaven knows I have paid enough to have the wool skirts and silk blouses mailed from Scotland and France. But next to Nina I've always felt dowdy.

This day she wore an elegant, light-blue dress that must have cost several thousand dollars. The color made her complexion seem even more perfect than usual and brought out the blue of her eyes. Her hair had gone as gray as mine, but somehow she managed to get away with wearing it long and tied back with a single barrette. It looked youthful and chic on Nina and made me feel that my short artificial curls were glowing with a blue rinse.

Few would suspect that I was four years younger than Nina. Time had been kind to her. And she had Fed more often.

She set down her cup and saucer and moved aimlessly around the room again. It was not like Nina to show such signs of nervousness. She stopped in front of the glass display case. Her gaze passed over the Hummels and the pewter pieces and then stopped in surprise.

"Good heavens, Melanie. A pistol! What an odd place to put an old pistol."

"It's an heirloom," I said. "A Colt Peacemaker from right after the War Between the States. Quite expensive. And you're right, it is a silly place to keep it. But it's the only case I have in the house with a lock on it and Mrs. Hodges often brings her grandchildren when she visits—"

"You mean it's *loaded?*"

"No, of course not," I lied. "But children should not play with such things . . ." I trailed off lamely. Nina nodded but did not bother to conceal the condescension in her smile. She went to look out the south window into the garden.

Damn her. It said volumes about Nina that she did not recognize that pistol.

◊◊◊

On the day he was killed, Charles Edgar Larchmont had been my beau for precisely five months and two days. There had been no formal announcement, but we were to be married. Those five months had been a microcosm of the era itself—naive, flirtatious, formal to the point of preciosity, and romantic. Most of all, romantic. Romantic in the worst sense of the word: dedicated to saccharine or insipid ideals that only an adolescent—or an adolescent society—would strive to maintain. We were children playing with loaded weapons.

Nina, she was Nina Hawkins then, had her own beau—a tall, awkward, but well-meaning Englishman named Roger Harrison. Mr. Harrison had met Nina in London a year earlier, during the first stages of the Hawkinses' Grand Tour. Declaring himself smitten—another absurdity of those times—the tall Englishman had followed her from one European capital to another until, after being firmly reprimanded by Nina's father (an unimaginative little milliner who was constantly on the defensive about his doubtful social status), Harrison returned to London to "settle his affairs." Some months later he showed up in New York just as Nina was being packed off to her aunt's home in Charleston in order to terminate yet another flirtation. Still undaunted, the clumsy Englishman followed her south, ever mindful of the pro-tocols and, restrictions of the day.

We were a gay group. The day after I met Nina at Cousin Celia's' June ball, the four of us were taking a hired boat up the Cooper River for a picnic on Daniel Island. Roger Harrison, seri-ous and solemn on every topic, was a perfect foil for Charles's irreverent sense of humor. Nor did Roger seem to mind the good-natured jesting, since he was soon joining in the laughter with his peculiar *haw-haw-haw*.

Nina loved it all. Both gentlemen showered attention on her, and although Charles never failed to show the primacy of his affection for me, it was understood by all that Nina Hawkins was one of those young women who invariably becomes the center of male gallantry and attention in any gathering. Nor were the social strata of Charleston blind to the combined charm of our four-some. For two months of that now-distant summer, no party was complete, no excursion adequately planned, and no occasion considered a success unless we four were invited and had chosen to attend. Our happy dominance of the youthful social scene was so pronounced that Cousins Celia and Loraine wheedled their parents into leaving two weeks early for their annual August sojourn in Maine.

I am not sure when Nina and I came up with the idea of the duel. Perhaps it was during one of the long, hot nights when the other "slept over" creeping into the other's bed, whispering and giggling, stifling our laughter when the rustling of starched uni-forms betrayed the presence of our colored maids moving through the darkened halls. In any case, the idea was the natural outgrowth of the romantic pretensions of the time. The picture of Charles and Roger actually dueling over some abstract point of honor relating to *us* thrilled both of us in a physical way that I recognize now as a simple form of sexual titillation.

It would have been harmless except for the Ability. We had been so successful in our manipulation of male behavior—a manipulation that was both expected and encouraged in those days—that neither of us had yet suspected that there was any-thing beyond the ordinary in the way we could translate our whims into other people's actions. The field of parapsychology did not exist then; or rather, it existed only in the rappings and knockings of parlor-game seances. At any rate, we amused ourselves for several weeks with whispered fantasies, and then one of us—or perhaps both of us—used the Ability to translate the fantasy into reality.

In a sense, it was our first Feeding.

I do not remember the purported cause of the quarrel, perhaps some deliberate misinterpretation of one of Charles's jokes. I can not recall who Charles and Roger arranged to have serve as seconds on that illegal outing. I do remember the hurt and confused expression on Roger Harrison's face during those few days. It was a caricature of ponderous dullness, the confusion of a man who finds himself in a situation not of his making and from which he cannot escape. I remember Charles and his mercurial swings of mood—the bouts of humor, periods of black anger, and the tears and kisses the night before the duel.

I remember with great clarity the beauty of that morning. Mists were floating up from the river and diffusing the rays of the rising sun as we rode out to the dueling field. I remember Nina reaching over and squeezing my hand with an impetuous excitement that was communicated through my body like an electric shock.

Much of the rest of that morning is missing. Perhaps in the intensity of that first, subconscious Feeding, I literally lost consciousness as I was engulfed in the waves of fear, excitement, pride—of *maleness*—emanating from our two beaus as they faced death on that lovely morning. I remember experiencing the shock of realizing, *this is really happening,* as I shared the tread of high boots through the grass. Someone was calling off the paces. I dimly recall the weight of the pistol in my hand—Charles's hand, I think; I will never know for sure—and a second of cold clarity before an explosion broke the connection, and the acrid smell of gunpowder brought me back to myself.

It was Charles who died. I have never been able to forget the incredible quantities of blood that poured from the small, round hole in his breast. His white shirt was crimson by the time I reached him. There had been no blood in our fantasies. Nor had there been the sight of Charles with his head lolling, mouth dribbling saliva onto his bloodied chest while his eyes rolled back to show the whites like two eggs embedded in his skull.

Roger Harrison was sobbing as Charles breathed his final, shuddering gasps on that field of innocence.

I remember nothing at all about the confused hours that followed. The next morning I opened my cloth bag to find Charles's pistol lying with my things. Why would I have kept that revolver? If I had wished to take something from my fallen lover as a sign of remembrance, why that alien piece of metal? Why pry from his dead fingers the symbol of our thoughtless sin?

It said volumes about Nina that she did not recognize that pistol.

◊◊◊

"Willi's here," announced Nina's amanuensis, the loathsome Miss Barrett Kramer. Kramer's appearance was as unisex as her name: short-cropped, black hair, powerful shoulders, and a blank, aggressive gaze that I associated with lesbians and criminals. She looked to be in her mid-thirties.

"Thank you, Barrett dear," said Nina.

Both of us went out to greet Willi, but Mr. Thorne had already let him in, and we met in the hallway.

"Melanie! You look marvelous! You grow younger each time I see you. Nina!" The change in Willi's voice was evident. Men continued to be overpowered by their first sight of Nina after an absence. There were hugs and kisses. Willi himself looked more dissolute than ever. His alpaca sport coat was exquisitely tailored, his turtleneck sweater successfully concealed the eroded lines of his wattled neck, but when he swept off his jaunty sports-car cap the long strands of white hair he had brushed forward to hide his encroaching baldness were knocked into disarray. Willi's face was flushed with excitement, but there was also the telltale capillary redness about the nose and cheeks that spoke of too much liquor, too many drugs.

"Ladies, I think you've met my associates, Tom Luhar and Jenson Reynolds?" The two men added to the crowd in my narrow hall. Mr. Luhar was thin and blond, smiling with perfectly capped teeth. Mr. Reynolds was a gigantic Negro, hulking forward with a sullen, bruised look on his coarse face. I was sure that neither Nina nor I had encountered these specific cat's-paws of Willi's before. It did not matter.

"Why don't we go into the parlor?" I suggested. It was an awkward procession ending with the three of us seated on the heavily upholstered chairs surrounding the Georgian tea table that had been my grandmother's. "More tea, please, Mr. Thorne." Miss Kramer took that as her cue to leave, but Willi's two pawns stood uncertainly by the door, shifting from foot to foot and glancing at the crystal on display as if their mere proximity could break some thing. I would not have been surprised if that had proved to be the case.

"Jense!" Willi snapped his fingers. The Negro hesitated and then brought forward an expensive leather attaché case. Willi set it on the tea table and clicked the catches open with his short, broad fingers. "Why don't you two see Mrs. Fuller's man about getting something to drink?"

When they were gone Willi shook his head and smiled apologetically at Nina. "Sorry about that, Love."

Nina put her hand on Willi's sleeve. She leaned forward with an air of expectancy. "Melanie wouldn't let me begin the Game with out you. Wasn't that *awful* of me to want to start without you, Willi dear?"

Willi frowned. After fifty years he still bridled at being called Willi. In Los Angeles he was Big Bill Borden. When he returned to his native Germany—which was not often because of the dangers involved—he was once again Wilhelm von Borchert, lord of dark manor, forest, and hunt. But Nina had called him Willi when they had first met in 1931 in Vienna, and Willi he had remained.

"You begin, Willi dear," said Nina. "You go first."

I could remember the time when we would have spent the first few days of our reunion in conversation and catching up with one another's lives. Now there was not even time for small talk.

Willi showed his teeth and removed news clippings, notebooks, and a stack of cassettes from his briefcase. No sooner had he covered the small table with his material than Mr. Thorne arrived with the tea and Nina's scrapbook from the sewing room. Willi brusquely cleared a small space.

At first glance one might see certain similarities between Willi

Borchert and Mr. Thorne. One would be mistaken. Both men tended to the florid, but Willi's complexion was the result of excess and emotion; Mr. Thorne had known neither of these for many years. Willi's balding was a patchy, self-consciously concealed thing—a weasel with mange; Mr. Thorne's bare head was smooth and unwrinkled. One could not imagine Mr. Thorne ever having *had* hair. Both men had gray eyes—what a novelist would call cold, gray eyes—but Mr. Thorne's eyes were cold with indifference; cold with a clarity coming from an absolute absence of troublesome emotion or thought. Willi's eyes were the cold of a blustery North Sea winter and were often clouded with shifting curtains of the emotions that controlled him—pride, hatred, love of pain, the pleasures of destruction.

Willi never referred to his use of the Ability as *Feedings*—I was evidently the only one who thought in those terms—but Willi sometimes talked of The Hunt. Perhaps it was the dark forests of his homeland that he thought of as he stalked his human quarry through the sterile streets of Los Angeles. Did Willi dream of the forest, I wondered. Did he look back to green wool hunting jackets, the applause of retainers, the gouts of blood from the dying boar? Or did Willi remember the slam of jack-boots on cobblestones and the pounding of his lieutenants' fists on doors? Perhaps Willi still associated his Hunt with the dark European night of the ovens that he had helped to oversee.

I called it Feeding. Willi called it The Hunt. I had never heard Nina call it anything.

"Where is your VCR?" Willi asked. "I have put them all on tape."

"Oh, Willi," said Nina in an exasperated tone. "You know Melanie. She's so old-fashioned. You know she wouldn't have a video player."

"I don't even have a television," I said. Nina laughed.

"Goddamn it," muttered Willi. "It doesn't matter. I have other records here." He snapped rubber bands from around the small, black notebooks. "It just would have been better on tape. The Los Angeles stations gave much coverage to the Hollywood Strangler, and I edited in the . . . Ach! Never mind."

He tossed the videocassettes into his briefcase and slammed the lid shut.

"Twenty-three," he said. "Twenty-three since we met twelve months ago. It doesn't seem that long, does it?"

"Show us," said Nina. She was leaning forward, and her blue eyes seemed very bright. "I've been wondering since I saw the Strangler interviewed on *Sixty Minutes*. He was yours, Willi? He seemed so—"

"*Ja, ja,* he was mine. A nobody. A timid little man. He was the gardener of a neighbor of mine. I left him alive so that the police could question him, erase any doubts. He will hang himself in his cell next month after the press loses interest. But this is more interesting. Look at this." Willi slid across several glossy black-and-white photographs. The NBC executive had murdered the five members of his family and drowned a visiting soap-opera actress in his pool. He had then stabbed himself repeatedly and written 50 SHARE in blood on the wall of the bathhouse.

"Reliving old glories, Willi?" asked Nina. "DEATH TO THE PIGS and all that?"

"No, goddamn it. I think it should receive points for irony. The girl had been scheduled to drown on the program. It was already in the script outline."

"Was he hard to Use?" It was my question. I was curious despite myself.

Willi lifted one eyebrow. "Not really. He was an alcoholic and heavily into cocaine. There was not much left. And he hated his family. Most people do."

"Most people in California, perhaps," said Nina primly. It was an odd comment from Nina. Years ago her father had committed suicide by throwing himself in front of a trolley car.

"Where did you make contact?" I asked.

"A party. The usual place. He bought the coke from a director who had ruined one of my—

"Did you have to repeat the contact?"

Willi frowned at me. He kept his anger under control, but his face grew redder. "*Ja, ja.* I saw him twice more. Once I just watched from my car as he played tennis."

"Points for irony," said Nina. "But you lose points for repeated contact. If he were as empty as you say, you should have been able to Use him after only one touch. What else do you have?"

He had his usual assortment. Pathetic skid-row murders. Two domestic slayings. A highway collision that turned into a fatal shooting. "I was in the crowd," said Willi. "I made contact. He had a gun in the glove compartment."

"Two points," said Nina.

Willi had saved a good one for last. A once-famous child star had suffered a bizarre accident. He had left his Bel Air apartment while it filled with gas and then returned to light a match. Two others had died in the ensuing fire.

"You get credit only for him," said Nina.

"*Ja, ja.*"

"Are you absolutely sure about this one? It could have been an accident.".

"Don't be ridiculous," snapped Will. He turned toward me. "*This* one was very hard to Use. Very strong. I blocked his memory of turning on the gas. Had to hold it away for two hours. Then forced him into the room. He struggled not to strike the match."

"You should have had him use his lighter," said Nina.

"He didn't smoke," growled Willi. "He gave it up last year."

"Yes," smiled Nina. "I seem to remember him saying that to Johnny Carson." I could not tell whether Nina was jesting.

The three of us went through the ritual of assigning points. Nina did most of the talking. Willi went from being sullen to expansive to sullen again. At one point he reached over and patted my knee as he laughingly asked for my support. I said nothing. Finally he gave up, crossed the parlor to the liquor cabinet, and poured himself a tall glass of bourbon from father's decanter. The evening light was sending its final, horizontal rays through the stained-glass panels of the bay windows, and it cast a red hue on Willi as he stood next to the oak cupboard. His eyes were small, red embers in a bloody mask.

"Forty-one," said Nina at last.

She looked up brightly and showed the calculator as if it verified some objective fact. "I count forty-one points. What do you have, Melanie?"

"*Ja,*" interrupted Willi. "That is fine. Now let us see your claims, Nina." His voice was flat and empty. Even Willi had lost some interest in the Game.

Before Nina could begin, Mr. Thorne entered and motioned that dinner was served. We adjourned to the dining room—Willi pouring himself another glass of bourbon and Nina fluttering her hands in mock frustration at the interruption of the Game. Once seated at the long, mahogany table, I worked at being a hostess. From decades of tradition, talk of the Game was banned from the dinner table. Over soup we discussed Willi's new movie and the purchase of another store for Nina's line of boutiques. It seemed that Nina's monthly column in *Vogue* was to be discontinued but that a newspaper syndicate was interested in picking it up.

Both of my guests exclaimed over the perfection of the baked ham, but I thought that Mr. Thorne had made the gravy a trifle too sweet. Darkness had filled the windows before we finished our chocolate mousse. The refracted light from the chandelier made Nina's hair dance with highlights while I feared that mine glowed more bluely than ever.

Suddenly there was a sound from the kitchen. The huge Negro's face appeared at the swinging door. His shoulder was hunched against white hands and his expression was that of a querulous child.

". . . the hell you think we are sittin' here like goddamned—" The white hands pulled him out of sight.

"Excuse me, ladies." Willi dabbed linen at his lips and stood up. He still moved gracefully for all of his years.

Nina poked at her chocolate. There was one sharp, barked command from the kitchen and the sound of a slap. It was the slap of a man's hand—hard and flat as a small-caliber-rifle shot. I looked up and Mr. Thorne was at my elbow, clearing away the dessert dishes.

"Coffee, please, Mr. Thorne. For all of us." He nodded and his smile was gentle.

◊◊◊

Franz Anton Mesmer had known of it even if he had not understood it. I suspect that Mesmer must have had some small touch of the Ability. Modern pseudosciences have studied it and renamed it, removed most of its power, confused its uses and origins, but it remains the shadow of what Mesmer discovered. They have no idea of what it is like to Feed.

I despair at the rise of modern violence. I truly give in to despair at times, that deep, futureless pit of despair that poet Gerard Manley Hopkins called carrion comfort. I watch the American slaughterhouse, the casual attacks on popes, presidents, and uncounted others, and I wonder whether there are many more out there with the Ability or whether butchery has simply become the modern way of life.

All humans feed on violence, on the small exercises of power over another. But few have tasted—as we have—the ultimate power. And without the Ability, few know the unequaled pleasure of taking a human life. Without the Ability, even those who do feed on life cannot savor the flow of emotions in stalker and victim, the total exhilaration of the attacker who has moved beyond all rules and punishments, the strange, almost sexual submission of the victim in that final second of truth when all options are canceled; all futures denied, all possibilities erased in an exercise of absolute power over another.

I despair at modern violence. I despair at the impersonal nature of it and the casual quality that has made it accessible to so many. I had a television set until I sold it at the height of the Vietnam War. Those sanitized snippets of death—made distant by the camera's lens—meant nothing to me. But I believe it meant something to these cattle that surround me. When the war and the nightly televised body counts ended, they demanded more, more, and the movie screens and streets of this sweet and dying nation have provided it in mediocre, mob abundance. It is an addiction I know well.

They miss the point. Merely observed, violent death is a sad and sullied tapestry of confusion. But to those of us who have Fed, death can be a *sacrament.*

◊◊◊

"My turn! My turn!" Nina's voice still resembled that of the visiting belle who had just filled her dance card at Cousin Celia's June ball.

We had returned to the parlor. Willi had finished his coffee and requested a brandy from Mr. Thorne. I was embarrassed for Willi. To have one's closest associates show any hint of unplanned behavior was certainly a sign of weakening Ability. Nina did not appear to have noticed.

"I have them all in order," said Nina. She opened the scrapbook on the now-empty tea table. Willi went through them carefully, sometimes asking a question, more often grunting assent. I murmured occasional agreement although I had heard of none of them. Except for the Beatle, of course. Nina saved that for near the end.

"Good God, Nina, that was you?" Willi seemed near anger. Nina's Feedings had always run to Park Avenue suicides and matrimonial disagreements ending in shots fired from expensive, small-caliber ladies' guns. This type of thing was more in Willi's crude style. Perhaps he felt that his territory was being invaded. "I mean . . . you were risking a lot, weren't you? It's so . . . damn it . . . so *public*."

Nina laughed and set down the calculator. "Willi *dear*, that's what the Game is *about*, is it not?"

Willi strode to the liquor cabinet and refilled his brandy snifter. The wind tossed bare branches against the leaded glass of the bay window. I do not like winter. Even in the South it takes its toll on the spirit.

"Didn't this guy . . . what's his name . . . buy the gun in Hawaii or someplace?" asked Willi from across the room. "That sounds like his initiative to me. I mean, if he was *already* stalking the fellow—"

"Willie dear." Nina's voice had gone as cold as the wind that raked the branches. "No one said he was *stable*. How many of yours are stable, Willi? But I made it *happen*, darling. I chose the place and the time. Don't you see the irony of the *place*, Willi? After that little prank on the director of that witchcraft movie a few years ago? It was straight from the script—"

"I don't know" said Willi. He sat heavily on the divan, spilling brandy on his expensive sport coat. He did not notice. The lamp light reflected from his balding skull. The mottles of age were more visible at night, and his neck, where it disappeared into his turtleneck, was all ropes and tendons. "I don't know."

He looked up at me and smiled suddenly, as if we shared a conspiracy. "It could be like that writer fellow, eh, Melanie? It could be like that."

Nina looked down at the hands in her lap. They were clenched and the well-manicured fingers were white at the tips.

◊◊◊

The Mind Vampires. That's what the writer was going to call his book.

I sometimes wonder if he really would have written anything. What was his name? Something Russian.

Willi and I received telegrams from Nina: COME QUICKLY YOU ARE NEEDED. That was enough. I was on the next morning's flight to New York. The plane was a noisy, propeller-driven Constellation, and I spent much of the flight assuring the overly solicitous stewardess that I needed nothing, that, indeed, I felt fine. She obviously had decided that I was someone's grandmother, who was flying for the first time.

Willi managed to arrive twenty minutes before me. Nina was distraught and as close to hysteria as I had ever seen her. She had been at a party in lower Manhattan two days before—she was not so distraught that she forgot to tell us what important names had been there—when she found herself sharing a corner, a fondue pot, and confidences with a young writer. Or rather, the writer was sharing confidences. Nina described him as a scruffy sort with a wispy little beard, thick glasses, a corduroy sport coat worn over an old plaid shirt—one of the type invariably sprinkled around successful parties of that era, according to Nina. She knew enough not to call him a beatnik, for that term had just become passé, but no one had yet heard the term *hippie,* and it wouldn't have applied to him anyway. He was a writer of the sort that barely ekes out a living, these days at least, by selling blood and doing novelizations of television series. Alexander something.

His idea for a book—he told Nina that he had been working on it for some time—was that many of the murders then being committed were actually the result of a small group of psychic killers, he called them *mind vampires,* who used others to carry out their grisly deeds.

He said that a paperback publisher had already shown interest in his outline and would offer him a contract tomorrow if he would change the title to *The Zombie Factor* and put in more sex.

"So what?" Willi had said to Nina in disgust. "You have me fly across the continent for this? I might buy the idea myself."

That turned out to be the excuse we used to interrogate this Alexander somebody during an impromptu party given by Nina the next evening. I did not attend. The party was not overly successful according to Nina but it gave Willi the chance to have a long chat with the young would-be novelist. In the writer's almost pitiable eagerness to do business with Bill Borden, producer of *Paris Memories, Three on a Swing,* and at least two other completely forgettable Technicolor features touring the drive-ins that summer, he revealed that the book consisted of a well-worn outline and a dozen pages of notes.

He was sure, however, that he could do a treatment for Mr. Borden in five weeks, perhaps even as fast as three weeks if he were flown out to Hollywood to get the proper creative stimulation.

Later that evening we discussed the possibility of Willi simply buying an option on the treatment, but Willi was short on cash at the time and Nina was insistent. In the end the young writer opened his femoral artery with a Gillette blade and ran screaming into a narrow Greenwich Village side street to die. I don't believe that anyone ever bothered to sort through the clutter and debris of his remaining notes.

◊◊◊

"It could be like that writer, *ja,* Melanie?" Willi patted my knee. I nodded. "He was mine," continued Willi, "and Nina tried to take credit. Remember?"

Again I nodded. Actually he had been neither Nina's nor Willi's. I had avoided the party so that I could make contact later without the young man noticing he was being followed. I did so easily. I remember sitting in an overheated little delicatessen across the street from the apartment building. It was over so quickly that there was almost no sense of Feeding. Then I was aware once again of the sputtering radiators and the smell of salami as people rushed to the door to see what the screaming was about. I remember finishing my tea slowly so that I did not have to leave before the ambulance was gone.

"Nonsense," said Nina. She busied herself with her little calculator. "How many points?" She looked at me. I looked at Willi.

"Six," he said with a shrug. Nina made a small show of totaling the numbers.

"Thirty-eight," she said and sighed theatrically. "You win again, Willi. Or rather, you beat *me* again. We must hear from Melanie. You've been so quiet, dear. You must have some surprise for us."

"Yes," said Willi, "it is your turn to win. It has been several years."

"None," I said. I had expected an explosion of questions, but the silence was broken only by the ticking of the clock on the mantel piece. Nina was looking away from me, at something hidden by the shadows in the corner.

"None?" echoed Willi.

"There was . . . one," I said at last. "But it was by accident. I came across them robbing an old man behind . . . but it was completely by accident."

Willi was agitated. He stood up, walked to the window, turned an old straight-back chair around and straddled it, arms folded. "What does this mean?"

"You're quitting the Game?" Nina asked as she turned to look at me. I let the question serve as the answer.

"Why?" snapped Willi. In his excitement it came out with a hard v.

If I had been raised in an era when young ladies were allowed to shrug, I would have done so. As it was, I contented myself with running my fingers along an imaginary seam on my skirt. Willi had asked the question, but I stared straight into Nina's eyes when I finally answered, "I'm tired. It's been too long. I guess I'm getting old."

"You'll get a lot *older* if you do not Hunt," said Willi. His body, his voice, the red mask of his face, everything signaled great anger just kept in check. "My God, Melanie, you *already* look older!

You look terrible. This is why we hunt, woman. Look at yourself in the mirror! Do you want to die an old woman just because you're tired of using *them?*" Willi stood and turned his back.

"Nonsense!" Nina's voice was strong, confident, in command once more. "Melanie's *tired,* Willi. Be nice. We all have times like that. I remember how *you* were after the war. Like a whipped puppy. You wouldn't even go outside your miserable little flat in Baden. Even after we helped you get to New Jersey you just sulked around feeling sorry for yourself. Melanie *made up* the Game to help you feel better. So quiet! *Never* tell a lady who feels tired and depressed that she looks terrible. Honestly, Willi, you're such a *Schwachsinniger* sometimes. And a crashing boor to boot."

I had anticipated many reactions to my announcement, but this was the one I feared most. It meant that Nina had also tired of the game. It meant that she was ready to move to another level of play.

It had to mean that.

"Thank you, Nina darling," I said. "I knew you would understand."

She reached across and touched my knee reassuringly. Even through my wool skirt, I could feel the cold of her fingers.

◊◊◊

My guests would not stay the night. I implored. I remonstrated. I pointed out that their rooms were ready, that Mr. Thorne had already turned down the quilts.

"Next time," said Willi. "Next time, Melanie, my little love. We'll make a weekend of it as we used to. A week!" Willi was in a much better mood since he had been paid his thousand-dollar prize by each of us. He had sulked, but I had insisted. It soothed his ego when Mr. Thorne brought in a check already made out to WILLIAM D. BORDEN.

Again I asked him to stay, but he protested that he had a midnight flight to Chicago. He had to see a prizewinning author about a screenplay. Then he was hugging me good-bye, his companions were in the hall behind me and I had a brief moment of terror.

But they left. The blond young man showed his white smile, and the Negro bobbed his head in what I took as a farewell. Then we were alone.

Nina and I were alone.

Not quite alone. Miss Kramer was standing next to Nina at the end of the hall. Mr. Thorne was out of sight behind the swinging door to the kitchen. I left him there.

Miss Kramer took three steps forward. I felt my breath stop for an instant. Mr. Thorne put his hand on the swinging door. Then the husky little brunette opened the door to the hall closet, removed Nina's coat; and stepped back to help her into it.

"Are you sure you won't stay?"

"No, thank you, darling. I've promised Barrett that we would drive to Hilton Head tonight."

"But it's late—"

"We have reservations. Thank you anyway, Melanie. I *will* be in touch."

"Yes."

"I mean it, dear. We must talk. I understand *exactly* how you feel, but you have to remember that the Game is still important to Willi. We'll have to find a way to end it without hurting his feelings. Perhaps we could visit him next spring in Karinhall or whatever he calls that gloomy old Bavarian place of his. A trip to the Continent would do wonders for you, dear."

"Yes."

"I *will* be in touch. After this deal with the new store is settled. We need to spend some time together, Melanie . . . just the two of us . . . like old times." Her lips kissed the air next to my cheek. She held my forearms tightly. "Good-bye, darling."

"Good-bye, Nina."

◊◊◊

I carried the brandy glass to the kitchen. Mr. Thorne took it in silence.

"Make sure the house is secure," I said. He nodded and went to check the locks and alarm system. It was only nine forty-five, but I was very tired. *Age,* I thought. I went up the wide staircase, perhaps the finest feature of the house, and dressed for bed. It had begun to storm, and the sound of the cold raindrops on the window carried a sad rhythm to it.

Mr. Thorne looked in as I was brushing my hair and wishing it were longer. I turned to him. He reached into the pocket of his dark vest. When his hand emerged a slim blade flicked out, nodded. He palmed the blade shut and closed the door behind him. I listened to his footsteps recede down the stairs to the chair in the front hall, where he would spend the night.

I believe I dreamed of vampires that night. Or perhaps I was thinking about them just prior to falling asleep, and a fragment had stayed with me until morning. Of all mankind's self-inflicted terrors, of all its pathetic little monsters, only the myth of the vampire had any vestige of dignity. Like the humans it feeds on, the vampire must respond to its own dark compulsions. But unlike its petty human prey, the vampire carries out its sordid means to the only possible ends that could justify such actions—the goal of literal immortality. There is a nobility there. And a sadness.

Before sleeping I thought of that summer long ago in Vienna. I saw Will young again—blond, flushed with youth, and filled with pride at escorting two such independent American ladies.

I remembered Willi's high, stiff collars and the short dresses that Nina helped to bring into style that summer. I remembered the friendly sounds of crowded *Biergartens* and the shadowy dance of leaves in front of gas lamps.

I remembered the footsteps on wet cobblestones, the shouts, the distant whistles, and the silences.

Willi was right; I had aged. The past year had taken a greater toll than the preceding decade. But I had not Fed. Despite the hunger, despite the aging reflection in the mirror, *I had not Fed.*

I fell asleep trying to think of that writer's last name. I fell asleep hungry.

◊◊◊

Morning. Bright sunlight through bare branches. It was one of those crystalline, warming winter days that make living in the South so much less depressing than merely surviving a Yankee Winter. I had Mr. Thorne open the window a crack when he brought in my breakfast tray. As I sipped my coffee I could hear children playing in the courtyard. Once Mr. Thorne would have brought the morning paper with the tray, but I had long since learned that to read about the follies and scandals of the world was to desecrate the morning. I was growing less and less interested in the affairs of men. I had done without a newspaper, telephone, or television for twelve years and had suffered no ill effects unless one were to count a growing self-contentment as an ill thing. I smiled as I remembered Willi's disappointment at not being able to play his video cassettes. He was such a child.

"It is Saturday is it not, Mr. Thorne?" At his nod I gestured for the tray to be taken away. "We will go out today," I said. "A walk. Perhaps a trip to the fort. Then dinner at Henry's and home. I have arrangements to make."

Mr. Thorne hesitated and half-stumbled as he was leaving the room. I paused in the act of belting my robe. It was not like Mr. Thorne to commit an ungraceful movement. I realized that he too was getting old. He straightened the tray and dishes, nodded his head, and left for the kitchen.

I would not let thoughts of aging disturb me on such a beautiful morning. I felt charged with a new energy and resolve. The reunion the night before had not gone well but neither had it gone as badly as it might have. I had been honest with Nina and Willi about my intention of quitting the Game. In the weeks and months, to come, they—or at least Nina—would begin to brood over the ramifications of that, but by the time they chose to react, separately, or together, I would be long gone. Already I had new (and old) identities waiting for me in Florida, Michigan, London, southern France, and even in New Delhi. Michigan was out for the time being. I had grown unused to the harsh climate. New Delhi was no longer the hospitable place for foreigners it had been when I resided there briefly before the war.

Nina had been right about one thing—a return to Europe would be good for me. Already I longed for the rich light and cordial *savoir vivre* of the villagers near my old summer house outside of Toulon.

The air outside was bracing. I wore a simple print dress and my spring coat. The trace of arthritis in my right leg had bothered me coming down the stairs, but I used my father's old walking stick as a cane. A young Negro servant had cut it for father the summer we moved from Greenville to Charleston. I smiled as we emerged into the warm air of the courtyard.

Mrs. Hodges came out of her doorway into the light. It was her grandchildren and their friends who were playing around the dry fountain. For two centuries the courtyard had been shared by the three brick buildings. Only my home had not been parceled into expensive town houses or fancy apartments.

"Good morning, Miz Fuller."

"Good morning, Mrs. Hodges. A beautiful day, isn't it?"

"It is that. Are you off shopping?"

"Just for a walk, Mrs. Hodges. I'm surprised that Mr. Hodges isn't out today. He always seems to be working in the yard on Saturdays."

Mrs. Hodges frowned as one of the little girls ran between us. Her friend came squealing after her, sweater flying. "Oh, George is at the marina already."

"In the daytime?" I had often been amused by Mr. Hodges's departure for work in the evening, his security-guard uniform neatly pressed, gray hair jutting out from under his cap, black lunch pail gripped firmly under his arm.

Mr. Hodges was as leathery and bowlegged as an aged cowboy. He was one of those men who were always on the verge of retiring but who probably realized that to be suddenly inactive would be a form of death sentence.

"Oh, yes. One of those colored men on the day shift down at the storage building quit, and they asked George to fill in. I told him that he was too old to work four nights a week and then go back on the weekend, but you know George. He'll never retire."

"Well, give him my best," I said.

The girls running around the fountain made me nervous.

Mrs. Hodges followed me to the wrought-iron gate. "Will you be going away for the holidays, Miz Fuller?"

"Probably, Mrs. Hodges. Most probably." Then Mr. Thorne and I were out on the sidewalk and strolling toward the Battery. A few cars drove slowly down the narrow streets, some tourists stared at the houses of our Old Section, but the day was serene and quiet.

I saw the masts of the yachts and sailboats before we came in sight of the water as we emerged onto Broad Street.

"Please acquire tickets for us, Mr. Thorne," I said. "I believe I would like to see the fort."

As is typical of most people who live in close proximity to a popular tourist attraction, I had not taken notice of it for many years. It was an act of sentimentality to visit the fort now. An act brought on by my increasing acceptance of the fact that I would have to leave these parts forever. It is one thing to plan a move; it is something altogether different to be faced with the imperative reality of it.

There were few tourists. The ferry moved away from the marina and into the placid waters of the harbor. The combination of warm sunlight and the steady throb of the diesel caused me to doze briefly. I awoke as we were putting in at the dark hulk of the island fort.

For a while I moved with the tour group, enjoying the catacomb silences of the lower levels and the mindless singsong of the young woman from the Park Service. But as we came back to the museum, with its dusty dioramas and tawdry little trays of slides, I climbed the stairs back to the outer walls. I motioned for Mr. Thorne to stay at the top of the stairs and moved out onto the ramparts.

Only one other couple—a young pair with a cheap camera and a baby in an uncomfortable-looking papoose carrier—were in sight along the wall.

It was a pleasant moment. A midday storm was approaching from the west and it set a dark backdrop to the still-sunlit church spires, brick towers, and bare branches of the city.

Even from two miles away I could see the movement of people strolling along the Battery walkway. The wind was blowing in ahead of the dark clouds and tossing whitecaps against the rocking ferry and wooden dock. The air smelled of river and winter and rain by nightfall.

It was not hard to imagine that day long ago. The shells had dropped onto the fort until the upper layers were little more than protective piles of rubble. People had cheered from tile rooftops behind the Battery. The bright colors of dresses and silk parasols must have been maddening to the Yankee gunners. Finally one had fired a shot above the crowded rooftops. The ensuing confusion must have been amusing from this vantage point.

A movement down below caught my attention. Something dark was sliding through the gray water—something dark and shark silent. I was jolted out of thoughts of the past as I recognized it as a Polaris submarine, old but obviously still operational, slipping through the dark water without a sound. Waves curled and rippled over the porpoise-smooth hull, sliding to either side in a white wake. There were several men on the tower. They were muffled in heavy coats, their hats pulled low. An improbably large pair of binoculars hung from the neck of one man, whom I assumed to be the captain. He pointed at something beyond Sullivan's Island. I stared. The periphery of my vision began to fade as I made contact. Sounds and sensations came to me as from a distance.

Tension. The pleasure of salt spray, breeze from the north, northwest. Anxiety of the sealed orders below. Awareness of the sandy shallows just coming into sight on the port side.

I was startled as someone came up behind me. The dots flickering at the edge of my vision fled as I turned.

Mr. Thorne was there. At my elbow. Unbidden. I had opened my mouth to command him back to the top of the stairs when I saw the cause of his approach. The youth who had been taking pictures of his pale wife was now walking toward me. Mr. Thorne moved to intercept him.

"Hey, excuse me, ma'am. Would you or your husband mind taking our picture?"

I nodded and Mr. Thorne took the proffered camera. It looked minuscule in his long-fingered hands. Two snaps and the couple were satisfied that their presence there was documented for posterity. The young man grinned idiotically and bobbed his head. Their baby began to cry as the cold wind blew in.

I looked back to the submarine, but already it had passed on, its gray tower a thin stripe connecting the sea and sky.

◊◊◊

We were almost back to town, the ferry was swinging in toward the ship, when a stranger told me of Willi's death.

"It's awful, isn't it?" The garrulous old woman had followed me out onto the exposed section of deck. Even though the wind had grown chilly and I had moved twice to escape her mindless chatter, the woman had obviously chosen me as her conversational target for the final stages of the tour. Neither my reticence nor Mr. Thorne's glowering presence had discouraged her. "It must have been terrible," she continued. "In the dark and all."

"What was that?" A dark premonition prompted my question. "Why, the airplane crash. Haven't you heard about it? It must have been awful, falling into the swamp and all. I told my daughter this morning—"

"What airplane crash? When?" The old woman cringed a bit at the sharpness of my tone, but the vacuous smile stayed on her face.

"Why last night. This morning I told my daughter—"

"Where? What aircraft are you talking about?" Mr. Thorne came closer as he heard the tone of my voice.

"The one last night," she quavered. "The one from Charleston. The paper in the lounge told all about it. Isn't it terrible? Eighty-five people. I told my daughter—"

I left her standing there by the railing. There was a crumpled newspaper near the snack bar; and under the four-word headline were the sparse details of Willi's death. Flight 417, bound for Chicago, had left Charleston International Airport at twelve-eighteen A.M. Twenty minutes later the aircraft had exploded in midair not far from the city of Columbia. Fragments of fuselage and parts of bodies had fallen into Congaree Swamp, where fishermen had found them. There had been no survivors. The FAA and FBI were investigating.

There was a loud rushing in my ears, and I had to sit down or faint. My hands were clammy against the green vinyl upholstery. People moved past me on their way to the exits.

Willi was dead. Murdered. Nina had killed him. For a few dizzy seconds I considered the possibility of a conspiracy—an elaborate ploy by Nina and Willi to confuse me into thinking that only one threat remained. But no. There would be no reason. If Nina had included Willi in her plans, there would be no need for such absurd machinations.

Willi was dead. His remains were spread over a smelly, obscure marshland. I could imagine his last moments. He would have been leaning back in first-class comfort, a drink in his hand, perhaps whispering to one of his loutish companions.

Then the explosion. Screams. Sudden darkness. A brutal tilting and the final fall to oblivion. I shuddered and gripped the metal arm of the chair.

How had Nina done it? Almost certainly not one of Willi's entourage. It was not beyond Nina's powers to Use Willi's own cat's-paws, especially in light of his failing Ability, but there would have been no reason to do so. She could have Used anyone on that flight. It *would* have been difficult. The elaborate step of preparing the bomb. The supreme effort of blocking all memory of it, and the almost unbelievable feat of Using someone even as we sat together drinking coffee and brandy.

But Nina could have done it. Yes, she *could* have. And the timing. The timing could mean only one thing.

The last of the tourists had filed out of the cabin. I felt the slight bump that meant we had tied up to the dock. Mr. Thorne stood by the door.

Nina's timing meant that she was attempting to deal with both of us at once. She obviously had planned it long before the reunion and my timorous announcement of withdrawal. How amused Nina must have been. No wonder she had reacted so generously! Yet, she had made one great mistake. By dealing with Willi first, Nina had banked everything on my not hearing the news before she could turn on me. She knew that I had no access to daily news and only rarely left the house anymore. Still, it was unlike Nina to leave anything to chance. Was it possible that she thought I had lost the Ability completely and that Willi was the greater threat?

I shook my head as we emerged from the cabin into the gray afternoon light. The wind sliced at me through my thin coat. The view of the gangplank was blurry, and I realized that tears had filled my eyes. For Willi? He had been a pompous, weak old fool. For Nina's betrayal? Perhaps it was only the cold wind.

The streets of the Old Section were almost empty of pedestrians. Bare branches clicked together in front of the windows of fine homes. Mr. Thorne stayed by my side. The cold air sent needles of arthritic pain up my right leg to my hip. I leaned more heavily upon father's walking stick.

What would her next move be? I stopped. A fragment of news paper, caught by the wind, wrapped itself around my ankle and then blew on.

How would she come at me? Not from a distance. She was somewhere in town. I knew that. While it is possible to Use someone from a great distance, it would involve great rapport, an almost intimate knowledge of that person. And if contact were lost, it would be difficult if not impossible to reestablish at a distance. None of us had known why this was so. It did not matter now. But the thought of Nina still here, nearby, made my heart begin to race.

Not from a distance. I would see my assailant. If I knew Nina at all, I knew that. Certainly Willi's death had been the least personal Feeding imaginable, but that had been a mere technical operation. Nina obviously had decided to settle old scores with *me,* and Willi had become an obstacle to her, a minor but measurable threat that had to be eliminated before she could proceed. I could easily imagine that in Nina's own mind her choice of death for Willi would be interpreted as an act of compassion, almost a sign of affection. Not so with me. I felt that Nina would want me to know, however briefly, that she was behind the attack. In a sense, her own vanity would be my warning. Or so I hoped.

I was tempted to leave immediately. I could have Mr. Thorne get the Audi out of storage, and we could be beyond Nina's influence in an hour—away to a new life within a few more hours. There were important items in the house, of course, but the funds that I had stored elsewhere would replace most of them. It would be almost welcome to leave everything behind with the discarded identity that had accumulated them.

No. I could not leave. Not yet.

From across the street the house looked dark and malevolent. Had I closed those blinds on the second floor? There was a shadowy movement in the courtyard, and I saw Mrs. Hodges's grand-

SOUTHERN BLOOD

daughter and a friend scamper from one doorway to another. I stood irresolutely on the curb and tapped father's stick against the black-barked tree. It was foolish to dither so—I knew it was—but it had been a long time since I had been forced to make a decision under stress.

"Mr. Thorne, please check the house. Look in each room. Return quickly."

A cold wind came up as I watched Mr. Thorne's black coat blend into the gloom of the courtyard. I felt terribly exposed standing there alone. I found myself glancing up and down the street, looking for Miss Kramer's dark hair, but the only sign of movement was a young woman pushing a perambulator far down the street.

The blinds on the second floor shot up, and Mr. Thorne's face stared out whitely for a minute. Then he turned away, and I remained staring at the dark rectangle of window. A shout from the courtyard startled me, but it was only the little girl—what was her name?—calling to her friend. Kathleen, that was it. The two sat on the edge of the fountain and opened a box of animal crackers. I stared intently at them and then relaxed. I even managed to smile a little at the extent of my paranoia. For a second I considered using Mr. Thorne directly, but the thought of being helpless on the street dissuaded me. When one is in complete contact, the senses still function but are a distant thing at best.

Hurry. The thought was sent almost without volition. Two bearded men were walking down the sidewalk on my side of the street. I crossed to stand in front of my own gate. The men were laughing and gesturing at each other. One looked over at me. *Hurry.*

Mr. Thorne came out of the house, locked the door behind him, and crossed the courtyard toward me. One of the girls said something to him and held out the box of crackers, but he ignored her. Across the street the two men continued walking. Mr. Thorne handed me the large front-door key. I dropped it in my coat pocket and looked sharply at him. He nodded. His placid smile unconsciously mocked my consternation.

"You're sure?" I asked. Again the nod. "You checked all of the rooms?" Nod. "The alarms?" Nod. "You looked in the basement?"

Nod. "No sign of disturbance?" Mr. Thorne shook his head.

My hand went to the metal of the gate, but I hesitated. Anxiety filled my throat like bile. I was a silly old woman, tired and aching from the chill, but I could not bring myself to open that gate.

"Come." I crossed the street and walked briskly away from the house. "We will have dinner at Henry's and return later." Only I was not walking toward the old restaurant. I was heading away from the house in what I knew was a blind, directionless panic. It was not until we reached the waterfront and were walking along the Battery wall that I began to calm down.

No one else was in sight. A few cars moved along the street, but to approach us someone would have to cross a wide, empty space. The gray clouds were quite low and blended with the choppy, white-crested waves in the bay.

The open air and fading evening light served to revive me, and I began to think more clearly. Whatever Nina's plans had been, they certainly had been thrown into disarray by my day-long absence. I doubted that Nina would stay if there were the slightest risk to herself. No, she would be returning to New York by plane even as I stood shivering on the Battery walk. In the morning I would receive a telegram, I could see it. MELANIE ISN'T IT TERRIBLE ABOUT WILLI? TERRIBLY SAD. CAN YOU TRAVEL WITH ME TO THE FUNERAL? LOVE, NINA.

◊◊◊

I began to realize that my reluctance to leave immediately had come from a desire to return to the warmth and comfort of my home. I simply had been afraid to shuck off this old cocoon. I could do so now. I would wait in a safe place while Mr. Thorne returned to the house to pick up the one thing I could not leave behind. Then he would get the car out of storage, and by the time Nina's telegram arrived I would be far away. It would be Nina who would be starting at shadows in the months and years to come. I smiled and began to frame the necessary commands.

"Melanie."

My head snapped around. Mr. Thorne had not spoken in twenty-eight years. He spoke now.

"Melanie." His face was distorted in a rictus that showed his back teeth. The knife was in his right hand. The blade flicked out as I stared. I looked into his empty, gray eyes, and I knew.

"Melanie."

The long blade came around in a powerful arc. I could do nothing to stop it. It cut through the fabric of my coat sleeve and continued into my side. But in the act of turning, my purse had swung with me. The knife tore through the leather, ripped through the jumbled contents, pierced my coat, and drew blood above my lowest left rib. The purse had saved my life.

I raised father's heavy walking stick and struck Mr. Thorne squarely in his left eye. He reeled but did not make a sound. Again he swept the air with the knife, but I had taken two steps back and his vision was clouded. I took a two-handed grip on the cane and swung sideways again, bringing the stick around in an awkward chop. Incredibly, it again found the eye socket. I took three more steps back.

Blood streamed down the left side of Mr. Thorne's face, and the damaged eye protruded onto his cheek. The rictal grin remained. His head came up, he raised his left hand slowly, plucked out the eye with a soft snapping of a gray cord, and threw it into the water of the bay. He came toward me. I turned and ran.

I *tried* to run. The ache in my right leg slowed me to a walk after twenty paces. Fifteen more hurried steps and my lungs were out of air, my heart threatening to burst. I could feel a wetness seeping down my left side and there was a tingling—like an ice cube held against the skin—where the knife blade had touched me. One glance back showed me that Mr. Thorne was striding toward me faster than I was moving. Normally he could have overtaken me in four strides. But it is hard to make someone run when you are Using him. Especially when that person's body is reacting to shock and trauma. I glanced back again, almost slipping on the slick pavement. Mr. Thorne was grinning widely. Blood poured from the empty socket and stained his teeth. No one else was in sight.

Down the stairs, clutching at the rail so as not to fall. Down the twisting walk and up the asphalt path to the street. Pole lamps flickered and went on as I passed. Behind me Mr. Thorne took the steps in two jumps. As I hurried up the path, I thanked God that I had worn low-heel shoes for the boat ride. What would an observer think seeing this bizarre, slow-motion chase between two old people? There were no observers.

I turned onto a side street. Closed shops, empty warehouses. Going left would take me to Broad Street, but to the right, half a block away, a lone figure had emerged from a dark storefront. I moved that way, no longer able to run, close to fainting. The arthritic cramps in my leg hurt more than I could ever have imagined and threatened to collapse me on the sidewalk. Mr. Thorne was twenty paces behind me and quickly closing the distance.

The man I was approaching was a tall, thin Negro wearing a brown nylon jacket. He was carrying a box of what looked like framed sepia photographs.

He glanced at me as I approached and then looked over my shoulder at the apparition ten steps behind.

"Hey!" The man had time to shout the single syllable and then I reached out with my mind and *shoved*. He twitched like a poorly handled marionette. His jaw dropped, and his eyes glazed over, and he lurched past me just as Mr. Thorne reached for the back of my coat.

The box flew into the air, and glass shattered on the brick sidewalk. Long, brown fingers reached for a white throat. Mr. Thorne backhanded him away, but the Negro clung tenaciously, and the two swung around like awkward dance partners. I reached the opening to an alley and leaned my face against the cold brick to revive myself. The effort of concentration while Using this stranger did not afford me the luxury of resting even for a second.

I watched the clumsy stumblings of the two tall men for a while and resisted an absurd impulse to laugh.

Mr. Thorne plunged the knife into the other's stomach, withdrew it, plunged it in again. The Negro's fingernails were clawing at Mr. Thorne's good eye now. Strong teeth were snapping in search of the blade for a third time, but the heart was still beating and he was still usable. The man jumped, scissoring his legs around Mr. Thorne's middle while his jaws closed on the muscular throat. Fingernails raked bloody streaks across white skin. The two went down in a tumble.

Kill him. Fingers groped for an eye, but Mr. Thorne reached up with his left hand and snapped the thin wrist. Limp fingers continued to flail. With a tremendous exertion, Mr. Thorne lodged his forearm against the other's chest and lifted him bodily as a reclining father tosses a child above him. Teeth tore away a piece of flesh, but there was no vital damage. Mr. Thorne brought the knife between them, up left, then right. He severed half the Negro's throat with the second swing, and blood fountained over both of them. The smaller man's legs spasmed twice, Mr. Thorne threw him to one side, and I turned and walked quickly down the alley.

Out into the light again, the fading evening light, and I realized that I had run myself into a dead end. Backs of warehouses and the windowless, metal side of the Battery Marina pushed right up against the waters of the bay. A street wound away to the left, but it was dark, deserted, and far too long to try.

I looked back in time to see the black silhouette enter the alley behind me.

I tried to make contact, but there was nothing there. Nothing. Mr. Thorne might as well have been a hole in the air. I would worry later how Nina had done this thing.

The side door to the marina was locked. The main door was almost a hundred yards away and would also be locked. Mr. Thorne emerged from the alley and swung his head left and right in search of me. In the dim light his heavily streaked face looked almost black. He began lurching toward me.

I raised father's walking stick, broke the lower pane of the window, and reached in through the jagged shards. If there was a bottom or top bolt I was dead. There was a simple doorknob lock and crossbolt. My fingers slipped on the cold metal, but the bolt slid back as Mr. Thorne stepped up on the walk behind me. Then I was inside and throwing the bolt.

It was very dark. Cold seeped up from the concrete floor and there was a sound of many small boats rising and falling at their moorings. Fifty yards away light spilled out of the office windows. I had hoped there would be an alarm system, but the building was too old and the marina too cheap to have one. I walked toward the light as Mr. Thorne's forearm shattered the remaining glass in the door behind me. The arm withdrew. A great kick broke off the top hinge and splintered wood around the bolt. I glanced at the office, but only the sound of a radio talk show came out of the impossibly distant door. Another kick.

I turned to my right and stepped to the bow of a bobbing in-oard cruiser. Five steps and I was in the small, covered space that passed for a forward cabin. I closed the flimsy access panel behind me and peered out through the Plexiglas.

Mr. Thorne's third kick sent the door flying inward, dangling from long strips of splintered wood. His dark form filled the doorway. Light from a distant streetlight glinted off the blade in his right hand.

Please. Please hear the noise. But there was no movement from the office, only the metallic voices from the radio. Mr. Thorne took four paces, paused, and stepped down onto the first boat in line. It was an open outboard, and he was back up on the concrete in six seconds. The second boat had a small cabin. There was a ripping sound as Mr. Thorne kicked open the tiny hatch door, and then he was back up on the walkway. My boat was the eighth in line. I wondered why he couldn't just hear the wild hammering of my heart.

I shifted position and looked through the starboard port. The murky Plexiglas threw the light into streaks and patterns. I caught a brief glimpse of white hair through the window, and the radio was switched to another station. Loud music echoed in the long room. I slid back to the other porthole. Mr. Thorne was stepping off the fourth boat.

I closed my eyes, forced my ragged breathing to slow, and tried to remember countless evenings watching a bowlegged old figure shuffle down the street. Mr. Thorne finished his inspection of the fifth boat, a longer cabin cruiser with several dark recesses, and pulled himself back onto the walkway.

Forget the coffee in the thermos. Forget the crossword puzzle. Go look!

The sixth boat was a small outboard. Mr. Thorne glanced at it but did not step onto it. The seventh was a low sailboat, mast folded down, canvas stretched across the cockpit. Mr. Thorne's knife slashed through the thick material. Blood-streaked hands

SOUTHERN BLOOD

pulled back the canvas like a shroud being torn away. He jumped back to the walkway.

Forget the coffee. Go look! Now!

Mr. Thorne stepped onto the bow of my boat. I felt it rock to his weight. There was nowhere to hide, only a tiny storage locker under the seat, much too small to squeeze into. I untied the canvas strips that held the seat cushion to the bench. The sound of my ragged breathing seemed to echo in the little space. I curled into a fetal position behind the cushion as Mr. Thorne's leg moved past the starboard port. *Now.* Suddenly his face filled the Plexiglas strip not a foot from my head. His impossibly wide grimace grew even wider. *Now.* He stepped into the cockpit.

Now. Now. Now.

Mr. Thorne crouched at the cabin door. I tried to brace the tiny louvered door with my legs, but my right leg would not obey. Mr. Thorne fist slammed through the thin wooden strips and grabbed my ankle.

"Hey there!"

It was Mr. Hodges's shaky voice. His flashlight bobbed in our direction.

Mr. Thorne shoved against the door. My left leg folded painfully. Mr. Thorne's left hand firmly held my ankle through the shattered slats while the hand with the knife blade came through the opening hatch.

"Hey—" My mind shoved. Very hard. The old man stopped. He dropped the flashlight and unstrapped the buckle over the grip of his revolver.

Mr. Thorne slashed the knife back and forth. The cushion was almost knocked out of my hands as shreds of foam filled the cabin. The blade caught the tip of my little finger as the knife swung back again.

Do it. Now. Do it. Mr. Hodges gripped the revolver in both hands and fired. The shot went wide in the dark as the sound echoed off concrete and water. *Closer, you fool. Move!* Mr. Thorne shoved again and his body squeezed into the open hatch. He released my ankle to free his left arm, but almost instantly his hand was back in the cabin, grasping for me. I reached up and turned on the overhead light. Darkness stared at me from his empty eye socket. Light through the broken shutters spilled yellow strips across his ruined face. I slid to the left, but Mr. Thorne's hand, which had my coat, was pulling me off the bench. He was on his knees, freeing his right hand for the knife thrust.

Now! Mr. Hodges's second shot caught Mr. Thorne in the right hip. He grunted as the impact shoved him backward into a sitting position. My coat ripped, and buttons rattled on the deck.

The knife slashed the bulkhead near my ear before it pulled away.

Mr. Hodges stepped shakily onto the bow, almost fell, and inched his way around the starboard side. I pushed the hatch against Mr. Thorne's arm, but he continued to grip my coat and drag me toward him. I fell to my knees. The blade swung back, ripped through foam, and slashed at my coat. What was left of the cushion flew out of my hands. I had Mr. Hodges stop four feet away and brace the gun on the roof of the cabin.

Mr. Thorne pulled the blade back and poised it like a matador's sword. I could sense the silent scream of triumph that poured out over the stained teeth like a noxious vapor. The light of Nina's madness burned behind the single, staring eye.

Mr. Hodges fired. The bullet severed Mr. Thorne's spine and continued on into the port scupper. Mr. Thorne arched backward, splayed out his arms, and flopped onto the deck like a great fish that had just been landed. The knife fell to the floor of the cabin, while stiff, white fingers continued to slap nervelessly against the deck. I had Mr. Hodges step forward, brace the muzzle against Mr. Thorne's temple just above the remaining eye, and fire again. The sound was muted and hollow.

◊◊◊

There was a first-aid kit in the office bathroom. I had the old man stand by the door while I bandaged my little finger and took three aspirin.

My coat was ruined, and blood had stained my print dress. I had never cared very much for the dress—I thought it made me look dowdy—but the coat had been a favorite of mine. My hair was a mess. Small, moist bits of gray matter flecked it. I splashed water on my face and brushed my hair as best I could. Incredibly, my tattered purse had stayed with me although many of the contents had spilled out. I transferred keys, billfold, reading glasses, and Kleenex to my large coat pocket and dropped the purse behind the toilet. I no longer had father's walking stick, but I could not remember where I had dropped it.

Gingerly I removed the heavy revolver from Mr. Hodges's grip. The old man's arm remained extended, fingers curled around air. After fumbling for a few seconds I managed to click open the cylinder. Two cartridges remained unfired. The old fool had been walking around with all six chambers loaded! *Always leave an empty chamber under the hammer.* That is what Charles had taught me that gay and distant summer so long ago when such weapons were merely excuses for trips to the island for target practice punctuated by the shrill shrieks of our nervous laughter as Nina and I allowed ourselves to be held, arms supported, bodies shrinking back into the firm support of our so-serious tutors arms. *One must always count the cartridges,* lectured Charles, as I half-swooned against him, smelling the sweet, masculine shaving soap and tobacco smell rising from him on that warm, bright day.

Mr. Hodges stirred slightly as my attention wandered. His mouth gaped, and his dentures hung loosely. I glanced at the worn leather belt, but there were no extra bullets there, and I had no idea where he kept any. I probed, but there was little left in the old man's jumble of thoughts except for a swirling tape-loop replay of the muzzle being laid against Mr. Thorne's temple, the explosion, the—

"Come," I said. I adjusted the glasses on Mr. Hodges's vacant face, returned the revolver to the holster, and let him lead me out of the building.

It was very dark out. We had gone six blocks before the old man's violent shivering reminded me that I had forgotten to have him put on his coat. I tightened my mental vise, and he stopped shaking.

The house looked just as it had . . . my God . . . only forty-five minutes earlier. There were no lights. I let us into the courtyard and searched my overstuffed coat pocket for the key. My coat hung loose and the cold night air nipped at me. From behind lighted windows across the courtyard came the laughter of little girls, and I hurried so that Kathleen would not see her grandfather entering my house.

Mr. Hodges went in first, with the revolver extended. I had him switch on the light before I entered.

The parlor was empty, undisturbed. The light from the chandelier in the dining room reflected off polished surfaces. I sat down for a minute on the Williamsburg reproduction chair in the hall to let my heart rate return to normal. I did not have Mr. Hodges lower the hammer on the still-raised pistol. His arm began to shake from the strain of holding it. Finally, I rose and we moved down the hall toward the conservatory.

Miss Kramer exploded out of the swinging door from the kitchen with the heavy iron poker already coming down in an arc. The gun fired harmlessly into the polished floor as the old man's arm snapped from the impact. The gun fell from limp fingers as Miss Kramer raised the poker for a second blow.

I turned and ran back down the hallway. Behind me I heard the crushed-melon sound of the poker contacting Mr. Hodges's skull. Rather than run into the courtyard I went up the stairway. A mistake. Miss Kramer bounded up the stairs and reached the bed room door only a few seconds after me. I caught one glimpse of her widened, maddened eyes and of the upraised poker before I slammed and locked the heavy door. The latch clicked just as the brunette on the other side began to throw herself against the wood. The thick oak did not budge. Then I heard the concussion of metal against the door and frame. Again.

Cursing my stupidity, I turned to the familiar room, but there was nothing there to help me. There was not as much as a closet to hide in, only the antique wardrobe. I moved quickly to the window and threw up the sash. My screams would attract attention but not before that monstrosity had gained access. She was prying at the edges of the door now. I looked out, saw the shadows in the window across the way, and did what I had to do.

Two minutes later I was barely conscious of the wood giving away around the latch. I heard the distant grating of the poker as it pried at the recalcitrant metal plate. The door swung inward.

Miss Kramer was covered with sweat. Her mouth hung slack,

and drool slid from her chin. Her eyes were not human. Neither she nor I heard the soft tread of sneakers on the stairs behind her.

Keep moving. Lift it. Pull it back—all the way back. Use both hands. Aim it.

Something warned Miss Kramer. Warned Nina, I should say; there was no more Miss Kramer. The brunette turned to see little Kathleen standing on the top stair, her grandfather's heavy weapon aimed and cocked. The other girl was in the courtyard shouting for her friend.

This time Nina knew she had to deal with the threat. Miss Kramer hefted the poker and turned into the hall just as the pistol fired. The recoil tumbled Kathleen backward down the stairs as a red corsage blossomed above Miss Kramer's left breast. She spun but grasped the railing with her left hand and lurched down the stairs after the child. I released the ten-year-old just as the poker fell, rose, fell again. I moved to the head of the stairway. I had to see.

Miss Kramer looked up from her grim work. Only the whites of her eyes were visible in her spattered face. Her masculine shirt was soaked with her own blood, but still she moved, functioned. She picked up the gun in her left hand. Her mouth opened wider, and a sound emerged like steam leaking from an old radiator.

"Melanie . . ." I closed my eyes as the thing started up the stairs for me.

Kathleen's friend came in through the open door, her small legs pumping. She took the stairs in six jumps and wrapped her thin, white arms around Miss Kramer's neck in a tight embrace.

The two went over backward, across Kathleen, all the way down the wide stairs to the polished wood below.

The girl appeared to be little more than bruised. I went down and moved her to one side. A blue stain was spreading along one cheekbone, and there were cuts on her arms and forehead. Her blue eyes blinked uncomprehendingly.

Miss Kramer's neck was broken. I picked up the pistol on the way to her and kicked the poker to one side. Her head was at an impossible angle, but she was still alive. Her body was paralyzed, urine already stained the wood, but her eyes still blinked and her teeth clicked together obscenely. I had to hurry. There were adult voices calling from the Hodgeses' town house. The door to the courtyard was wide open. I turned to the girl. "Get up." She blinked once and rose painfully to her feet.

I shut the door and lifted a tan raincoat from the coatrack.

It took only a minute to transfer the contents of my pockets to the raincoat and to discard my ruined spring coat. Voices were calling in the courtyard now.

I kneeled down next to Miss Kramer and seized her face in my hands, exerting pressure to keep the jaws still. Her eyes had rolled upward again, but I shook her head until the irises were visible. leaned forward until our cheeks were touching. My whisper was louder than a shout.

"I'm coming for you, Nina."

I dropped her head onto the wood and walked quickly to the conservatory, my sewing room. I did not have time to get the key from upstairs; so I raised a Windsor side chair and smashed the glass of the cabinet. My coat pocket was barely large enough.

The girl remained standing in the hall. I handed her Mr. Hodges's pistol. Her left arm hung at a strange angle and I wondered if she had broken something after all. There was a knock at the door, and someone tried the knob.

"This way," I whispered, and led the girl into the dining room. We stepped across Miss Kramer on the way, walked through the dark kitchen as the pounding grew louder, and then were out, into the alley, into the night.

◊◊◊

There were three hotels in this part of the Old Section. One was a modern, expensive motor hotel some ten blocks away, comfortable but commercial. I rejected it immediately. The second was a small, homey lodging house only a block from my home. It was a pleasant but nonexclusive little place, exactly the type I would choose when visiting another town. I rejected it also. The third was two and a half blocks farther, an old Broad Street mansion done over into a small hotel, expensive antiques in every room, absurdly overpriced. I hurried there. The girl moved quickly at my side. The pistol was still in her hand, but I had her remove her sweater and carry it over the weapon. My leg ached, and I frequently leaned on the girl as we hurried down the street.

The manager of the Mansard House recognized me. His eyebrows went up a fraction of an inch as he noticed my disheveled appearance. The girl stood ten feet away in the foyer, half-hidden in the shadows.

"I'm looking for a friend of mine," I said brightly. "A Mrs. Drayton."

The manager started to speak, paused, frowned without being aware of it, and tried again. "I'm sorry. No one under that name is registered here."

"Perhaps she registered under her maiden name," I said. "Nina Hawkins. She's an older woman but very attractive. A few years younger than I. Long, gray hair. Her friend may have registered for her . . . an attractive, young, dark-haired lady named Barrett Kramer—"

"No, I'm sorry," said the manager in a strangely flat tone. "No one under that name has registered. Would you like to leave a message in case your party arrives later?"

"No," I said. "No message.

I brought the girl into the lobby, and we turned down a corridor leading to the restrooms and side stairs. "Excuse me, please," I said to a passing porter. "Perhaps you can help me."

"Yes, ma'am." He stopped, annoyed, and brushed back his long hair. It would be tricky. If I was not to lose the girl, I would have to act quickly.

"I'm looking for a friend," I said. "She's an older lady but quite attractive. Blue eyes. Long, gray hair. She travels with a young woman who has dark, curly hair."

"No, ma'am. No one like that is registered here."

I reached out and grabbed hold of his forearm tightly. I released the girl and focused on the boy. "Are you sure?"

"Mrs. Harrison," he said. His eyes looked past me. "Room 207. North front."

I smiled. *Mrs. Harrison.* Good God, what a fool Nina was. Suddenly the girl let out a small whimper and slumped against the wall. I made a quick decision. I like to think that it was compassion, but I sometimes remember that her left arm was useless.

"What's your name?" I asked the child, gently stroking her bangs. Her eyes moved left and right in confusion. "Your name!"

"Alicia." It was only a whisper.

"All right, Alicia. I want you to go home now. Hurry, but don't run.

"My *arm* hurts," she said. Her lips began to quiver. I touched her forehead again and *pushed*.

"You're going home," I said. "Your arm does not hurt. You won't remember anything. This is like a dream that you will forget. Go home. Hurry, but do not run." I took the pistol from her but left it wrapped in the sweater. "Bye-bye, Alicia."

She blinked and crossed the lobby to the doors. I handed the gun to the bellhop. "Put it under your vest," I said.

◊◊◊

"Who is it?" Nina's voice was light.

"Albert, ma'am. The porter. Your car's out front, and I'll take your bags down."

There was the sound of a lock clicking and the door opened the width of a still-secured chain. Albert blinked in the glare, smiled shyly, and brushed his hair back. I pressed against the wall.

"Very well." She undid the chain and moved back. She had already turned and was latching her suitcase when I stepped into the room.

"Hello, Nina," I said softly. Her back straightened, but even that move was graceful. I could see the imprint on the bedspread where she had been lying. She turned slowly. She was wearing a pink dress I had never seen before.

"Hello, Melanie." She smiled. Her eyes were the softest, purest blue I had ever seen. I had the porter take Mr. Hodges's gun out and aim it. His arm was steady. He pulled back the hammer and held it with his thumb. Nina folded her hands in front of her. Her eyes never left mine.

"Why?" I asked.

Nina shrugged ever so slightly. For a second I thought she was going to laugh. I could not have borne it if she had laughed—

that husky, childlike laugh that had touched me so many times. Instead she closed her eyes. Her smile remained.

"Why Mrs. Harrison?" I asked.

"Why, darling, I felt I owed him *something*. I mean, poor Roger. Did I ever tell you how he died? No, of course I didn't. And you never asked." Her eyes opened. I glanced at the porter, but his aim was steady. It only remained for him to exert a little more pressure on the trigger.

"He *drowned*, darling," said Nina. "Poor Roger threw himself from that steamship—what was its name?—the one that was taking him back to England. So strange. And he had just written me a letter promising marriage. Isn't that a *terribly* sad story, Melanie? Why do you think he did a thing like that? I guess we'll never know, will we?"

"I guess we never will," I said. I silently ordered the porter to pull the trigger.

Nothing.

I looked quickly to my right. The young man's head was turning toward me. *I had not made him do that.* The stiffly extended arm began to swing in my direction. The pistol moved smoothly like the tip of a weather vane swinging in the wind.

No! I strained until the cords in my neck stood out. The turning slowed but did not stop until the muzzle was pointing at my face. Nina laughed now. The sound was very loud in the little room.

"Good-bye, Melanie *dear*," Nina said, and laughed again. She laughed and nodded at the porter. I stared into the black hole as the hammer fell. On an empty chamber. And another. And another.

"Good-bye, Nina," I said as I pulled Charles's long pistol from the raincoat pocket. The explosion jarred my wrist and filled the room with blue smoke. A small hole, smaller than a dime but as perfectly round, appeared in the precise center of Nina's forehead. For the briefest second she remained standing as if nothing had happened. Then she fell backward, recoiled from the high bed, and dropped face forward onto the floor.

I turned to the porter and replaced his useless weapon with the ancient but well-maintained revolver. For the first time I noticed that the boy was not much younger than Charles had been. His hair was almost exactly the same color. I leaned forward and kissed him lightly on the lips.

"Albert," I whispered, "there are four cartridges left. One must always count the cartridges, mustn't one? Go to the lobby. Kill the manager. Shoot one other person, the nearest. Put the barrel in your mouth and pull the trigger. If it misfires, pull it again. Keep the gun concealed until you are in the lobby."

We emerged into general confusion in the hallway.

"Call for an ambulance!" I cried. "There's been an accident. Someone call for an ambulance!" Several people rushed to comply. I swooned and leaned against a white-haired gentleman. People milled around, some peering into the room and exclaiming. Suddenly there was the sound of three gunshots from the lobby. In the renewed confusion I slipped down the back stairs, out the fire door, into the night.

◊◊◊

Time has passed. I am very happy here. I live in southern France now, between Cannes and Toulon, but not, I am happy to say, too near St. Tropez.

I rarely go out. Henri and Claude do my shopping in the village. I never go to the beach. Occasionally I go to the townhouse in Paris or to my pensione in Italy, south of Pescara, on the Adriatic. But even those trips have become less and less frequent.

There is an abandoned abbey in the hills, and I often go there to sit and think among the stones and wild flowers. I think about isolation and abstinence and how each is so cruelly dependent upon the other.

I feel younger these days. I tell myself that this is because of the climate and my freedom and not as a result of that final Feeding. But sometimes I dream about the familiar streets of Charleston and the people there. They are dreams of hunger.

On some days I rise to the sound of singing as girls from the village cycle by our place on their way to the dairy. On those days the sun is marvelously warm as it shines on the small white flowers growing between the tumbled stones of the abbey, and I am content simply to be there and to share the sunlight and silence with them.

But on other days—old, dark days when the clouds move in from the north—I remember the shark-silent shape of a submarine moving through the dark waters of the bay, and I wonder whether my self-imposed abstinence will be for nothing. I wonder whether those I dream of in my isolation will indulge in their own gigantic, final Feeding.

It is warm today. I am happy. But I am also alone. And I am very, very hungry.

Dan Simmons is the best-selling and award-winning author of *The Hollow Man*, *Phases of Gravity*, *Children of The Night*, *Song of Kali*, *Hyperion*, *Lovedeath*, and many other works.

*Long live the King! There have been many reports of
Elvis sightings throughout the years. Now you'll why!*

Blessed by His Dying Tongue

BY TRACY A. KNIGHT

1.

Under midnight's shroud, the man darted through the
shadows of Graceland, sprinting from tree to tree until
finally, he arrived at the front door. As prearranged, he
knocked sharply three times, following then with a series of
five light taps. He hadn't noticed before, but the rhythm his
knocks created sounded like the beat behind "Don't Be
Cruel." He smiled to himself.

The door opened slightly. A burly bodyguard peered through
the crack and growled, "You the guy the Colonel sent for?"

"I am," said the man, lifting himself on the balls of his feet and
touching the brim of his black fedora.

The bodyguard opened the door wide. The man followed him
through a narrow hallway and into a garishly decorated room.
Opposing walls were yellow and black, the ceiling mirrored.
Three televisions, each tuned to a different station, sat along one
wall, their ghostly images strobing through the room. A white

ceramic monkey, with wide onyx eyes, squatted in the middle of a coffee table.

Elvis slouched in the plush, velvety cushions of the couch. He looked up, weary eyes peeking out from beneath sagging lids. He flicked a finger toward the man. "This the fella we been waiting for?"

"Sure is," said the bodyguard. "You want me to leave you two alone?"

"Might as well," said Elvis, only the faintest vestige of his smooth voice evident. His black hair was disheveled, traces of gray glittering at the roots. He wore a thick white terrycloth bathrobe, "TCB" stitched above one pocket. Elvis was over-weight and even though he was resting when the man arrived, beads of sweat shone on his forehead.

The bodyguard left the room. The man removed his fedora and carefully laid his briefcase on the floor. He waited reverently, hands clasped in front of him, until Elvis invited him to sit on the couch.

"I'm not sure what this is about," Elvis said, "but the Colonel told me it'd be good for me to meet with you, sir."

A blush spread across the man's stark cheekbones. "'Sir' isn't necessary, not from you, Mr. Presley. My name's Cal. Cal Fincher."

"Fine, Cal. Call me Elvis." They shook hands. Elvis smiled, albeit weakly.

The visitor crossed one bony leg over the other and interlocked his fingers over a knee. "I'm honored to be here . . . Elvis. I met the Colonel some months ago, and he told me what you needed. I'm more than happy to . . ."

"What did he say I needed?" Elvis asked, pinching his eyebrows and frowning slightly.

"Time. Rest. He said you're worried about dying. And that you need privacy. I guess privacy's pretty hard for you to come by these days, eh?"

Elvis let his body sag farther into the couch, and sighed. "I just need a break, but the Colonel doesn't see it that way. He says I need to keep working, to stay in the public eye. But I'm tired, Cal . . . so tired. The Colonel told me you could work something out, satisfy the both of us. That right?"

Cal smiled. "You bet, Elvis. You bet. You can rest—recharge your batteries—and make a comeback anytime you want, whether it's several months or several years. In the meantime, you'll have all the peace you need and want. See? You get your break, the Colonel is assured of the most fabulous comeback tour in history. Everybody wins. How many times in life can we say that?"

Elvis narrowed his eyes, obviously intrigued. "Hmm. So what do I have to do?"

Cal snapped open his briefcase. He removed a small vial and a hypodermic needle. He punched the needle through the vial's top and began pulling its contents into the syringe. "Just relax. This will only take a moment."

"Ah, you a doctor, then, Cal? That's good. I trust doctors."

Elvis rolled up the sleeve of his bathrobe, exposing his arm,and lay down on the couch.

"Will this hurt?" Elvis asked.

"Not a bit."

Cal injected Elvis with the solution. The King fluttered his eyelids briefly. Then his eyes rolled upward as he sank into unconsciousness.

Cal replaced the syringe and closed his briefcase. He turned back to Elvis and bent down over his white, pulsing neck.

2

Elvis awoke with a splitting headache, the slightest movements leading to clangorous pain. As his eyesight cleared, he saw that he was sprawled on a tattered couch in a small, dimly lit house. The windows were open and a fresh, playful evening breeze pirouetted through the living room.

He propped himself up on one arm. Each muscle fiber seemed to protest with grating insistence. He ached all over, but above this dull dolor shimmered an odd tingling, the likes of which he'd never felt before.

Elvis looked down at his stomach and was surprised to notice he was significantly thinner than before Cal's visit.

Soft footsteps approached. Elvis looked up to see Cal Fincher entering the room, carrying a large decanter and a crystal goblet.

"Ah, you're awake," Cal said quietly. "How're you feeling?"

"Kinda strange, but not bad . . . I guess."

Cal pointed toward Elvis's now-flat abdomen. "Nice weight loss, eh?" said Cal. "What do you think of that?"

"How did it happen . . . so quick?"

Cal set the decanter on an end table and sat down beside Elvis. "I know it seems like yesterday when we were talking at Graceland, but it's been three months, Elvis."

"Three months." He frowned through his haze. "How?"

Cal shrugged. "All part of the treatment. Nothing to worry about. We kept you nourished. You're in good, no, *excellent* health."

"And I can have my break from things?"

"Long as you want, Elvis." Cal opened a drawer in the endtable and pulled out a newspaper. He unfolded it and presented it to Elvis.

It was a tabloid rag. On its cover was a large black and white photo of Elvis in his casket. "Jesus God!" Elvis exclaimed, tossing the newspaper to the floor and stomping it, as if Cal had thrown him a live snake. "What's that?"

"That's you, Elvis. Remember I gave you that shot? It simulated death. We were able to carry off the funeral without anyone knowing any better. The Colonel knows, sure, and we had a couple of physicians help us with the paperwork . . . but nobody else knows."

"Lisa Marie? Daddy?"

Cal's smile was warm and empathic. He shook his head. "Had to be done, Elvis, for this to be a success. Look at it this way: You can take a long vacation, the one you've always wanted and needed. Away from the crowds, the business, the noise. When you're ready, you can make a comeback, a true career resurrection. Imagine the response!"

Elvis hung his head. "This ain't what I wanted. I didn't want Lisa Marie to hurt, or Daddy, or my fans."

Laying his hand on Elvis' shoulder, Cal said, "Don't worry. The Colonel'll see they're well taken care of. And someday—when you're ready—you *can* go home again." Cal stood up and put his hands on his hips. "Meanwhile, you're a free man, as free as you've ever been. While you were unconscious, I took the liber-

ty of dyeing your hair red—I hope you don't mind the crewcut—
and trimming you a nice beard. People won't recognize you,
bother you. So Elvis . . . what you want to do? How do you want
to spend tonight, your first night of freedom?"

Elvis fell silent for a few moments. Finally he nodded to himself
and said, "Church. I think I want to go to a church. That's something I always wanted to do, never could really do it comfortably,
you know?"

Cal cleared his throat. "Church? How about going downtown
to a night club, maybe see a movie?"

Elvis walked calmly to Cal and grabbed him by the collar."You
said I was free, right? I want to go to church! Now . . ." He
released Cal. "Where's a mirror? I want to take a look at myself."

"No mirrors here, Elvis. Not a one." Cal took a couple of steps
backward.

"What a rathole!" Elvis stormed from the room and out the
front door.

3

Elvis walked six blocks before spying a tall white steeple illuminated by floodlights. As he neared the church, he saw the sign out
front: "First United Methodist Church of Elmwood. Before that
moment, he hadn't known what state he was in, much less the
city. Elmwood. Had a nice sound to it. Relaxing.

It must have been past midnight. No one else seemed to be out
and around. The surrounding homes were dark.

Elvis walked up the concrete steps of he church and tried the
door. It was open.

After he stepped inside, he smiled to himself and basked in the
warm, gentle silence that caressed him. Such a rare feeling.

He walked through another door and saw row upon row of
empty wooden pews. He saw the majestic organ, its pipes extending up the wall, almost to the ceiling. At that moment, he felt so
free, so relaxed, so empowered, he wanted to belt out a nice
gospel tune.

Then, on the far wall, he saw the cross.

He felt faint, fell to one knee. Reaching up and clutching the back of a pew, Elvis tried to pull himself to his feet. Energy drained from his body and, against his will, one of his hands sprang up before his eyes.

Feeling he might vomit at any moment, and not wanting to soil the beautiful crimson carpeting, Elvis lurched from the room and stumbled back out into the night.

4

"What's going on? You tell me or I'll hurt you, I swear it!" Elvis had returned to the house, and when he saw the smiling Cal waiting for him, he lunged at the man and threw him to the floor. Elvis' hands were locked around Cal's neck. "Tell me!"

"Vam . . . pire," Cal said, choking between syllables.

"What're you talkin' about?"

"Let me up!"

Slowly, Elvis removed his hands from Cal's neck and stood over him.

Cal coughed several times, then said, "You're a vampire, Elvis. So am I."

"What's that supposed to mean?"

Cal struggled to his feet and continued, softly, "I've been a fan of yours from the beginning of your career. I always wanted to meet you, and one night I got the chance to talk with the Colonel. He told me how exhausted you were getting, how you wanted to get away, but how important it was that you keep performing. I told him I had the solution. Elvis, if I hadn't stepped in when I did, I'm sure you'd be dead. Remember how you felt? How you looked? Death was lurking around the corner, my friend. Believe me—I can smell death."

Elvis rubbed his neck and fingered the small lumps of scar tissue there.

"Look," Cal said, standing up to face the King. "People've been feeding off of you for a long time now, all sorts of people. You might as well have been a vampire's victim all those years. I just wanted you to have some peace—hell, to have eternal life. You can take as long or as short a break from everything that you need, and make a return to all the fame you had, and more. I'm here for you, at your service. I'm a fan. Always." Cal stepped to the end table and picked up the decanter that still sat there. "You thirsty yet?"

"What is that?"

"Blood, Elvis. That's what keeps us alive now."

Elvis sat on the couch, clasped his hand over his mouth. He began to cry softly. "I can't live like this. I can't."

Cal poured Elvis a cup of the clotting liquid and offered it to him. "You have to, Elvis. Don't worry: You'll never have to hurt anyone, I promise. I'll take care of you. I'll supply the blood."

Elvis stared at the glass. Reluctantly, he took the cup and gulped down the contents.

5

For the next six months, Elvis made an honorable effort to adjust to his new life. He got hired as a night watchman at a local factory, which at least allowed him to make some human contact, even if it was only with fellow guards and the occasional interloper. He tried to forget what he was.

Nonetheless, his depression continued and deepened. Despite the fact he was still trim, his body felt heavy, bloated. He walked slowly, almost a shamble. He sounded like a fool whenever he tried to make small talk, to turn sluggish thoughts into words.

Then one night, during a glorious midnight shift, he met a new fellow worker, Tricia.

Tricia Farner was a divorced mother of two and had taken the security job as a way to make ends meet. When Elvis first saw her bright red hair, her comely shape, glowing under the mercury vapor lamps outside the factory, he was smitten. For the first time since he had awakened into his new life, Elvis thought, *Maybe this'll work.*

After all, he reasoned, he had successfully scaled most of the barriers his new life represented: He had forced himself to adjust to drinking blood, though he did it by imagining the liquid to be bad pudding; He had gotten used to sleeping in the darkened house all day, rising only at night; he had even become accustomed to never seeing himself in a mirror.

But until that moment, until he saw Tricia, he hadn't realized how deep his true craving was, the craving that was more basic, more powerful than the blood-thirst. It was the hunger to hold and be held, to talk to someone, to listen. Sure, Cal kept him company and all, but he seemed little more than a valet or a bodyguard. Not a friend, not really.

Before meeting Tricia, Elvis had never been certain that when a woman was interested in him, she honestly was attracted to *him*—the human—and not merely drawn to worship at the feet of the cultural icon named Elvis.

During the 2:00 A.M. break, Elvis introduced himself as "Aaron Johnson," and even before they'd finished their first cup of coffee, Tricia and Elvis were chatting and laughing like classmates at a high school reunion.

Discovering they both had Saturday night off, and feeling an innocent excitement he thought had died within him years ago, Elvis invited Tricia to his house for the evening.

<h1 style="text-align:center">6</h1>

"I've had my eye on you since we first met, Aaron," Tricia said, flipping back her long red hair. "You've got the dreamiest eyes I've ever seen."

The next moment found Elvis discovering that vampires can blush. "Nice of you to say, ma'am."

"Tricia. Please." She scooted closer to him on the couch. "You have anything to drink in here?" She wrapped an arm around the King's shoulders.

"Yes'm. In the refrigerator. I bought some wine before I came home."

She kissed him on the cheek, got up, and walked into the kitchen. After she was out of sight, Elvis doubled over, wrapped his arms around his stomach. It felt like he'd been shot in the gut with a cannonball. He thought he might pass out.

Cal had been gone for two days. When he left, he promised Elvis he'd be gone a few hours at most, that it was time for the monthly "harvest," that soon he'd return with the nourishment Elvis required. Cal had never made Elvis wait before. This feeling—this gnawing, squirming hunger—was new.

Just then, Tricia returned to the room. She wasn't holding a drink, however. She was clutching her open purse, and a camera she'd pulled from it.

"I know who you are." Tricia said, smiling. "You can grow a beard and lose weight and dye your hair. But you can't hide those eyes.

Elvis was pushing so hard against the hunger, he was unable to respond. He couldn't muster an incredulous denial, couldn't point out the impossibility of a dead celebrity working as a night watchman in a small town.

Tricia raised the camera to her eye and pressed the shutter release. The flash was blinding; Elvis covered his eyes and turned his head.

He remained in that position, looking away from the woman who, until now, had seemed to represent a potential cornerstone in the construction of a new life.

The next sounds Elvis heard were, first, a surprised whimper, then a muffled cry.

He opened his eyes. When he turned back to Tricia, he saw the hand reaching around her face, and the blood running freely down her neck, painting a thick red vee between her breasts.

Cal stood behind her. As he smiled, streams of Tricia's blood rolled from his mouth's corners. He twisted Trica's neck to one side, and Elvis heard the dull, sickening crack as it broke. Her eyes, wide and amber, drifted in their sockets as if they were independently searching for something, anything to look at, to take her away from this.

"Don't worry, boss," Cal said. "There isn't any way you would've appeared on the picture. Uses mirrors, you know? We don't reflect, remember?"

Inside, Elvis' yearning for Tricia, the warm love and compassion she seemed to promise was all mixed up with anger—at Tricia for misleading him, at Cal for killing her. At the world, at fate, at life.

And he was hungry.

He leaped to Tricia, who was still being held up by Cal, and began lapping at the blood that spurted from her neck.

"I can't help it," Elvis managed between licks.

Blessed by His Dying Tongue   193

Soon his hunger abated and Elvis said, evenly, sincerely, "I won't be able to have no friends, ever, will I? 'Cept for you."

"That's pretty close to it, boss."

Elvis wiped his forearm across his mouth. "This life ain't no good, Cal. Ain't got no meaning."

Cal dragged Tricia's body into the next room. Elvis heard a door open and Tricia's body flopping down the wooden steps to the basement. Then, Cal's voice: "When you're done down there, come on up. I think we're almost ready."

7

After Cal returned to the living room, he sported the most confident, self-assured smile Elvis had ever seen. Cal sat down on the couch, crossed his arms, and began tapping his foot.

Elvis didn't know whether he should laugh along or slap Cal across the mouth. "What're you so self-satisfied about? You look like the cat that ate the canary."

"Ah, it's so much better than that, Elvis. So much better."

"So what's the deal here? Why'd you toss that girl down and then go yellin' into the basement?"

Cal shook his head, apparently committed to not revealing anything of value. He asked, "Elvis, if you could have anything in the world, what would you choose? What would make your life complete?"

"Rest. A little peace and quiet. A woman to love."

"Nonsense, boss. In case you haven't noticed, you've been resting like never before these past months. You've had peace and quiet. You tried to date that woman tonight. You can't believe you're going to find what you're looking for. And you know why? I'm not sure you know what you're really looking for. What's really been missing."

"So you tell me, Cal. You tell me, smart guy."

"That wouldn't be any good, boss. You'll know soon enough. Just promise me you'll remember what a good friend Cal Fincher was to you."

At that moment, Gladys Presley walked into the living room.

8

"Momma!" Elvis cried. He stumbled to her and fell to his knees, hugging her legs as tightly as he could. "Momma!"

Gladys, dressed in a large print dress, wearing an over coat and pillbox hat, smiled down at her son. She looked the same, exactly the same as Elvis remembered her. Except she looked less . . . haunted. In the years before her death, Elvis had noticed the deepening dark bags beneath her eyes, the expression of inconsolable sadness that seemed always on her face. Tonight, her eyes were bright and she smiled broadly.

"I've been waitin' for this moment, son. For a long time."

"I thought you were dead," Elvis said, still hugging her, still weeping.

"I probably would've been, but Cal here came to me. He asked me what I wanted and I told him I wanted to see you grow up. So he did for me what he did for you."

Elvis rose to his feet and now hugged Gladys around the neck. "How have you stood it all these years, Momma, livin' like this? It's about to drive me crazy."

"I had somethin' to wait for, son. And so did you. And now—here we are."

"But what can we do?"

"We can go where we're supposed to, son. Back to Graceland."

9

After taking a final midnight ride on Rising Sun, his favorite horse, Elvis joined Gladys and Cal next to the tombs.

He gave his Momma a warm, final hug and helped Cal secure her. Now it was his turn.

"You sure this is what you want?" Cal asked as he heaved up the tomb's cover.

"Yep." said the King.

"Like I told your Momma before we put her in, we built in some things so you'll have a little air, I hope enough for awhile. But as far as we know, you'll die sooner or later . . . That is, if the hunger doesn't get to you first and you find your way back out . . ."

"I can control my hunger." Elvis hopped over the lip of the tomb, grabbed the sides, and then dropped down to the casket. "Don't close it up until I'm in the coffin."

"You got it, boss." Cal said, his smile surrounded by a face full of sweet sadness.

Soon Elvis shouted up, "You were a real friend, Cal!"

And the coffin lid thudded shut.

Cal replaced the cover of the tomb. Then he transformed himself into a bat and fluttered away.

10

For the next several months, Elvis and his mother chatted away through the suffocating darkness. They cried and laughed, reviewing their lives together and apart, telling each other the things they always had intended.

When the darkness gave way to hallucinations, Elvis actually thought his Momma was cradling him, just like when he was a baby. Life was never so perfect.

One day, Momma's voice was no longer there, and Elvis understood. He couldn't think of a lullaby, so he sang "Amazing Grace" to her.

Until the day he finally died, Elvis lay relaxed and smiling in the dark, cushioned space. His hearing became increasingly sharp, so sharp in fact that he could hear his fans as they filed by his tomb. He could hear the questions they asked, the blessings they offered. At times, he even heard the gentle *tip-taps* of their falling tears.

Occasionally, Elvis sang to himself there in the coffin, crooning the gospel songs he loved so much. And to each fan who whispered his or her blessing or question, Elvis whispered an answer.

Tracy A. Knight's fiction also appears in *The UFO Files* and *Cat Crimes at the Holidays*.

*She was a nice girl—everything a guy could want in a wife.
There was just one small matter. . . .*

She Only Goes
Out at Night

BY WILLIAM TENN

*I*n this part of the country, folks think that Doc Judd carries magic in his black leather satchel. He's *that* good.

Ever since I lost my leg in the sawmill, I've been all-around handyman at the Judd place. Lots of times when Doc gets a night call after a real hard day, he's too tired to drive, so he hunts me up and I become a chauffeur too. With the shiny plastic leg that Doc got me at a discount, I can stamp the gas pedal with the best of them.

We roar up to the farmhouse and, while Doc goes inside to deliver a baby or swab grandma's throat, I sit in the car and listen to them talk about what a ball of fire the old Doc is. In Groppa County, they'll tell you Doc Judd can handle *anything.* And I nod and listen, nod and listen.

But all the time I'm wondering what they'd think of the way he handled his only son falling in love with a vampire. . . .

It was a terrifically hot summer when Steve came home on vacation—real blister weather. He wanted to drive his father around and kind of help with the chores, but Doc said that after the first tough year of medical school anyone deserved a vacation.

"Summer's a pretty quiet time in our line," he told the boy. "Nothing but poison ivy and such until we hit the polio season in August. Besides, you wouldn't want to shove old Tom out of his job, would you? No, Stevie, you just bounce around the countryside in your jalopy and enjoy yourself."

Steve nodded and took off. And I mean took off. About a week later, he started coming home five or six o'clock in the morning. He'd sleep till about three in the afternoon, lazy around for a couple of hours and, come eight-thirty, off he'd rattle in his little hot-rod. Road-houses, we figured, or maybe some girl. . . .

Doc didn't like it, but he'd brought up the boy with a nice easy hand and he didn't feel like saying anything just yet. Old buttinsky Tom, though—I was different. I'd helped raise the kid since his mother died, and I'd walloped him when I caught him raiding the ice-box.

So I dropped a hint now and then, kind of asking him, like, not to go too far off the deep end. I could have been talking to a stone face for all the good it did. Not that Steve was rude. He was just too far gone in whatever it was to pay attention to me.

And then the other stuff started and Doc and I forgot about Steve.

Some kind of weird epidemic hit the kids of Groppa County and knocked twenty, thirty, of them flat on their backs.

"It's almost got me beat, Tom," Doc would confide in me as we bump-bump-bumped over dirty back-country roads. "It acts like a bad fever, yet the rise in temperature is hardly noticeable. But the kids get very weak and their blood count goes way down. And it stays that way, no matter what I do. Only good thing, it doesn't seem to be fatal—so far."

Every time he talked about it, I felt a funny twinge in my stump where it was attached to the plastic leg. I got so uncomfortable that I tried to change the subject, but that didn't go with Doc. He'd gotten used to thinking out his problems by talking to me, and this epidemic thing was pretty heavy on his mind.

He'd written to a couple of universities for advice, but they didn't seem to be of much help. And all the time, the parents of the kids stood around waiting for him to pull a cellophane-wrapped miracle out of his little black bag, because, as they said in Groppa County, there was nothing could go wrong with a human body that Doc Judd couldn't take care of some way or other. And all the time, the kids got weaker and weaker.

Doc got big, bleary bags under his eyes from sitting up nights going over the latest books and medical magazines he'd ordered from the city. Near as I could tell he'd find nothing, even though lots of times he'd get to bed almost as late as Steve.

And then he brought home the handkerchief. Soon as I saw it, my stump gave a good, hard, extra twinge and I wanted to walk out of the kitchen. Tiny, fancy handkerchief, it was, all embroidered linen and lace edges.

"What do you think, Tom? Found this on the floor of the bedroom of the Stopes' kids. Neither Betty nor Willy have any idea where it came from. For a bit, I thought I might have a way of tracing the source of infection, but those kids wouldn't lie. If they say they never saw it before, then that's the way it is." He dropped the handkerchief on the kitchen table that I was clearing up, stood there sighing. "Betty's anemia is beginning to look serious. I wish I knew . . . wish . . . Oh, well." He walked out to the study, his shoulders bent like they were under a sack of cement.

I was still staring at the handkerchief, chewing on a finger-nail, when Steve bounced in. He poured himself a cup of coffee, plumped it down on the table and saw the handkerchief.

"Hey," he said. "That's Tatiana's. How did it get here?"

I swallowed what was left of the fingernail and sat down very carefully opposite him. "Steve," I asked, and then stopped because I had to massage my aching stump. "Stevie, you know a girl who owns that handkerchief? A girl named Tatiana?"

"Sure, Tatiana Latianu. See, there are her initials embroidered in the corner—T. L. She's descended from the Rumanian nobility, family goes back five hundred years. I'm going to marry her."

"She the girl you've been seeing every night for the past month?"

He nodded. "She only goes out at night. Hates the glare of the sun. You know, poetic kind of girl. And Tom, she's so beautiful. . . ."

For the next hour, I just sat there and listened to him. And I felt sicker and sicker. Because I'm Rumanian myself, on my mother's side. And I knew why I'd been getting those twinges in my stump.

She lived in Brasket Township, about twelve miles away. Tom had run into her late one night on the road when her convertible had broken down. He'd given her a lift to her house—she'd just rented the old Mead Mansion—and he'd fallen for her, hook, line and whole darn fishing rod.

Lots of times, when he arrived for a date, she'd be out, driving around the countryside in the cool night air, and he'd have to play cribbage with her maid, an old beak-faced Rumanian biddy, until she got back. Once or twice, he'd tried to go after her in his hot-rod, but that had led to trouble. When she wanted to be alone, she had told him, she wanted to be alone. So that was that. He waited for her night after night. But when she got hack, according to Steve, she really made up for everything. They listened to music and talked and danced and ate strange Rumanian dishes that the maid whipped up. Until dawn. Then he came home.

Steve put his hand on my arm. "Tom, you know that poem—The Owl and the Pussy-Cat? I've always thought the last line was beautiful. 'They danced by the light of the moon, the moon, they danced by the light of the moon.' That's what my life will be like with Tatiana. If only she'll have me. I'm still having trouble talking her into it."

I let out a long breath. "The first good thing I've heard," I said without thinking. "Marriage to that girl—"

When I saw Steve's eyes, I broke off. But it was too late.

"What the hell do you mean, Tom: that girl? You've never even met her."

I tried to twist out of it, but Steve wouldn't let me. He was real sore. So I figured the best thing was to tell him the truth.

"Stevie. Listen. Don't laugh. Your girlfriend is a vampire."

He opened his mouth slowly. "Tom, you're off your—

"No, I'm not." And I told him about vampires. What I'd heard from my mother who'd come over from the old country, from Transylvania, when she was twenty. How they can live and have all sorts of strange powers—just so long as they have a feast of human blood once in a while. How the vampire taint is inherited, usually just one child in the family getting it. And how they go out only at night, because sunlight is one of the things that can destroy them.

Steve turned pale at this point. But I went on. I told him about the mysterious epidemic that had hit the kids of Groppa County—and made them anemic. I told him about his father finding the handkerchief in the Stopes' house, near two of the sickest kids. And I told him—but all of a sudden I was talking to myself. Steve tore out of the kitchen. A second or two later, he was off in the hot-rod.

He came back about eleven-thirty, looking as old as his father. I was right, all right. When he'd wakened Tatiana and asked her straight, she'd broken down and wept a couple of buckets-full. Yes, she was a vampire, but she'd only got the urge a couple of months ago. She'd fought it until her mind began to break when the craving hit her. She'd only touched kids, because she was afraid of grownups—they might wake up and be able to catch her. But she'd kind of worked on a lot of kids at one time, so that no one kid would lose too much blood. Only the craving had been getting stronger. . . .

And still Steve had asked her to marry him! "There must be a way of curing it," he said. "It's a sickness like any other sickness." But she, and—believe me—I thanked God, had said no. She'd pushed him out and made him leave. "Where's Dad?" he asked. "He might know."

I told him that his father must have left at the same time he did, and hadn't come back yet. So the two of us sat and thought. And thought.

When the telephone rang, we both almost fell out of our seats. Steve answered it, and I heard him yelling into the mouthpiece.

He ran into the kitchen, grabbed me by the arm and hauled me out into his hot-rod. "That was Tatiana's maid, Magda," he told me as we went blasting down the highway. "She says Tatiana got hysterical after I left, and a few minutes ago she drove away in her convertible. She wouldn't say where she was going. Magda says she thinks Tatiana is going to do away with herself."

"Suicide? But if she's a vampire, how—" And all of a sudden I knew just how. I looked at my watch. "Stevie," I said, "drive up to Crispin Junction. And drive like holy hell!"

He opened that hot-rod all the way. It looked as if the motor was going to tear itself right off the car. I remember we went around curves just barely touching the road with the rim of one tire.

We saw the convertible as soon as we entered Crispin Junction. It was parked by the side of one of the three roads cross the town. There was a tiny figure in a flimsy nightdress standing in the middle of the deserted street. My leg stump felt like it was being hit with a hammer.

The church clock started to toll midnight just as we reached her. Steve leaped out and knocked the pointed piece of wood out of her hands. He pulled her into his arms and let her cry.

I was feeling pretty bad at this point. Because all I'd been thinking of was how Steve was in love with a vampire. I hadn't looked at it from her side. She'd been enough in love with him to try to kill herself the only way a vampire could be killed—by driving a stake through her heart on a crossroads at midnight.

And she was a pretty little creature. I'd pictured one of these siren dames: you know, tall, slinky, with a tight dress. A witch. But this was a very frightened, very upset young lady who got in the car and cuddled up in Steve's free arm like she'd taken a lease on it. And I could tell she was even younger than Steve.

So, all the time we were driving back, I was thinking to myself these kids have got plenty trouble. Bad enough to be in love with a vampire, but to be a vampire in love with a normal human being. . . .

"But how can I marry you?" Tatiana wailed. "What kind of home life would we have? And Steve, one night I might even get hungry enough to attack you!"

The only thing none of us counted on was Doc. Not enough, that is.

Once he'd been introduced to Tatiana and heard her story, his shoulders straightened and the lights came back on in his eyes. The sick children would be all right now. That was most important. And as for Tatiana—

"Nonsense," he told her. "Vampirism might have been an incurable disease in the fifteenth century, but I'm sure it can be handled in the twentieth. First, this nocturnal living points to a possible allergy involving sunlight and perhaps a touch of photophobia. You'll wear tinted glasses for a bit, my girl, and we'll see what we can do with hormone injections. The need for consuming blood, however, presents a somewhat greater problem."

But he solved it.

They make blood in a dehydrated, crystalline form these days. So every night before Mrs. Steven Judd goes to sleep, she shakes some powder into a tall glass of water, drops in an ice cube or two and has her daily blood toddy. Far as I know, she and her husband are living happily ever after.

William Tenn is the author of many popular story collections, including The Human Angle, The Square Root of Man, The Wooden Star, and Of All Possible Worlds, among others.

Look for other books in
THE AMERICAN VAMPIRE SERIES!

Blood Lines

**EDITED BY
LAWRENCE SCHIMEL
AND MARTIN H. GREENBERG**

New Englanders have a sense of lineage unmatched in any other region of America. To this day those whose ancestors were the first Europeans to settle here tend to regard families whose first ancestors arrived as early as 200 years ago as newcomers. This New England fondness for lineage is akin to the longevity of the vampire, whose life (or unlife) is extended by draining the lives and blood of others.

The stories in *Blood Lines* explore the ancient mysteries of vampirism, along with the rich literary tradition begun with Lord Byron and with Bram Stoker's Dracula, first published in 1871 long after the aristocratic blood lines were established.

**FROM CUMBERLAND HOUSE
PUBLISHERS**